Finding Ginny

Jen Dodrill

Copyright © 2026 by Jen Dodrill

Printed in the United States of America

All rights reserved.

No part of this publication may be reproduced, distributed, or transmitted in any form or by any means, including photocopying, recording, or other electronic or mechanical methods, without the prior written permission of the publisher, except as permitted by U.S. copyright law. For permission requests, contact the author at jend@jendodrillwrites.com.

Paperback ISBN 979-8-9944721-1-8

ebook ISBN 979-8-9944721-0-1

Editors: Jessica Gwyn & Teresa Lynn

Proofreader: Sarah Harmon

Cover design by Jen Dodrill

The story, all names, characters, and incidents portrayed in this production are fictitious. No identification with actual persons (living or deceased), places, buildings, and products is intended or should be inferred.

NO AI TRAINING: Without in any way limiting the author's exclusive rights under copyright, any use of this publication to "train" generative artificial intelligence (AI) technologies to generate text is expressly prohibited. The author reserves all rights to license uses of this work for generative AI training and development of machine learning language models.

Preface

I wrote *Finding Ginny* as a loved one of an addict—for the family members and friends who often find themselves searching for steadiness while loving someone in pain. This story is offered as a gesture of hope and encouragement, a reminder that even in the confusion and heartache that addiction brings, no one has to walk alone.

What I have learned is that navigating recovery takes time, patience, and a great deal of hard work. It is rarely simple, rarely fast—but it is deeply worth it. I cannot speak for the experience of addiction itself. I can only speak as someone learning how to live, grow, and heal alongside it. For me, recovery has been a day-by-day practice of letting go, showing up honestly, and choosing progress over perfection.

This book exists because of the people who taught me those lessons—the ones who listened, shared their stories, and reminded me to keep the focus where it belongs. Where would I be without my family group? Their presence made space for hope when mine felt thin, and their courage helped me trust that healing, in all its forms, is possible. It is in that spirit that this story is told.

For those who love someone battling addiction—your patience, courage, and steady hope matter more than you know. And for those in recovery, whose daily work to heal, choose honesty, and begin again is an act of quiet bravery. This book is for all of you.

Contents

1. Chapter 1   1
2. Chapter 2   12
3. Chapter 3   22
4. Chapter 4   32
5. Chapter 5   41
6. Chapter 6   50
7. Chapter 7   58
8. Chapter 8   66
9. Chapter 9   74
10. Chapter 10   83
11. Chapter 11   92
12. Chapter 12   101
13. Chapter 13   110
14. Chapter 14   119
15. Chapter 15   128
16. Chapter 16   137
17. Chapter 17   146
18. Chapter 18   156

19.	Chapter 19	165
20.	Chapter 20	174
21.	Chapter 21	183
22.	Chapter 22	192
23.	Chapter 23	202
24.	Chapter 24	212
25.	Chapter 25	222
26.	Chapter 26	231
27.	Chapter 27	240
28.	Chapter 28	250
29.	Chapter 29	260
30.	Chapter 30	270
31.	Chapter 31	279
32.	Chapter 32	290
33.	Chapter 33	300
	Fullpage image	305
	Acknowledgements	306
	About the author	307
	Also by Jen Dodrill	308

Chapter 1

Virginia Beach, VA

The morning my life changed started like any other. My alarm buzzed. I yanked out the plug and tossed the thing into my closet as if banishing a bad habit. Two months of summer stretched before me like an empty beach with endless possibilities.

After getting ready for the day, I sat at the table on the sunporch, a cup of coffee before me, contemplating what to do with all my time. Heavy spring rains had flooded my backyard, turning it into a jungle. Hiring a yard guy topped my list.

The garage was a problem too. Just the other day, the tail end of something whipped around the corner into the cluttered space. If it were a snake, I'd have to move. At the memory, the hairs on my arms stood at attention.

On to more pleasant things. I opened my Pinterest app to search for color schemes for my bedroom, finally settling on a pale green with crisp white trim. My fingers itched to take out my sewing machine and whip up some long, flowy window coverings. Now to find the exact color paint, less mint and more seafoam.

A rusty sedan crunching up my pebbled driveway snagged my attention. It shimmied and sputtered to a halt. The driver's door opened. A young woman stepped out. My hand jerked, spilling hot coffee everywhere. The last time I'd seen her, she was sixteen, her face beet red, accusations and cruel words spewing out of her mouth.

I did some spewing myself.

For years, I worried she might be dead. Made myself accept the possibility I'd never know. But I often dreamed about reuniting with her.

Funny how I never imagined how I'd react in real life. Everything around me slowed—my heartbeat, her movements, my thoughts. For a second, I wondered what she wanted, but then the world sped back up. I raced out the front door, tripping down the porch steps, catching myself on the chipped wrought-iron railing at the last moment. "Becky?"

Could she hear the desperation in my voice? Did it matter anymore?

"Hi, Mom." She wiggled her fingers before winding her arms around her waist.

I pulled up short, clamping my hands over my mouth. My Becky was here. I rushed to her, grabbed her close, and held on tight. She smelled like an ashtray, and her stringy, overly bleached blonde hair clung to her pallid face.

"Eight years," I said, leaning back to study her. Disheveled clothes—a stained T-shirt and raggedy shorts—sagged on her skinny frame, contrasting with my memories of her still round teenage face, trendy clothes, and shiny hair. There wasn't any teenager left in the woman before me. I ran my hands down her arms and tugged her close for another hug.

"Yep, it's been a while." Becky wriggled out of my grip and opened the car's back door. A little girl climbed out, her thumb in her mouth, her forehead furrowed. She hid behind Becky, who reached back and gave her a slight shove toward me. "Ginny, this is your Grandma Kat."

Grandma? Wait, what? I was Grandma Kat? I backed up, my legs hitting the car. My breath whooshed out even as I attempted to hold all my feelings close. I reminded myself to breathe.

"Wow." I rubbed my chin. "How, when ..."

Becky smirked, one eyebrow cocked up.

Ginny's wavy light brown hair and jagged bangs resembled her mom's at that age. Her eyes, wary and peering from me to the house and back, were the same shade of brown as mine. I reached for my daughter's bony shoulder. "She reminds me of you."

"Yeah." She drew the word out.

The child's brows remained scrunched, but she removed her thumb. She popped a hand on her hip. "You don't look like my mama."

Everything inside me screamed to hug her. I squatted to study her face. "Well, I'm her mama, but she looks more like her daddy."

"I don't have a daddy." She crossed her arms once more.

Becky grunted.

Okay, then.

I stood and held out my hand to Ginny. "Want to go inside? We'll have some sweet tea. Oh, and there's chocolate milk." Her eyes narrowed, but she slipped her hand into mine. This moment, something I'd never allowed myself to dream about, felt ... surreal.

"I'm not staying." Becky's harsh tone sliced into me.

"But, honey, you just got here." In seconds, I regretted my whiny words.

She pulled out a small tote from the car's back seat. "Here, Ginny, take this."

Ginny reached for the bag, an agonizing expression of betrayal on her face. "Mama? Why?"

Her pleading penetrated my heart like a knife.

Becky ignored her. She jerked open the driver's door. Through gritted teeth, she said, "Mom, please keep her. I'll be back." She slammed the door, backed up, and squealed off.

I raised my hand. "Wait. When?" My words blew away on the summer breeze.

My thoughts seesawed between hot anger at my daughter and wondering what I'd do with her little girl until she came back. A scream, the best way to express my current wild, careening feelings, worked its way up my throat. I bit my tongue to keep it in check. *Control yourself, Kat.*

Ginny—my granddaughter—stared at me, her tote clenched in her fist. Her gaze went to the street with a longing for her mother that broke my heart all over again.

"Come on, sweetie. Let's put your things in your room." I forced a smile, coaxing her toward the house. "Here, I'll take your clothes."

She shoved the bag behind her back and followed me up the steps, sniffling and wiping her nose with the hem of her shirt.

I held open the front door. "How old are you?"

"Six." She stared at her feet as she stepped inside. Silent tears tracked down her cheeks. "My mama won't come back, will she?"

I pulled the storm door closed. "Sure, honey. She said she would." She wriggled away when I touched her shoulder.

She traipsed after me to the guest room. I pushed open the door to twin beds covered with lightweight bedspreads and a nightstand in between, all in dull shades of brown. It wasn't exactly a room for a six-year-old, but I didn't have anything else.

"It's kinda ugly in here." She set her tote down and ran her hand over one of the bedspreads. "I never had my own bedroom." Her little shoulders drooped.

"Hang on." I grabbed several tissues from the bathroom. "Here, blow."

She did so with a loud honk.

"Any better?"

She shrugged one shoulder.

"Want to put away your clothes?"

"No." She pointed to the bed. "Can I sit on it?"

"Sure, honey. This is your room now."

She climbed up, her legs dangling off the side. She lay her head on the pillow, stretching out like a little starfish. "We stayed at a motel last night. I couldn't touch the sides of that bed."

"I'm sure you liked that." Where did she and Becky drive from if they stayed in a motel?

She jumped down. "Nah, it was stinky." She pulled a ragged brown teddy bear out of her bag, hugging it close. "What's next?" Her thumb crept back toward her mouth.

Her quick change of subject startled me. "Are you hungry?"

She shook her head.

"Okay, how about a tour?" She ignored my outstretched hand and walked out of the room.

We inspected the bathroom situated between my bedroom and hers.

She tapped the black-and-white tile floor with her foot, her toes hanging over the end of her dirty sandals. "It's like a checkerboard."

I nodded at her comment. "That's what I thought."

When I moved in, the tiles were in good shape, so I added a bright red shower curtain with a matching valance over the window to tie the room together. The bathroom ended up being one of my favorite rooms in the house.

What did that say about me?

In my bedroom, Ginny ran her fingers over the knick-knacks on my dresser and rifled through my costume jewelry. She slipped a bulky ring on her small finger, tipping it this way and that. Her reflection in the mirror reminded me again of Becky as a little girl.

She gestured to a picture on my nightstand. "Who's that?"

"Your Grandpa Joe. Your mama's dad."

"Is he here?"

"No, honey." I sat on the bed and picked up the picture, tracing Joe's face with my finger. "He died when your mama was a baby."

"Did he use drugs?"

"Uh, no." I set down the frame, blowing out a quiet breath. What had this child endured? What had she seen? "Let's go upstairs. It gets hot, but you'll like it. You can see your mama's bedroom."

"'kay."

She hustled up the stairs in front of me. The large room was paneled, dark, hot, and musty. I turned on the small window air conditioner and opened the blinds while Ginny explored. She peeked into the closet before examining the tiny bathroom.

"My mama stayed here?"

"Yes, she moved upstairs after she turned fifteen." *Before she ran away.*

"Can *I* sleep up here?"

I tapped my chin, considering her request. "I don't think so. Not yet, anyhow."

She scrunched her nose, turned, and stomped down the stairs.

I resisted the urge to stomp down them like she had. I found her in the kitchen and showed her the sunporch, my other favorite room. She peeked out the jalousie windows at the backyard.

She tapped the glass panes. "What's this?"

"These are louvered windows." I demonstrated how to open and close them. "They need to be replaced, but I like how they work. My family lived here for years. Your mama and I moved in when she was a baby. We lived with my mom, your great-grandmother, after Grandpa Joe died. So some things are old."

She practiced opening them. A slight breeze floated through the porch, bringing the salty scent of the ocean. "Now what?"

Good question. I didn't have any toys for kids, especially six-year-olds. We made our way to the front porch, where Ginny plopped onto the free-standing glider, her feet swinging.

A family walked up the street, carrying folding chairs and totes stuffed with brightly colored towels. Inflated floats slowed them down. "Where're they goin'?"

"The beach is just past the parking lot, over those steps." I joined her on the glider.

"We lived in Miss'ippi one time. Mama said the beach was dirty. I don't 'member it." She edged forward, using her toe to swing us.

"This one is clean. We can search for shells. We'll go tomorrow morning, okay? I'm on summer break from teaching, so I have lots of time." *Quit babbling. She'll think you're crazy.* "You lived in Mississippi?" How many places did I search for Becky? How many years did I wait to hear something, anything? And then I gave up.

"Yep." She pushed harder with her foot.

I gripped the armrest, dragging my sandal to slow us. "Where do you live now?"

"Tenn'ssee."

"You stayed in a motel last night?"

"It stunk." She pinched her nose shut. "Mama said I looked like an urchin and made me wash my hair." She shook her head in dismay. "What's an urchin?"

I covered my grin. "She wanted you to be clean."

"Why'd she leave me here?" She rubbed her eyes. "I wanna go home."

"I'm happy you're here." What an understatement. I couldn't begin to describe all the crazy feelings flying through my brain and body. I already loved her, and I didn't even know her.

She squirmed back on the seat. "Mama never left me this far away before." Her thumb made its way back into her mouth.

Wait, what?

Needing to stop my thoughts before anger took over again, I stood, gesturing for her to follow me inside. We unpacked her tote and tucked her meager belongings—two pairs of worn shorts, three faded T-shirts, a nightgown, and a ratty hairbrush—into the three-drawer dresser. I'd already seen the shape her sandals were in.

Ginny nixed my first dinner offer of burgers and voted for spaghetti. She ate two full bowls, yawning through the second. After a bath, she climbed into bed. I stopped myself from brushing the curls off her forehead, settling for pulling the covers under her chin. I handed her the stuffed teddy bear.

I racked my brain trying to come up with things to do together. "Do you still want to go to the beach tomorrow?"

"Yes!" Her eyes lit up for an instant before her forehead wrinkled in a frown. "What if my mama comes while we're gone?"

"We'll leave a note taped to the front door for her, okay?"

Clutching her bear, she nodded and turned onto her side.

I pulled the door almost closed. Fatigue hit me. My legs felt like they weighed a hundred pounds each. The day began with a sense of excitement, but it turned into something I'd never considered. Not fully. My heart felt as if it would burst thinking about Ginny. I shoved thoughts of Becky to the dark recesses of my mind.

As much as I hated to admit it, a tiny sense of injustice wiggled through my heart.

My plans for the summer, tentative as they might be, flew out the window with everything that happened in this one day. Where did I go from here?

Goodness, woman. Get over yourself! Don't be so selfish. I hadn't lost anything, but Ginny sure had.

When she snored, the cutest sound I'd heard in a while, I grabbed my cell phone and searched for an open pack of cigarettes. I headed to the sunporch and tipped the windows open before dropping into a chair. Calling Sugar took the last of my energy.

"Why are you breathing hard?" she asked.

Too bad my best friend couldn't read my mind. "I'm not. I'm smoking." I took another puff, holding it in my lungs. "There's a good reason." I exhaled.

"Are you sick?" Concern colored her words. "Did someone die?"

"No." Tears burned my eyes.

"Kat, what happened? You're scaring me."

"It's Becky." My voice came out high-pitched. My emotions, held in all day, poured down my cheeks. I set the cigarette in the ashtray and grabbed a napkin, wiping my face with force.

She gasped. "What?" A chair creaked. I pictured her plopping into it. *Probably as in shock as I am. There's more, Sugar. Hold on tight.*

"It's really about her? Did she call? Is she back?" Her breath whooshed out. "After all this time, I didn't think we'd ever hear from her again."

Her questions made my head spin. I forced my shoulders down. "Me neither. She showed up out of the blue. She looks rough, so rough. Skinny and tired and smelling like cigarettes."

Sugar snorted.

"And guess what? She brought her daughter." After all those years of worrying about Becky, wondering why she left, whether she was still alive—eight years without contact. The knot in my stomach twisted.

Before she spoke, I added, "She's six. Reminds me of Beck at that age. All arms and legs. Remember when she cut her bangs?" I hiccupped. "She has my eyes. She saw Joe's picture and asked if he died from drugs. What in the world? Where has this kid been? Where has my daughter been?" I clenched my hands into fists.

"Oh, Kat." Sugar's sad tone echoed my feelings. "Are they still there? Can I come see them?"

"Becky left as soon as she got here. She didn't even come inside. She dropped Ginny off with some old clothes and drove away without explaining anything." Irritation tinged my words. I wanted to scream loud and long. "We have to go shopping tomorrow, but we're going to the beach in the morning. Want to go with us?"

"Of course. I want to meet her." She huffed. "Becky always liked drama. Doesn't sound like she's changed. I wonder how much Ginny can tell us. Think we can ask her questions?"

"Maybe, but she's so young, I hate to put all this on her."

"Yeah. She's not responsible for what her mom does."

She spoke the truth. I wasn't angry with my granddaughter. Thinking about her brought warm, fuzzy feelings to my heart. But it didn't stamp out my frustration with her mother.

The fatigue gave way to exhaustion. I ground out my cigarette, the first one I'd smoked in weeks. After Sugar and I hung up, I pushed myself up from the table on shaky legs. I left the windows tipped open to air out the sunporch and flipped off the kitchen light. My bed called, even though I doubted I'd sleep. If I learned anything from today, I figured tomorrow would be anything but calm—so much for my peaceful, boring life.

Chapter 2

The next morning, when the sun peeked through my bedroom curtains, I gave up pretending to sleep. I dressed and headed to the garage. Five old, slightly bent, "Keep Off the Lawn" signs were tucked into a corner. I grabbed them, along with a hammer, and carried them to the curb.

My narrow street didn't have sidewalks. Beach goers parked wherever possible, some with no regard for homeowners, and the tiny parking lot at the base of the steps to the beach filled quickly.

I'd pounded the last sign into the ground and brushed off my hands when Sugar's voice startled me. My friend trudged up the street, her short, dark hair ruffling in the early June breeze. "Morning," she called.

"Hey, you're awake early," I said.

"Couldn't sleep, so I've been working on a painting. I figured I'd grab some coffee with you before the beach." She stopped, her eyes searching my face. "How are you this morning? You don't seem like you slept any more than I did."

"Nope. I have tons of questions, and I'm wondering about school in the fall." I picked up the hammer. "How could Becky do this? She's thrown my life into a tailspin for sure." I hooked my arm in Sug's, and we walked toward the garage. "Nothing against Ginny. She's something else. Wait till you meet her. She's a feisty one. But I can't help wondering what she's been around."

Sugar squeezed my arm. "Yeah, I thought about that. Let's grab some coffee and a notebook. We can try to work out answers to our questions."

My friend liked lists.

I closed the garage door and set the hammer on the dryer. We peeked in on Ginny, still asleep and clutching her bear.

Sug's eyebrows rose into her bangs. "That thing is ratty."

She followed me to the kitchen, where I started the coffee pot. "That *thing* is 'Bearhoven,' and she loves him. He is quite ratty, though. Missing an eye and a bit of fur on his tummy."

"Bearhoven? Creative name. Sounds Irish."

"Sounds like something Becky would make up." I crossed my arms and leaned against the counter. "What am I going to do?" My voice broke. "Does she have any idea what she's done? How can she just show up and expect me to jump back into her life? It's not fair." I wanted to stomp my feet.

Sug filled our mugs and gestured to the sunporch. "Let's talk out here so we don't wake the kiddo."

I found paper and a pencil and joined her at the table. We spent half an hour writing questions before splitting them into two pages. One for Becky—like where she'd been for the last eight years, and when she might return this time. And one page for Ginny—what she liked to do, and my responsibilities regarding her living with me.

"Bet we could think of tons more for my daughter." I sipped my coffee and grimaced. I liked it cold or hot, never lukewarm.

Sug pushed back from the table. "Probably, but she's not here, and your granddaughter is." She held up a finger, went to the kitchen, and returned with the coffee pot. "There's nothing we can ask Becky until she comes back." She refilled my cup, topped hers off, and set the carafe on a trivet.

"*If* she shows up. We have no idea what she's going to do." I propped my chin on my hand.

"Be careful, or I'll think you're too positive a friend for me." She softened her words with a wink.

Ginny appeared in the doorway to the sunporch, rubbing her eyes, hair askew, and skinny arms and legs poking out of a too-short, faded nightgown.

I rose and patted her shoulder. "Morning, honey. This is Sugar, my best friend." I gestured to Sug, thankful Ginny didn't shrug away from my hand.

"Oh, honey." Sug's eyes glittered with tears. "Can I hug you? Please? I knew your mom when she was your age." She held her arms open.

Ginny walked into the hug. I squashed down the jealousy that reared up.

Sug held her tight. "You can call me Ms. Sug, okay?"

My standoffish granddaughter giggled.

"What's so funny, kiddo?"

"What kinda name is Sugar?" Her eyes twinkled. "Did your mama name you that?"

"I don't have a mom."

Ginny's mouth dropped open, and she stepped back.

"It's okay. You didn't know. I had a great daddy, though."

Ginny twisted the bottom of her nightgown. "I don't have a daddy."

"I know, baby." Sugar pulled her in for another hug. "Now you have a grandma and a Ms. Sug." She turned her around. "Sounds like we're headed to the beach this morning. Go get dressed."

Ginny scurried off, and I faced my friend. "Thank you. You're making this an easier morning for sure."

She held up her hands. "I loved Becky like she was mine. That girl is her mom all over again."

"It's kind of eerie, isn't it? I keep reminding myself she's not a mini-Becky." I blew out a breath. "And how she hugged you. Gracious, I can barely touch her."

"She's going to act out more because you're her grandmother." Sug swiped our mugs from the table. "Let me pack a breakfast picnic. You find towels and a blanket, and we'll introduce her to our beach."

I scribbled a note for Becky and read it aloud to Ginny. After she gave her approval, we taped it to the front door as we left.

Sugar and I spread the blanket in the sand and anchored it with our flip-flops and the picnic basket. We sat side by side while Ginny tiptoed along the shoreline. Contentment filled me as she played in the mild Atlantic surf. Did I have a second chance? Could I help this child and do it right this time?

Hope mingled with the knot in my stomach. I couldn't decide if it was nausea or excitement.

"Wonder who her daddy is?"

Sug's words brought me back to the present. "No idea. I don't want to ask, either. She's already told me twice she doesn't have one."

"Yeah, that's got to be rough."

"People asked you about your mom. How did you handle it?" We didn't often talk about her mother, who'd left Sugar and her dad when Sug was an infant.

"You remember my dad. He just seemed enough for me. He was so matter-of-fact about all the changes. You know, in my body." Her cheeks flushed. "He explained everything, and he made it all okay. There was one girl, though. Misty Brown. What a mean girl. She'd talk about my mama, tease me, you know? I slugged her once, and Daddy said I could slug her again if she kept bugging me."

"I don't remember that."

"Yeah, in eighth grade."

I nudged her shoulder with mine. "You old meanie."

She chuckled. "A woman has to have her secrets."

Ginny skipped at the water's edge, digging her toes into the coarse, wet sand. She yanked her foot out and kicked at the water before stepping further into the surf.

As a kid, I loved the feeling of the water going out and my feet being sucked down into the sand. I pretended quicksand trapped me and pulled them out quickly. Memories of taking Becky here as a young child made me smile. Getting sunscreen on her wasn't fun, but once she got in the water, I couldn't get her out. She swam like a little fish.

I leaned back on my hands, tipping my face toward the sky. Sunshine warmed my bones. I took deep breaths, in and out, letting the end-of-school-year stress and the pain of seeing Becky drain into the sand. I pictured it all leaving my body, as I whispered prayers for restoration and healing.

What would that even be like?

A squeal startled me. I opened one eye.

"Ah, she met her first crab." Sug pushed herself up and brushed the sand off her hands. "I'll help her. Stay here. Relax."

After Sug made hand motions of crab pincers and finished consoling her, Ginny ran to the blanket, kicking sand and shaking her wet hair on me.

"I got bitted."

"Bitten," the teacher in me corrected. She ignored me and stuck her foot in my face. "Yes, you sure did. You okay?"

"Yep." She plopped on the blanket, pulled her foot around, and peered at it. "It's not like the time Smitty got me on the ankle. See?" She shoved her foot back at me and pointed to a tiny, faded scar.

I handed her a towel to dry off, making a mental note to work on her manners.

Sug sat and pulled the picnic basket toward her. "Who is Smitty?"

"Our stinky dog. He died. Choked on a chicken bone and went to doggy heaven." Ginny rubbed her tummy. "I'm hungry."

I bit my lip to hide my grin.

Sugar unpacked our breakfast. We munched on blueberry muffins and clementines while Ginny told us about her dog and his chicken bone, complete with details of her mom trying to fish it out of the dog's mouth. Sug's shoulders shook, and she snickered, clamping her hand over her mouth.

She cleared her throat. "Well, all right then." She repacked the leftovers. "This was fun, but I have a painting commissioned that I need to finish." She pointed to Ginny. "I paint beach scenes. Want to come over one day and see what I do?"

Her face lit up. "Sure."

Sug turned to me. "What are y'all doing today?"

We needed to shop, but maybe later. "After we clean up, we could go to the lighthouse."

Interest flickered across Ginny's face. "I've never been to one of those."

"Then it's time, kiddo. You can see forever from the top." Sugar leaned over, kissed her temple, and tapped me on the head. "I'll catch up with you later." She leaned closer and whispered, "This is a chance for a new beginning, Kat. It's time to face what's happened. It's way past time, if you ask me. Ginny will get you out of your rut."

I rolled my eyes. She wasn't singing a new song, just another verse. She might be right, or at least she thought so, but I didn't see a quick resolution. I knew nothing about Becky's life. Who knew where she had been for the past eight years? How was I supposed to deal with that? Did I even want to know? And what about an apology? How Becky dropped her daughter without explanation or apology baffled me.

"I'm not in a rut."

Sug's eyebrow twitched. She shook her head and headed up the dune to the stairs, a hand lifted in a wave. "Bye, you two. Have fun."

"Can I see my mama from the lighthouse?" Ginny's question interrupted my musings about ruts and Becky.

I pushed myself off the blanket and held out my hand. "No, sweetie, but come on. Have you ever used an outdoor shower? Your Grandpa Joe put it in years ago."

"Nope." She trudged off, leaving me with our blanket, her towel, and the picnic basket.

Okay then, I'm up to this. I can do this. I picked up our bundle of things. She waited on the curb in the parking lot.

"Which house is yours?" she asked.

I passed her a towel and pointed it out. "The shower is on the side of the garage."

Ginny ran through the yards to my house and danced in the outdoor shower, still wearing her shorts and T-shirt, getting wet but not very clean. She'd have to take a bath later to remove the sand from the tricky places.

She dressed and sat on my bed while I fixed my hair. "Grandma?"

I grabbed a comb and sat behind her to untangle her curls. "What's up, kiddo?"

"Why did my mama leave me here?"

Her voice was small. In the mirror over my dresser, I saw her bottom lip trembling. Fat tears rolled down her cheeks. I hesitated, then wrapped her in my arms, inhaling her warm scent of sunscreen and saltwater.

People leave, and she was too young to hear that. Joe and Becky left me. I couldn't say anything to make it better, but I didn't want this tiny girl to grow up thinking everyone did that.

"I won't leave you, honey." I kissed the top of her head.

I held Becky responsible for her daughter's pain. Who knew how this might play out, what Becky's plans were, or how long Ginny would be in my life? My granddaughter didn't deserve any of this.

She pulled away, turned around, and wiped her face on my shirt. I pretended to growl. "Now I have to change again."

She giggled and hopped off the bed, surprising me with her quick change of emotions.

"Go wash your face and blow your nose. I'll put on a clean shirt, and we can explore the lighthouse."

"The first Cape Henry Lighthouse was built after the Revolutionary War." I pulled into the parking lot. "It's ninety feet above the water table. Do you know what octagonal means?"

"Nope." Ginny craned her neck, peering up at the lighthouse.

I explained its eight-sided shape. Just looking at the historic, brown-bricked landmark encouraged me. It was solid, strong, grounded—everything I wanted to be.

Ginny ran up the stone steps at the lighthouse's base and danced from foot to foot. I took my time climbing them. Forty-nine might not be old, but the last day or two had taken something from me.

She peered up the spiral staircase as we entered. "We're goin' up that far?"

"Of course we are. That's why we're here."

She shook her head. "That's a long way."

"Let's try to spot dolphins from the top."

That spurred her on, even when her energy flagged before we were halfway. She let me lift her onto one of the windowsills, and she pressed her nose against the glass.

"No dolphins."

"No, we have to walk higher up."

She hopped down and hurried up the steps. I found her with her small hand cupped to a window. "Look, a dolphin. I think?" Her little face wrinkled in question.

I patted my chest, waiting for my heart to stop racing. "You're right. You've never seen one?"

She shook her head and walked around the room, narrating a blow-by-blow description of what she saw out the windows. "Grass, water, parking lot, cars, another lighthouse." She turned to me. "Why's there another one?"

"The Coast Guard uses it."

"Can we climb it?" she asked.

"No, just this one."

Her nose wrinkled. "Wasteful."

I snorted a laugh. She had a point. "Are you ready to go? We'll stop on the way home and buy crab to boil for dinner."

Ginny cocked an eyebrow, resembling Joe and Becky so much it stole my breath. "I'd like to eat the one that bit my toe."

"Well, we'll stick to the ones at the grocery store for today, but we can go crabbing soon."

As we descended the steep stairs, she muttered, "I'm gonna chow down on that crab."

Chapter 3

Ginny chose the crabs at the grocery store, and I loaded our buggy with tomatoes, lettuce, and cucumbers before we headed to the freezer aisle, where I studied the variety of frozen desserts.

"Do you like chocolate ice cream? My mom's old dog loved chocolate. My favorite is the kind with peanuts and lots of fudge."

A wail startled me. I turned to see Ginny crouched on the floor, pounding her little fists, her face red and tears streaming down her cheeks.

"Chocolate's bad for dogs." She glared at me, continuing to sob. "Your dog died from it. Smitty's dead. Everyone dies." Her small body crumpled on the hard floor. "Everybody leaves."

She whispered her last words.

All my teacher training deserted me. This was my granddaughter. She had every right to be furious and sad all at the same time. Ignoring the people staring at us, I sat beside her and patted her back. The store manager approached. My raised hand stopped him.

When Joe died, I cried. Then, our chocolate-ice-cream-loving dog passed away a few months later, and I bawled like a baby. Sometimes feelings explode. Ginny deserved this time to process what she'd been through. She'd been handed a raw deal, being left with a woman she'd never met. Of all people, she had earned the right to fall apart.

After several minutes, she sniffled and heaved a loud sigh. I brushed her tears away with my thumbs. She used her shirt sleeve to wipe her nose.

"Feel better?"

She shrugged.

We checked out and took our crabs, salad fixings, and strawberry ice cream home. I sent her out back to explore. While the water for the crabs boiled, I made coffee and nibbled on vanilla wafers. Ginny found a stick in the backyard and walked the perimeter, banging it on the chain-link fence with each step.

My granddaughter needed my help. I needed to figure out what to do. Everything was up in the air. Who knew when Becky would come to pick up Ginny? It might be tomorrow, next week, or eight years from now. She'd given me no clue. I had to plan with nothing to plan around.

Life revolved around Becky. I rolled my shoulders, took a deep breath, and blew it out. It took me years to find my way after she left the last time. In one day, she threatened the peace I'd carefully cultivated.

Sug would tell me to find paper and pencil again. Her words from the beach came back to me. This was a time for a new beginning. A chance to cope with what happened. An opportunity to help my granddaughter adjust.

At the desk in the kitchen, I flipped past the questions we'd written earlier. They weren't getting me anywhere. I headed three columns: Summer, Fall, and Winter Plans. We would sightsee and explore. Ginny could help paint my room, and I'd hire someone to mow the lawn. Do a couple of the things I'd planned for my break. Then, if she lived with me in the fall, I'd enroll her in Seaside Elementary School, where I worked.

It was a start.

Ginny came in for supper and scarfed down the crab and two bowls of salad. While we enjoyed our ice cream, she offered ideas for the Summer Plans list.

"We gotta go to the saltwater taffy shop and go crabbing. But we gotta wear sneakers. I don't wanna get bit again." She checked her injured foot. "Mama said there's some kind of 'musement park here." She licked her ice cream spoon and dropped it into the bowl. "That true?"

I scribbled her ideas on the paper. "Yes, we have two here." I added Neptune's Park and Atlantic Fun Park. I yawned and stretched my arms over my head. "It's late, and I'm tired. Go take a bath, and then I'll read to you."

"I don't have a book," she whined.

"My bookshelves are full." I waved her toward the bathroom. "I'll pick one out." I knew exactly which one I'd choose. Her mom's favorite, *Artie and the Princess*, still sat on the shelf in the living room. I curled up in the big chair, plucked it out, and opened it in my lap.

That old book smell—worn paper, years of hands holding it and turning the pages—enveloped me. A present on my eighth birthday, it was well-loved, even though Becky ripped a couple of edges as a child. Ginny would love the little dragon, Artie, and his friend, Princess Pandy.

Ten minutes passed before I realized the bathtub water wasn't running. Setting the book aside, I discovered Ginny on the bathroom rug, sound asleep. A long day of playing at the beach, getting chomped on by a crab, climbing almost two hundred steps, and having a meltdown wore her plumb out. After I managed to nudge her up enough for her to stumble to bed, I tucked Bearhoven under her chin.

I kissed her forehead. "I love you, baby girl." Pulling the door closed, I went back to the book. *Artie and the Princess* was my favorite too. I read it through before going to bed.

We had time to read, buy saltwater taffy, and enjoy amusement parks. A sense of possibility—grins and giggles and plenty of time to get to know my granddaughter—filled me.

The sliver of hope I went to bed with evaporated like mist the following day when I remembered Becky hadn't mentioned when she would return.

"Grandma?" Ginny chewed her cereal with her mouth open. "Grandma?" She snapped her fingers in front of my face.

I waved her hand away. "Hmm?"

"Can we go to the beach? I wanna swim today." She pushed her bowl toward me. "I'm done eatin'."

I had a secret I didn't want to tell her. The beach, with its sand, birds, shells, and sunshine, was amazing. But not saltwater. I never liked how it tasted or dried on my skin. Not to mention my healthy fear of biting crabs.

But Ginny wanted to learn to swim, so I'd have to go in the water. A little crab or salt-laden water wouldn't keep me from my granddaughter's wishes. I would be brave.

"Sure." I placed our breakfast dishes in the sink. "We have to go shopping first, though."

"Why?" She pouted.

"You don't have a swimsuit, and I need a new one." Last time I'd looked, mine had dry-rotted.

We headed to one of the department stores at the mall. Before visiting the swimsuit section, we found another nightgown, underwear, two pairs of shorts, several T-shirts, and sandals for Ginny. She picked out a plain blue one-piece swimsuit, tried it on, and threw it over my arm along with the rest of her new clothes.

She rubbed her hands together. "Now can we go?"

"I need a swimsuit, too, remember?" I ruffled her hair and held my breath. She didn't pull away.

Tiny victories.

My bathing suit choices were bikinis or what Ginny called "old lady" suits. Those were fine with me, but Ginny kept pushing skimpy bikinis my way.

"Mama would like this one." She held up the tiniest pink string bikini ever made.

"I'm a bit older than your mom. She's only twenty-four."

She squinted and looked me up and down. "Well, yeah, you're pretty old. You're a grandma, so maybe seventy?"

"Ha-ha, funny girl." I grabbed a blue suit similar to hers but with a skirt-style bottom. "This will do."

"Try it on." She crossed her arms and stood in my way.

No way. If she thought I was seventy, wait until she saw my stretched-out, jiggly tummy. "No, honey, it'll fit." *I hope.* "Let's go change and head to the beach."

My words persuaded her to leave.

At home, we put her clothes in her room and quickly changed. As we walked to the beach, I told her what I knew about bodysurfing, even though I couldn't remember the last time I'd done it. I swallowed more water than Ginny. While she gracefully surfed to shore, I washed the mountain of golden, pebbly sand out of the bottom of my suit. After I gave up surfing, I stood ankle-deep in the water, watching her.

"Where'd you find the kid, Kat?"

My heart beat triple time. I grabbed my friend's arm. "Oh my, Mac, where did you come from? Don't scare me like that."

"Just taking my daily beach stroll."

Mac Walsh, a fellow teacher at Seaside Elementary, was pale as chalk and covered in freckles. He dodged the sun and always begged me to take his class out for recess so he wouldn't burn. But today he wore a sunhat and sunglasses, skin slick with sunscreen, nose striped with zinc.

Something was up. I smelled gossip. "Mac?" I narrowed my eyes.

"The kid, Kat. Where'd she come from?"

"Who sent you?" Two could play this game. I wasn't giving any information until he did. First.

He took off his sunglasses and blinked his pale blue eyes. "What do you mean? I was walking and saw you teaching that girl to bodysurf." He pointed to Ginny. "I'm just curious." He crossed his arms, his short-sleeved Madras shirt pulling against his biceps.

I could wait him out, but I'd taught at Seaside Elementary for years. He knew about Becky. Ginny ended our stalemate.

She ran to me, shaking her wild, wet hair and showering us in cold water droplets. "Come back in, Grandma." She grabbed my hand and tugged.

Mac's eyes widened. "Grandma?"

"Ginny, give me a minute." I put my hand on her head and gestured to Mac. "This is my friend, Mr. Walsh. Mac, this is my granddaughter, Ginny. She's Becky's little girl."

Surprise lit his face, but he stuck out his hand to shake Ginny's. She stared, slapped it, and ran back into the water.

I would put learning manners at the top of our Summer Plans list. The expressions flashing across his face were comical. Almost.

"Becky's back? Wow, that's great." A thoughtful expression crossed his face. "It is great, right?"

My shoulders drooped. Mac was my friend, not a gossip. He lived two streets over and probably saw us, wondering who I had with me. "Becky isn't here. She left Ginny with me the other day."

His mouth dropped open. "Wait. She left her here? How long? Is she coming back? Did she ever tell you that you had a granddaughter?"

So many questions. Where to start?

"Yes, she stopped by and left her with me. I'd never heard about Ginny before then. I don't have a clue where Becky is now or when she'll be back." I shaded my eyes and kept an eye on Ginny.

He whistled. "That is crazy. Just so ... Becky."

I couldn't help but chuckle. "True, very true. You never know, do you? She looked rough and skinny. Ginny said they'd been in Mississippi, but they now live in Tennessee. She mentioned being near Graceland, so I'm guessing Memphis." I picked at my fingernail. "I'm not sure. Becky didn't give me any information or a phone number. I'm clueless."

Hands on his hips, he shook his head. "I'm sorry." He scuffed his foot in the sand. "Sorry about Becky. I don't understand how she can treat you like that."

"Not your fault. It's okay to ask about her. I suppose I have to accept it for what it is." The words stuck in my mouth. Why did I have to accept this? I'd been a grandmother for six years and didn't even know.

"I'm not sure about that." He patted my shoulder. "I'm heading home. Call me if you want some company, okay?"

"Thanks, Mac." After he left, I watched Ginny and thought about what I told him. Accepting what happened made me more than mad.

Livid best described how I felt. It seemed like I'd been angry forever. Mad at Joe for dying. Mad at Becky for leaving. Angry because things happened to me, and I didn't take any action. I shoved my feelings down where I didn't have to deal with them. I'd become complacent and gotten used to my "rut," as Sug called it.

Enough was enough.

I would take control, deal with my feelings, and quit being a victim of other people's decisions and bad choices.

Later in the week, Sug joined Ginny and me for dinner. While Ginny played outside, I told her what I'd discussed with Mac.

"So, what will you do?" She put napkins and forks on the table on the sunporch while I dished out the spaghetti.

"I'm not sure." I put two bowls on the table and went back for the third. "I haven't taken an active role in my life in a long time. And I'm tired of being angry." I set down the last bowl. "I want to help Ginny. Give her the kind of life she deserves."

Sug grabbed a stick of margarine, a knife, and a loaf of bread. "Helping her is a great goal. But you're being hard on yourself about not taking an active role. You've done the best you could in a hard situation."

I leaned on the back of one of the chairs. "I'm trying to be realistic. First, I need to contact Becky. Ginny asks about her every day. I don't know what to tell her. I should have a way to contact her. Don't you think?"

"Of course you should."

"Can you keep her one afternoon? I'll go to the library and find phone books and phone numbers." I frowned. "Do libraries still have those? If

Becky is listed, I can talk to her. Her Instagram account is private, and she's not active on any other social media platforms. I can't even message her on Instagram. I thought a phone book might be the best place to start."

Sug touched my arm. "I can watch Ginny anytime. No problem."

"I want to ask her a few more questions. I've tried to listen when she mentions something, but I need to talk to my daughter." I opened the back door and called Ginny inside. After I sent her off to wash her hands, I turned back to Sugar. "She told me her mom has left her with other people too."

Sug's eyes widened.

Dinnertime conversation revealed more insight into my granddaughter's life. Aside from remembering Graceland, she said it took a whole day, a night, and half a day to drive to my house. That sounded right if they drove from West Tennessee.

"Do you have a phone at your house?" I asked.

"We don't have a house, Grandma." She slurped her noodles. One smacked her in the nose, and she giggled.

"What?" Sug and I asked at the same time.

Ginny twirled more noodles with her fork. "Nah, we live in a trailer."

"Oh?" *That's okay. Better than nothing at all.*

"Mhm." She held out her bowl. "More psghetti?"

"Please." I scooped out a second helping and returned to the table. "Where you live, is it around other people?"

"Mhm. Lotsa people. Ours is green. My friend Jack's is white. Till the fire. Now it's kinda brownish white."

A fire. My granddaughter and daughter lived in a trailer park, maybe near Elvis's mansion, and one of the trailers caught on fire. I wasn't sure I wanted to hear anything else.

My expression must have given away my panic, because Sug laid her hand on mine. "Honey, what's your last name?"

"Johnson." Ginny sat straight in her chair, chest puffed out. "Virginia Morgan Johnson is my name. My birthday is May twenty-fifth. I'm six. I'll go to first grade this year."

Sug kept her hand pressed over mine. "What school do you go to?"

"Gardenview." Ginny slurped more noodles.

"Is that in Memphis?"

"Near Graceland." She pointed her fork at me. "I told you."

She did. She sure did. This child told me things I didn't even realize. Gardenview Elementary in Memphis. Surely, I could find a phone number.

Chapter 4

Monday afternoon found me heading for the library, not for books, but for answers. Ginny told me the trailer didn't have a landline, and her mom's cell phone—when she had it—was unreliable. "Not always, though," she told me. "I think she loses it sometimes."

Couldn't pay for it, more likely.

Getting to the Oceanfront Area Library took me less than ten minutes. I entered, steeling myself for whatever I would discover. I wanted time to myself and a chance to find answers. The answers themselves, or my imagination of what they might be, were another matter. What-ifs consumed me.

It had been a long time since anyone, let alone a little girl, lived with me night and day. Figuring out how to be a grandparent to a child who hadn't had much parenting was stressful. New gray hairs popped out daily. I avoided my magnifying mirror. The wrinkles must be worse.

One of the librarians steered me to the computers and showed me how to access phone books online. I found the one for Memphis, Tennessee. My hands shook as I wrote the information for Gardenview Elementary. Then I searched for Becky's phone number. Finding cell numbers was nearly impossible, but I hoped she still had a landline.

What if it were listed? Would I have the courage to call?

No listing appeared for Becky or Rebecca Johnson. I even checked for a "Johnson, B." or "Johnson, R." with no luck. I shoved my disappointment down and ignored the tiny bit of relief rushing through me. With my notebook under my arm, I headed for the children's section.

A display of new nonfiction books situated beside the checkout counter caught my eye—one of the titles, *Addiction,* written in large red letters on the front of the book, tempted me. Should I learn more about addiction? I never had before. Just saying Becky had a drug problem and that she might be an addict was hard enough.

I overrode my many questions and added the book to my stack. This was my summer of revelation. Maybe I'd find answers to my questions and solve my problems.

At home, I found Sug and Ginny in my bedroom. My furniture stood in the middle of the room. Sug cleaned the baseboards while Ginny chased dust bunnies with the broom.

"Having fun?" I leaned against the doorframe and held out the children's books. "Here you go, kiddo. I found these for you. One's on shells, and the other is about sea creatures."

"Oh, yay!" She dropped the broom, took the books, and headed for the living room. "I'm gonna read in the big chair."

"Sure, honey. That's fine."

Sugar rocked back on her heels. "Any luck? Did you find any numbers?"

"One for the school but nothing for Becky." I showed her the book I'd checked out. "Did you know they had books on addiction?"

She rolled her eyes. "Well, it is a library, Kat."

"Ha-ha." I gestured to my room. "What are y'all doing in here? I thought you'd still be at your house."

"Ginny lost interest in my project pretty fast. She wanted to paint, so we came here since you planned to redo your bedroom this summer."

"You're the best. Let me grab the vacuum. Ginny only stirred the dust around."

That weekend, we painted my bedroom the faintest shade of purple. Ginny insisted on a soft lavender with fresh white trim instead of the pale green I'd imagined. I found fabric for the two windows facing the front yard. It took a few evenings with my sewing machine to make the curtains how I wanted. Ginny helped me hang them, and afterward, we surveyed the finished room.

"I'm glad you and Ms. Sug helped me with this. It topped my list of things to do this summer." I hugged her to my side.

"Know what's on my list, Grandma?"

"The taffy shop," we said at the same time.

The week after my trip to the library, I woke up, poured some coffee, and settled down to read the news on my phone. When I went for a second cup, it dawned on me that Ginny still hadn't gotten up. I knocked on her door and peeked into her room. She wasn't in her bed.

"Ginny?" I checked the bathroom and called her name again. I opened the door to the second floor. The oppressive air hit me in the face. Would she have slept up there?

I traipsed up the steep staircase, calling her name. At the top, I turned left into the open bedroom, but I only found dust motes floating in the hazy heat. A peek under the double bed, in the closet, and in the tiny bathroom revealed nothing.

I hurried down the stairs and jerked open the front door. "Ginny? Ginny, are you out here?" I looked around both sides of the house and opened the gate to the backyard. "Ginny! Virginia Johnson!"

No answer. I called Sug.

"Ginny's missing." My hands shook, and my heart raced. I panted, trying to catch my breath.

"Missing?"

"I've checked everywhere. Upstairs, in the backyard, out front, even in the garage." I drew in a deep breath and blew it out slowly.

"Would she have gone to the beach without you?"

"Oh, no. No, no." My stomach dove into a free fall before surging up into my throat. I clasped my hand over my mouth. Ginny was six. Would she go to the beach—a short walk from my house, not far down my road, and over the steps—by herself? She knew how to get there.

"How was she last night?" Sug's question interrupted my panicked thoughts.

"She cried at bedtime. She gets whiny at night and cries."

"I'm sure. Poor kid. She's had to deal with a lot."

"I know. Can you come help me look?" I racked my brain, trying to remember what Ginny wore to bed the night before. What if we had to involve the police? What would I tell them?

"Yes, give me a few minutes, and I'll be there." She hung up.

I dropped my head in my hands. Where hadn't I looked? My neighbor had a small guest apartment next door, but Ginny didn't know about it.

Oh Lord, where is my girl?

My cell rang. I jumped, grabbed it, and stabbed the accept call button.

"Kat, Ginny is here. She ... she's curled up in the rocker on my front porch," Sug stammered.

"Oh, thank You, Lord." Relief battled confusion. "Is she okay? How did she get to your house?"

"She's fine. She said she left early this morning, snuck out her window, and walked here."

I smacked myself on the forehead. I hadn't checked the windows. "I'm glad she didn't go to the beach. What else did she say? Why did she leave?"

"She's missing her mom, I think. I sent her to the bathroom to wash up, and then we'll talk about moms and running away."

"I'm just glad she's okay." I blew out a breath. "I think this took ten years off my life."

"Me too." Several seconds passed before she added, "Apparently, she remembered I didn't have a mom and wanted to ask me some questions. I'll bring her home after our chat."

"Thank you, Sug. Tell Ginny I love her."

I replayed what happened, filtering through all the what-ifs and reminding myself they hadn't come true. Ginny's decision to run away had nothing to do with me and everything to do with her mom. She lost trust and faith in her mom. She didn't know what to do, where to turn, or if she could trust me. I'd have to show her.

Consistent actions and love. That's all I came up with.

This grandparenting thing was tough. I'd been coordinating so many aspects of our lives. I tried to keep Ginny from being sad, make sure everything went her way, and get her to respond emotionally to me. It was time to back off and let her learn to adjust to life with me in her own way. If she was standoffish, so be it. I couldn't entertain her every second of every day. That wasn't healthy for either of us.

On sunny mornings, Ginny and I ate our breakfast out back. Several days after she ran away to Sugar's, I was updating my calendar while she crunched on her toast. I still needed to hire someone to mow my yard.

Otherwise, one of my neighbors would complain. And I wanted to clean out my garage. I hadn't forgotten my resolutions from just a few weeks ago.

I tapped my pen on the calendar. Ginny stood beside me, running her finger over the boxes for each day.

"Can we put my birthday on your calendar?" Her sweet expression melted my heart.

"Of course." I flipped to May and wrote her name on the twenty-fifth.

"When's your birthday?" she asked.

I grimaced. My birthday wasn't something I liked to acknowledge. "Next week on July fourth."

Ginny beamed. "The Fourth of July? Were you there when they made it the Fourth? You know, when they signed the paper thingy? The declaring thing?"

"The Declaration of Independence?"

"Yeah, that one. We watched a play about it."

A snort popped out. "No, dear, I am not that old."

She asked for a pen. "Can you put it on the right month?" She gestured to the calendar and circled the fourth. "Let's have a party." Ginny bounced from foot to foot. "We can invite Ms. Sug and Mr. Mac and, and ..." She narrowed her eyebrows. "Grandma, do you have any other friends?"

We saw Sugar most days. Mac often joined us at the beach. Other than that, nope, no other friends. "Not really, but we can invite them and have a party. Just the four of us. It'll be fun." *What was I saying?* The words kept coming. "We can eat out here at the picnic table."

"And have boiled crab and balloons." She darted into the kitchen, returned to the table with my notebook, and shoved it toward me. "Here, make a list."

I dreaded the Fourth of July. The fireworks were fantastic, but getting older was not my idea of fun. The wrinkles were a little deeper. The aches and pains lasted a little longer. But Friday morning, I woke with a lightness in my spirit. I stretched and thought about the day ahead—my fiftieth birthday. I never thought I'd be this content to celebrate it.

I never imagined I would have my granddaughter with me either.

Ginny pattered down the hall and burst into my room, singing, "Happy birthday, Grandma. Happy birthday to you." She climbed onto my bed and offered a rare hug.

Warmth radiated throughout my body.

"You gotta get up, Grandma. We gotta get ready." She bounced on the bed, her hair flying around her face.

"I'm up, I'm up." I waved her out of the room. "Let me put some clothes on, okay?"

We planned the party for a late lunch. Then we would head to the boardwalk to watch the fireworks. Sug was making the cake, and Mac said he'd bring a fruit salad. I bought crabs and stuck them in the pot to boil. Ginny insisted on blowing up balloons. Once I twisted them closed, she kicked them around the room. Then, she asked for posterboard to make a "Happy Birthday" sign.

"I have some tucked behind the chest in the living room," I said, thankful she could use my leftover school supplies.

She pulled out a few sheets, picked her favorite color, and brought it to the table.

"Grandma, how do you spell 'happy'?" She frowned, her nose scrunched up. Her tongue stuck out to one side. "What letter makes the *huh*?"

"H." I lowered the flame under the pot and joined her on the porch. She managed an "H" and looked up.

"What else?"

I spelled the rest of "happy" and then "birthday" for her. She ran her finger under each word, sounding them out.

"Can you write your name on it?" I asked.

When she finished, we hung the poster out back. Besides saying 'Happy Birthday,' it had sketches of crabs with pincers wide open, bug-eyed looking fish, starfish dancing around the edges, and her name scribbled in the corner.

She helped me tie balloons to strings. I explained that, without helium, the balloons wouldn't fly. We tied a bunch to a low-hanging tree limb near the picnic table.

Ginny clapped. "They look like big lightbulbs."

"Yes, they do. Let's add some streamers. Ms. Sug and Mr. Mac should be here soon."

Sug arrived with my favorite German chocolate cake. I swiped a finger of frosting when she wasn't looking.

"I saw that," she said.

"You have eyes in the back of your head."

Mac walked around the side of the house carrying a bowl full of fruit. "Who does?"

I pointed at Sug. "Hang on, I'll get the rest of the food. Ginny, can you help me?"

We carried the crabs and a bowl of melted butter to the picnic table and sat down to a feast fit for a birthday girl. I thanked God for my friends and Ginny.

She sat beside me. We ate until we were stuffed. She coughed several times and cleared her throat. I leaned down and watched her. Her lips were puffy, and panic flared in her eyes.

"Ginny? Ginny, what's wrong?"

Chapter 5

Ginny covered her mouth and continued coughing. Each cough sounded raspier than the one before.

Sugar turned pale. "Kat, call 911." She helped Ginny into the house while I rushed in behind them and searched for my cell phone.

"Kat, tell them it's an allergic reaction." Sug's voice stayed calm and controlled.

"I know, I know." I found my cell phone on the coffee table. My hands shook as I entered the three numbers. At the call taker's answer, it took everything in me to calm down enough and explain the situation. The person volunteered to stay on the phone until help arrived, but I hung up. "Sugar, they're coming." My voice trembled.

"Good. Grab your antihistamine. You have some from last summer when you got poison ivy."

Thank God she knew me so well. I took the medicine box from the linen closet where I'd stashed it after Ginny moved in. Rummaging through it, I found a bottle of little pink pills. "They're for adults. Can she take these?"

Sug examined the label. "One, I think." She sat Ginny in a chair and handed her a cup of water along with the pill.

Ginny's breathing still sounded funny. Her face and lips were even more swollen. The faint sound of sirens blared from up the road.

Mac ran out front and directed the ambulance to my yard. Emergency Medical Technicians hurried into my living room. One EMT reached into a black bag and removed various instruments. He checked Ginny's pulse, temperature, and blood pressure.

While he worked, another EMT asked questions.

"We were eating. It's my birthday. We were eating out back." My words stumbled over each other.

Sugar took over, explaining what Ginny had eaten and what medicine we'd given to her. The EMT started an IV. I crouched down by Ginny, taking her hand.

She gripped mine hard. "I want my mama." Her words came out in a whisper. She lifted her chin, straining to breathe.

"I know, honey." What else could I say? Every child wants their mother when they're hurt or sick. I smoothed back her hair.

"Okay, Mom, we're going to take her to the hospital." The EMTs raised the stretcher's rails and rolled it to the front door.

"I'm her grandma." I followed them outside.

"Grandma, right. No problem. Where's Mom? We'll need her consent to treat."

"I, I have no idea where she is." Would they refuse to help Ginny? Why hadn't I insisted that Becky give me a way to contact her?

"No problem. We'll work things out, but let's get going. You can ride with us. We'll take her to Princess Anne Hospital."

I nodded, climbing inside the ambulance. Sug handed my purse to me.

As the doors closed, I heard her say, "Mac, put the food away. I'll follow Kat to the hospital."

It took forever to get Ginny into a room. Sug and I tried to distract her, but she wasn't having it. Once inside, we waited and waited for the doctor to arrive. I kept telling myself that if they thought it was an emergency, they'd have rushed in to help. But after pacing the tiny room over and over, I opened the door and peered into the hall.

"Where's the doctor? I want to know what he's going to do."

"Grandma, I'm all right." Ginny's husky voice frightened me, but the swelling in her face and lips had lessened. "I'm sorry I was grumpy."

Her strength floored me.

"Oh, honey." I sat beside her and brushed the hair off her forehead, trailing my fingers down her cheek. "I'm sorry. You're so brave. The doctor will be here soon. We'll find out how to spring you from this place."

Her eyes fluttered closed, and her wheezing eased a bit more.

"The medicines are working." Sug blew out a breath. "Whew, that scared me." She wrapped her arms around herself and rocked in her chair.

It scared me too. What in the world was I doing, pretending I could take care of this child? I couldn't even contact Becky and find out if Ginny had other allergies.

The doctor knocked and entered, bringing my racing thoughts to an end. "Mrs. Johnson? Nice to see you again."

"Dr. Fulsom, hi. This is my granddaughter, Ginny, and my friend, Sugar." I turned to Sug. "His son was in my class last year."

The doctor read Ginny's chart. "What happened here?"

I answered his questions, adding that she had eaten crab before, but he interrupted.

"It sounds like the culprit was the crab, the coconut in the German chocolate cake, or one of the fruits in the fruit bowl. She needs an appointment with an allergist, Mrs. Johnson. Here." He scribbled on a piece of paper and handed it to me. Peering over the top of his glasses, he added, "Make sure she gets this checked out. She had a severe reaction. Next time might be worse."

"I will. I don't have any information for the hospital, though. My daughter didn't tell me how to contact her. And I don't have Ginny's birth certificate or social security number."

He tapped his pen on the chart. "Give the nurse your name and contact information. I'll help you straighten it out. We'll also send you home with a prescription for an EpiPen. Fill it right away. The nurse will explain how to use it."

"Thank you," I said.

After two more hours of observation, they let me take my girl home. As we drove down Laskin Road, the fireworks started at the boardwalk.

"Ginny." She dozed in the backseat. I nudged her. "Ginny, look, fireworks."

Her eyes shot open. "Oh, they're so pretty." She turned to me. "Happy birthday to you, Grandma."

My heart swelled. "Thank you, sweetie. Thank you."

It would be a long time before Ginny ate crab, mixed fruit, or German chocolate cake again. Her allergic reaction strengthened my resolve to find answers. I wanted to talk to Becky. At this point, I didn't care about her coming to get Ginny, giving her a second chance to be in my life, or rebuilding a relationship with her.

I only cared about helping my granddaughter.

My head throbbed thinking about calling Ginny's school in Memphis. Our days were filled with fun adventures. Ginny was settling in. I rarely saw her thumb in her mouth, and most of the time she accepted my hugs. But I had to take responsibility.

Monday after lunch, while Ginny played in the backyard, I sat inside at the table with my cell phone in one hand, flipping through my notebook for the phone number I needed with the other. With my heart in my throat and shaking hands, I punched in the numbers.

"Gardenview Elementary, this is Principal Patterson speaking."

"Oh, hi." Why was the principal answering? "Um, this is Katherine Johnson. My granddaughter Ginny, Virginia Johnson, attends Gardenview, I think." *Get a grip, woman. You sound like an idiot.*

"Yes?"

"She does?" I asked.

"Well, you said she does." The woman's exasperation came through the line.

I rolled my eyes. "I think she does. Can you confirm that?"

Paper rustled on the other end, followed by tapping on a keyboard. "You're her grandmother?"

"Yes, I'm Kat Johnson. Ginny is staying with me this summer. I live in Virginia Beach. I'm trying to contact my daughter, Becky Johnson, Ginny's mom."

"You don't have your daughter's number? Mrs. Johnson, I can't give out that information." Her words washed away any hope I had. "I don't normally answer the phone, but I'm the only one in today. Since it's summer." The last sentence held a bit of snark.

Now she wondered why I was calling in the summer. Great. "Please, Mrs. Patterson. I need some help here." I told her everything, including Ginny's trip to the hospital, hoping it would convince her to help me.

"I understand, Mrs. Johnson." She paused and cleared her throat. "The best I can do is contact your daughter and give her your information. I'm sorry, but I can't give you her number."

"Thank you. I understand. Please give Becky my information as soon as you can."

"Of course, I'll do my best." Her tone softened. "Ginny is a sweet girl. She liked kindergarten here. But her mom ..."

I leaned forward, hoping to learn more.

"She's your daughter, so I hate to say anything against her. Ginny often came to school with dirty clothes and tangled hair. Her teacher talked to me several times about having someone visit their home, but she never saw any bruises or anything. The teacher said Ginny is as smart as a whip. Being dirty is not a crime. She just felt things weren't ... ideal ... at home."

It wasn't ideal, and they did nothing about it. As a teacher, I knew they needed concrete reasons to ask for a home visit, but these people let my granddaughter slip through the cracks. I attempted to keep my frustration out of my voice. "Have you met my daughter, Mrs. Patterson? Have you seen her?"

"No. I've spoken with Ginny's teacher and have her notes from Ginny's file in front of me."

I gritted my teeth and held in a groan. The principal offered to contact Becky, which was my best bet. I blew out a slow breath and asked her again to contact my daughter as soon as possible, stressing Ginny's allergic reaction and the need for more information. Then I hung up.

Thoughts of what I should have done whirled through my mind. How could I fault the school? They might not be going above and beyond, but neither had I. I stopped searching for Becky years ago. I didn't even know about Ginny until last month.

I banged my hand on the table. Doing nothing brought me to this place of frustration and grief. But I could fix this.

I wouldn't lose Ginny like I'd lost her mom.

I finally made an appointment with an allergist for Ginny. Then I came up with a brilliant idea—a dog. A dog would solve my problems. Ginny would fall in love with it. I'd heard how she talked about Smitty. The dog would be hers. She'd learn responsibility, take him for walks, and tell him her secrets.

Without revealing our destination, I drove to the animal shelter. When we got out of the car, Ginny pinched her nose.

"It stinks. Why are we here?"

"Well, I thought we'd look for a dog." I swung my purse strap over my shoulder. It did stink outside. No getting around it.

Ginny followed me in, her fingers still clamped on her nose.

A receptionist greeted us. "Hello. What can I do for you?" Several candles burned. Bottles of room deodorizing spray sat on her desk.

"We're looking for a dog," I said.

"Grandma." Ginny tugged on my shirt. She sounded funny with her nose plugged. "Grandma, I like that one." She pointed down the hall.

I turned to see the dog in the first cage. His fur, white and matted, stuck out in all directions. And he was huge. That dog had love handles.

"How about something not quite so big, Ginny. Maybe a puppy?"

She approached the cage and made kissing noises at the mutt. His heavy tail thumped on the floor, and he jumped up.

"Oh, Grandma." She kneeled on the floor by the cage. "Can I pet him? He's so cute."

"No one's ever called him cute." The receptionist took out a key chain and opened the cage.

"Wait, I think a smaller dog might be good. Don't you, Ginny?" This was less a dog and more a miniature horse. Ginny and the lady both ignored me. The dog sat when told to. When his crate opened, his tail swished on the ground. His rump wriggled too.

Ginny held the back of her hand to him as the lady instructed. He sniffed and licked it. Even his tongue was large.

He must eat a bag of food a day.

"How long has he been here?" Maybe he'd just been picked up and was waiting for his owner to arrive.

Ginny crawled into the cage and sat cross-legged beside him, combing his tangled fur with her fingers. One of his eyes had what looked like doggy eyeliner encircling it, while the other had only a bit.

"Oh, Oliver's been here a couple of months, haven't you, boy?" The receptionist cooed and slipped him a treat.

"A couple of months. No one's gotten him?"

"Well, yes." Her lips twitched. "Someone adopted him, but they brought him back."

Ah, the story changed. "Why?" I imagined he tore up their door, dug up their bushes, or ate the couch.

She smirked. "Allergies."

Oh, well.

"Grandma." Ginny climbed out of the crate, grabbed my hand, and pulled me closer to the dog. "He likes his ears rubbed. Try it. You'll love it. He's soft."

Part of the stink in the building came from him, but I petted his gigantic head and rubbed his ear. His fur left my fingers greasy. I wouldn't call it soft.

"We'll even give him a bath before you take him," the receptionist said, pulling out all the stops.

"Please, Grandma." Ginny hugged me, leaning her head into my belly. "They'll wash him, and he'll smell great." She turned to Oliver and scratched him under his chin. "Won't you, boy?"

I doubted one bath would cure this odor, but Ginny's hug melted my heart.

"We'll take him. But please bathe him first."

And that's how I got a dog.

Chapter 6

We shortened the dog's name to Ollie, and he played the role of our built-in doorbell. Any car using my driveway to turn around caused a deep, beagle-type bay to roar out of his huge lungs. Sometimes it made us giggle, but on weekends, it became annoying with the heavy beach traffic.

Ginny loved him, but he followed me around. Most likely because I fed him every morning. After going back to the store for more chow twice in one week, I called Mac to help with the biggest bag of dog food I could find.

Mac took one look at him and snickered. "He's white."

"Yes, I noticed that."

"You know white dogs are prone to allergies?"

Allergies? Oh. Now I understood. The dog had allergies, not the previous owners. *Hmm.*

Mac pointed to where Ollie lay on the cool linoleum in the kitchen, panting. "That's why his tummy is irritated, and probably the inside of his ears." He flipped Ollie's ear back, revealing a bright pink.

"He pulls himself across the carpet to scratch himself," I said. He was tearing up my rug, not to mention the holes he dug in the backyard and the way he'd rounded the edges of my picnic table with his teeth.

"Yeah." Mac rubbed Ollie. The dog groaned with contentment, rolling onto his back and almost knocking Mac over. "Take him to the vet, Kat. They can give him allergy medicine or shots." He patted Ollie again and stood. "You might consider ordering his food and having it delivered. Then you won't have to pick it up."

"Okay, I'll do that right away." I couldn't help but laugh. This wasn't why I adopted a dog. He was supposed to be Ginny's friend, not a money pit. And bringing him home from the animal shelter was not fun. Not only did Ollie have allergies, but he also got car sick.

"We can take him to the vet in my truck if that would help," Mac said.

"Yes to the truck. Bring a towel. Trust me on this."

I flipped through the pages of the book on addiction. After renewing it once at the library, I wanted to complete it and move on. If I understood Becky's issues, I'd explain what she was doing and convince her to change.

That is, when I talked to her. If she came back. If she acknowledged what she did, she would stop. I would make it happen. And she'd apologize. And maybe I'd be able to trust her.

And maybe donkeys would fly.

None of that took my feelings into account. I didn't think I would ever trust her. Guilt flushed through me. Then I reminded myself that Becky hadn't earned my trust in years. Eight years.

Our last fight flashed through my mind. The desperate look in her eyes was why I let her back into my life this summer. She wore the same expression as when I'd bandaged her scraped knee as a little girl. It was just the two of us, and I could make things better. Then she decided I couldn't, and she left.

With a sigh, I grabbed my pack of cigarettes, a cup of coffee, and a lighter, and joined Ginny outside. I wanted to ask her if she'd heard about the "Just Say No" or DARE programs. She couldn't think drugs were good. If people could "just say no," why didn't Becky?

How could it be that hard? That's what I didn't understand.

"Ginny, did they have 'Just Say No' people at your school when you were in kindergarten? Or the DARE program?" I lit my cigarette and waited for her answer.

She scrunched her face, mouth skewed to one side. "Somethin' like that. Saying no to drugs?" She collected sticks and stacked them.

"Yes. What did you think of it?"

She looked up, her little eyebrows knitted. "Drugs are bad."

"Yes, yes, they are." At least she understood—one less hurdle to jump. She went back to her sticks. "Mama said it's stupid."

"Wait, what? What's stupid? Drugs?"

She stood and placed her hands on my shoulders. "Drugs aren't bad, Grandma. Some people are bad, but not drugs. I tried telling them what Mama said at school, but no one listened."

She reminded me of Becky as a teenager. I'd tried to reason with her, but Becky said I should have an open mind and be "cool."

Words escaped me. Why would Becky tell her daughter that drugs weren't harmful? Now it was up to me to explain that her mother had it all wrong. This added to the long list of things I wanted to say to my daughter. If I ever got ahold of her.

I still hadn't received a call back from the principal at Ginny's school. Or a call from Becky. I tried the school again, hoping to talk to Mrs. Patterson, but no one answered. Seaside Elementary closed for part of the summer. Schools in Tennessee might have done the same. I'd wait another week and try again.

Ginny's appointment with the allergist was approaching, and they required specific medical information. Only my daughter could answer my questions.

In late July, the day before Ginny's allergy appointment, Ollie bayed, and I ignored him. There were still plenty of beachgoers. My signs to keep people off my lawn still stood, although a couple were bent and leaning.

Ginny was changing after our morning walk while I prepared a light lunch. Ollie stood on the sunporch, howling.

"Ollie, shush." After several rounds of his baying, I wiped my hands on the kitchen towel, went to the porch, and glanced through the windows.

Déjà vu. The same rusty car sat in the driveway. The driver's door opened. Becky emerged as skinny as she'd been eight weeks earlier. I put Ollie out back and went into the garage. Swinging the door open brought me face-to-face with my daughter. Thoughts swirled in my head. In a split second, my emotions cycled through relief, pain, and anger, settling on fear.

"Hi, Mom." Becky pushed her sunglasses on top of her head.

"Hi, Beck." On the outside, I was cool as a cucumber. Inside, my heart raced. I wanted to grab Ginny, run, and hide. "You're here." It wasn't a question.

"Yep, Ginny needs to go back for school." She picked at the cuticle on her thumb.

School. "Did the principal call you?" My fingernails dug into my palms.

"Yeah, so here I am." Becky shrugged as if driving nearly nine hundred miles was no big deal.

I just wanted a phone call. She didn't have to come. Things were under control. "Well, come on in." I gestured to the house. "Ginny's getting dressed."

She turned and walked back to the car. "Tell her to grab her things. I'll wait."

"Becky." The words stuck. How could she do this? I had so much to tell her—beach trips, Ginny bodysurfing, climbing the lighthouse, picking Ollie, the hospital, the questions Sug and I wrote, what I learned about addiction. It all twisted together in my head.

I had to try. "Becky, come on in for a minute. We need to talk."

Her nostrils flared. "No, Mom. Just send her out."

My good judgment flew out the window. I stamped my foot. "No, you listen to me, young lady. I need to talk to you. There are things you need to know." My voice ended in a growl. I wrapped my arms around my waist.

"Really, Mom?" Her lip curled. "You don't change, do you? Send *my* daughter out. Now." She slid into the car and started the engine, keeping her eyes averted.

In one summer, my world changed. My heart expanded and then exploded. My long-lost daughter returned, and I met my amazing granddaughter. Now, my summer was over. They left, and I was alone.

Again.

The last few weeks of summer dragged on. Ginny lived with me for two months, but life without her now was unthinkable. Unbearable. And I had to keep going, one foot in front of the other, not knowing if I'd ever see her again.

I was broken in a way I'd never been, even when Becky left for so long. It felt like trying to breathe underwater.

Ollie tagged after me everywhere and checked Ginny's room each evening. Then he'd plant himself outside her door and stare in like he thought she'd appear the same way she left. Sometime during the night, he came to my room and slept on the floor beside my bed, snoring and chasing bunnies. He made me smile, even when I didn't want to.

August ranked as the hottest on record in Virginia Beach. I closed my windows tight and pulled my curtains against the relentless sun.

School started the day after Labor Day. Ollie spent most days outside. I left him with plenty of water, and he slept under the picnic table. Each day after school ended, I hurried home to let him in, then holed up until I repeated the process the next day. Weekends were spent in my room or the living room. I avoided the sunporch. Too much light. Too many memories.

Sug pestered me to go out and do something. Take a walk on the beach or have dinner with her and Mac. But I couldn't. How could I enjoy the beach without Ginny? Mac would pop into my classroom at odd times and tell me corny jokes or stories about his disastrous dates.

One afternoon, after the students were gone, he visited my room. "Hey, Kat. Got a question. What do you call a pig that does karate?"

I cocked an eyebrow and continued grading math tests.

"Come on, Kat."

I groaned and laid down my pencil. "No idea. What?"

"Pork chop!" He slapped his thigh, braying with laughter.

"That's about as funny as the last date you told me about."

He shook his head and turned one of the student chairs backward, attempting to perch on it. "I guess I have bad taste in women."

"What about Sugar?" I chewed my pencil's eraser, debating another grade.

"Kat."

I looked up. "What?"

"You two are like my sisters." Mac scratched his head. "Seriously. Y'all are, well, you're a bit older than me."

"Excuse me?"

The tops of his ears reddened. He stood, backing out of my room. "I'll see you soon, okay? Have fun grading papers."

Sisters. Well, at least that answered my question about Sugar.

I went back to my papers. Grading, never a favorite job, had become tedious.

So had life.

On a Saturday morning in the middle of October, someone knocked on my front door, and Ollie bayed. I cracked open the door to find Sugar and Mac.

"Hey, you two. What's going on?"

They exchanged looks. "We're worried about you," Sug said.

"Worried?"

"You're not the same, Kat. Since Ginny left." Mac's mouth pulled to the side.

He had a point. My house was messier than ever. I kept Ollie and myself fed, but that's about it. Every day I'd teach, come home, and mope.

"I've tried to cheer you up with my stupid jokes, but ..." He lifted his hands.

Sug pushed her way inside. "What's going on, Kat?"

I plopped onto the couch, cradling my head in my hands. "I just don't know what to do. What if I never see Ginny again? I keep wondering how she is or where she is. And Becky ..." I looked at my friends and wiped my eyes. "Will they ever come back?" I wanted to sit on the floor, cry, and beat it with my fists like Ginny did that day at the grocery store, but I didn't have the energy.

Mac shut the door. Sugar sat on one side of me, Mac on the other, and Ollie curled up on my feet. Sugar pulled me into her shoulder and let me cry.

"Kat, I think you need help." Mac patted my back. "Can we help you?"

I drew in a deep breath and held it for several seconds. My sadness felt like a black hole with no way out. I wanted to get better and be stronger, but I didn't know how. Ginny still wouldn't be here. Did it even matter if I felt better? I let my breath out slowly.

"Kat." Sug turned my face toward her. "You have an appointment this afternoon."

"What? I ... what?"

She stood and reached down to me. "Come on, you need a shower." She toed Ollie away, pulled me to my feet, and pushed me toward the bathroom. "You're kind of smelly."

She helped me into the shower and brought me clean pants and a T-shirt. After I dressed, she stood behind me and combed my hair.

I looked at her in the mirror. "What kind of appointment did you make?"

She set the comb on the counter, wrapped her arms around me, and whispered in my ear. "A psychiatrist friend of mine can work you in today. I love you, my dear friend. Let us help you."

Chapter 7

I doubted anyone could help me, but I went without argument. The doctor's office was a small storefront located between a cramped used bookstore and a flower shop. Browsing the bookstore didn't even tempt me.

Dr. Rush met us in the lobby, introduced herself, and gestured to her office. She showed me to a chair. "No couch." Her bright smile didn't faze me.

I sat in the colorful plush armchair and forced my lips up. Faking feelings had become second nature.

She pulled up a chair beside me. "Sugar told me a bit of what happened. Can you fill me in?"

"I'm just, I don't know. Sad?"

She jotted notes in her notebook. "Sad? Can you explain that?"

I couldn't stop a frustrated grunt from escaping. I had to tell her the whole thing—all about my summer and my Ginny. I took a deep breath and blurted everything out.

"What about your daughter?"

"What about her?" What did this woman know about my daughter?

She tilted her head. "You haven't mentioned her except to say she left your granddaughter and then took her back."

I chewed on my lower lip. I wanted to roll my eyes, but that wouldn't be polite. "Becky is Becky. I've lost her." *No*, my brain screamed. *Now you've done it!*

She forced me to talk about my daughter.

After half an hour, I was exhausted. "Please don't make me say anything else. It won't make a difference. Nothing will."

She stood and retrieved a notepad from her desk. She scribbled on it. When she handed me the slip of paper, she said, "Try this, and I'll see you in two weeks. Wait,"—she wrote a name and number on another piece of paper—"make an appointment with her."

"Okay. Thanks." I tucked the papers in my purse.

She touched my shoulder. "I can help you, okay? Call me if you need to, and be sure to call the counselor."

I nodded and left, overwhelmed and tired to my bones. The shower alone was more than I usually managed. Visiting the psychiatrist took the last bit of my energy. We picked up my prescription, and Sugar watched as I called and left a message for the counselor.

She made me a toad-in-the-hole and handed me one of my pills before sitting beside Mac at the table.

"Thank you for going today, Kat," she said. "That was very brave."

I stuffed another bite into my mouth. The egg cooked in the toast was buttery, warm, and yummy. "Thank you both." I pointed at them with my fork. "Y'all are the best a girl could ask for."

Sugar cleaned the kitchen before the two of them left. I locked the door behind them and headed to bed. The tiniest light of hope peered through the black hole.

The holiday season arrived much sooner than I was prepared for. Mac and Sugar helped, but I floundered more days than I liked. My medication had to be tweaked, and my counselor advised me to take my time and not try to tackle a huge holiday alone. Sug invited me over on Christmas Day. Mac stopped by that evening.

I held my own as well as I could. Breathing became a little easier. I could draw a deep breath without feeling like my heart would shatter. I imagined covering the cracks with duct tape. Sometimes, I'd picture adding a little more and pressing it down just so.

Having a schedule when school started again in January helped. More light glimmered through the blackness, but I still missed my Ginny.

March brought heavy rains to Virginia Beach, followed by the warmest spring I could remember. Ollie's allergies were back in full force, making me wonder for the thousandth time how Ginny was doing. Had Becky taken her to the allergist? I did my best with Ollie and tried to keep him as comfortable as possible. I bathed him every week, and many nights he enjoyed a scoop of strawberry ice cream while I ate mine with vanilla wafers.

Before school let out in early June, Sug helped me list ideas to fill my summer. The house needed more paint inside and out. Ollie and the rain made a mess of the backyard. I planned to hire neighborhood teens to fill in the holes and maintain the grass, something I never got around to the previous summer. Several boards on the front porch had rotted and needed to be replaced. As much as I wanted to hold my grief inside, I also wanted to push it away and bury myself in busyness.

The weekend after school ended, I climbed a ladder, paintbrush in hand. The sofa and bookshelves stood in the middle of the front room. I painted the walls a soothing pale peach color to complement the pattern of my couch.

"Knock, knock." Mac tapped on the screen door and opened it. "Why are you on a ladder, Kat?"

I waved my paintbrush. "I'm painting, duh."

He leaned against a yet-to-be-painted wall and crossed his arms. He wore Hawaiian swim trunks and sported zinc on his nose. The coconut scent of his sunscreen wafted to me.

"You headed to the beach? Park in my driveway if you want."

"Yes, and thank you, but I walked over. Will you go with me?"

I stopped mid-brushstroke. "To the beach?" My words came out in a semi-screech. I cleared my throat.

"Yep." He tapped his nose. "That's why I put this awesome stuff on."

I turned back to painting. "No, thanks. I'm going to finish this." If I worked all weekend, I could move to the kitchen.

He grimaced and opened the screen door. "Suit yourself." The door thwapped shut.

I winced. He wanted to help. He and Sugar encouraged me to return to the beach, one of my favorite places. I took my medication every day and still saw my counselor regularly. But I couldn't manage the beach. Not yet.

Painting helped in a different way. "Bye, Mac." I didn't want him to be mad. I just wanted to work through things on my own, at my own pace.

By the end of the day, I was a sweaty mess. As I headed for the shower, planning what to make for dinner, Ollie started baying at the front screen door. He wouldn't stop, even after I shushed him.

"Dog! Ollie, cut it out." He kept howling, and I gripped his collar. "Sit, Ollie, sit." My firm commands flew in one of his shaggy ears and out the other.

He finally obeyed, panting and drooling on the floor. I grabbed a paint rag and wiped up the slobber before one of us slipped. As I stood, I spotted a car in the driveway—a small, rusty sedan. Adrenaline flashed through my body.

Ginny. Did Becky bring her back? Could it be? I shoved open the screen door, and Ollie barged past me, almost knocking me over. He hoofed it to the car, jumping on the passenger door and barking with abandon. I followed as quickly as I could, avoiding the rotten boards on the porch, hands over my mouth, blinking back tears.

Ginny's little face, sporting a broad grin, appeared in the back window. *She was here. My girl came back.*

Joy flooded my body. I nudged Ollie off the car with my hip and tugged the door open. Ginny leaped into my arms. Ollie danced around us, adding a few yips and barks.

"Grandma, I'm back!" She hugged me hard and then petted a frantic, happy Ollie.

Becky stepped around the car. She offered a tentative side hug. "Hi, Mom."

"Hi. Thank you for bringing Ginny." I shook my head. "I've missed her so much. And you, too," I added.

"Yeah." Becky watched Ginny and Ollie play.

"How has she been? Did she ever go to an allergist?" I had many other questions, but I wasn't sure how long Becky would stay. I clenched my fists, determined not to hurl ugly words again.

She cocked her head. "Allergist? No, why should she? Can I go in and use the bathroom?"

I forced myself not to react. If I wanted answers, I had to be patient. "Of course. Just watch your step. A few of the boards are bad." I called Ginny and the dog. "Y'all come on in too."

I picked up my painting supplies and shoved them in the corner. The paint wasn't dry, so I herded Ginny and Ollie onto the sunporch, where I opened the windows to allow a breeze inside. Ginny looked good. Taller, but still all arms and legs. Sugar needed to see her and Becky. I grabbed my cell, hoping she could run over before Becky left.

When she answered, I cupped my hand and lowered my voice. "Sug, Sug, they're here. Come over here now."

"Who? Who's there? Why are we whispering?"

"Becky and Ginny. Come over." The bathroom door opened. "Hurry." I hung up and busied myself getting three glasses of ice water and a box of vanilla wafers.

Becky entered the kitchen, and I passed her two glasses, tipping my chin to the porch. "Let's sit out there." I picked up my water and the wafers.

"I can't stay long, Mom." She perched on the edge of a chair and sipped her water.

Harsh words flew into my head. I bit my lip to keep from saying any of them, reminding myself how she'd reacted when I confronted her before.

Ginny dug into the box of cookies. "I can stay all summer, Grandma."

I looked at my daughter, eyebrows raised. My heart soared, and in my mind, I did handsprings and yelled, "Yahoo!"

"Yeah, is that okay? I mean, you kept her last summer, and she's bugged me all year to see you again." Becky bummed a cigarette from my pack on the table.

"Of course she can." I leaned forward to light her cigarette. "Those things are bad for you." I meant the cigarettes, but I also meant the drugs. Her complexion had a worrying yellowish tint.

She exhaled and waved the smoke away. "Yeah, Mom, yeah. I know." She stood. "I'll grab her stuff from the car."

"You can stay for supper, can't you? After my shower, I'll make something."

She leaned over and set her cigarette on the side of the ashtray. "No, I need to get back on the road. Can I go through the garage?"

"Sure, honey." I had so many things I still wanted to discuss with her. Were they worth another argument?

She pushed open the garage door and headed for her car, where she pulled out two plastic bags. Ginny's Bearhoven hung out of one.

I turned to my granddaughter and clapped my hands. "I'm so glad you're here. I've missed you."

"Me too, Grandma. What are we gonna do this summer?"

Over her head, I saw Becky heading back inside. Behind her, Sug speed-walked up the street. I couldn't wait for them to see each other.

"I have lots of painting to do." I tapped Ginny's nose. "Want to help?"

She nodded, her smile stretching from ear to ear.

Becky came back into the house and dropped the bags on the table. She held out her arms. "Give me a hug, Ginny."

As she turned to leave, Sug opened the door. Her face lit up, and she grabbed Becky in a bear hug. My daughter, who rarely acknowledged my hugs, melted into my friend's arms.

They were both crying when they parted. Sug wiped Becky's tears with her thumbs. "Girl, I have missed you."

"I missed you too." Becky's voice shook.

Sug held onto her arms and peered deep into her eyes. "Where have you been?"

Ginny tugged on her mom's hand, interrupting the moment. "Mama, how do ya know Ms. Sug?"

"I've known her forever, honey." The two of them shared a laugh. My heart filled with joy at seeing my daughter relax. Maybe she'd stay longer now.

Ginny giggled and joined them in a group hug.

"I'll start some spaghetti. That won't take long. Sound good?" I turned toward the kitchen.

"Yum, I love psghetti. Grandma's is the best, Mama."

Becky picked up her keys. "I really can't stay, honey. Grandma's spaghetti is yummy. Next time I'll stay, okay?"

At least this time, she'd come inside, and Sug got to see her.

I pulled her close, and for once, she leaned into me. "I love you, honey. Thank you for bringing Ginny."

This time, Becky gave me a phone number and warned me she might not answer. I got the message. But at least I had some way to contact her. If I wanted to.

Chapter 8

Ginny insisted we write a Summer Plans list again. This time, besides trips to the saltwater taffy shop and the amusement park, I added a visit to Jamestown. She could also help me clean out the garage. I made my own list, which included getting her in to see an allergist. She wouldn't fall through the cracks on my watch. We would confront things head-on this summer, and whenever Becky showed up again, I'd have information for her. I'd do my best for my granddaughter, no matter what.

We read together every night before bedtime. I helped her sound out the big words in her favorite books, which were *Artie and the Princess* and *Harry the Dirty Dog*.

"We should have named Ollie 'Harry,'" Ginny said one night as I tucked her into bed. "He's dirty like Harry."

I combed her hair with my fingers. So far this summer, I hadn't seen her thumb in her mouth, and she'd welcomed my hugs. "He already had his name, though. Someone else owned him first and named him Ollie."

She stared at the ceiling. "Grandma, can I live with you? Kind of like Ollie does. All the time?"

Her question caught me off guard. "But your mom would miss you."

"Yeah, I guess." She picked at a thread on her nightgown.

"What's up, pumpkin? You can tell me." Every tiny hair on the back of my neck jumped to attention. The worst things imaginable tumbled through my mind.

"We moved," she said, her voice soft and low.

"Yes, your mom told me."

"We live in a apartment now."

"An," I corrected.

She ignored me. "I miss the trailer park. There were cats and dogs, but now we can't have any at the apartment." Tears welled in her eyes. "I want to live here. With Ollie and you."

The clench in my gut eased. "You're here now, sweetie. You have Ollie and me for the summer, okay?"

"I guess." Ginny snuggled against me. "I missed you a lot."

I tucked Bearhoven under her arm and rubbed her back until she slept. "I missed you a lot too," I whispered, blinking away tears. My girl was back for the summer, and she finally opened up to me.

We made a deal that we'd go to the saltwater taffy shop after we finished painting the living room. We cleaned up the last paint supplies on a hot, late June afternoon and headed to Forbes Candies on Atlantic Avenue.

When I opened the door, the scent of sugar smacked me in the face. My mouth watered at the thought of my favorite taffy mix—orange and chocolate. Ginny looked through the kitschy gifts and found a seashell-covered hula girl that swayed when you touched it. We joined the throng of tourists and locals in line to buy it and our sweets.

"Grandma," Ginny leaned around the couple waiting in front of us, "that's what I want." She gestured to three different flavors—pink, green, and yellow.

After we checked out, I stuck the hula girl on my car's dashboard, and we drove down to Atlantic Fun Park. The Ferris wheel circled, and the scent of oil from the bumper cars brought back childhood memories.

"Can we ride something, Grandma?" Her eyes sparkled. Pink taffy stuck to her front teeth, making her words sound funny.

I wedged the rest of our candy inside my purse. "Of course."

She pulled me toward the "baby" roller coaster.

"This was your mom's favorite when she was little," I said.

"Really?" Surprise lit her eyes.

We boarded the coaster, and I told her about the big wooden one in Ocean View. She begged me to take her.

"They blew up that wooden roller coaster when I was a young girl."

"Why?" she asked.

"They used it in a movie and needed to demolish it." I patted her arm. "My mom, your great-grandma, rode it as a teenager. She said it scared her."

Ginny pointed to another area of the amusement park. "When we're done, let's go there."

The bumper cars she'd indicated were more my speed. I snugged her against my side as we were jostled from all directions. She giggled and steered wildly while I attempted to control our speed with one foot.

We finished the day with cotton candy.

Ginny bounced on her tiptoes. "This was the best day ever."

I ruffled her hair. "I told you you'd love painting."

"Funny, Grandma. I mean the taffy, the coaster, and the bumper cars."

"Don't forget the cotton candy."

She yanked another bite of pink fluff off the paper holder. "Yum. Can we go down the boardwalk?"

"Yes, we can, but then we need to head back. Ollie will dig to China if we leave him out back for a long time."

"Can he really? Dig all the way to China?" Her expression made me wish for a camera to save the moment. Wide-eyed innocence, cotton fluff stuck to the corner of her mouth, and the sun setting over the ocean water. What a beauty, my granddaughter.

"No, honey, but he will try, and that's the problem." We walked until the streetlamps clicked on. "Come on, let's head home. We can eat a sandwich before bed. I'm not sure taffy and cotton candy make the best dinner."

"It was good, though." Ginny licked her lips and skipped back to where I'd parked.

The tourists were out in droves, hurrying across the street to play miniature golf or to visit the ice cream shop. They drove slowly down Atlantic Avenue, gaping at all the sights. I followed behind an old VW bus before turning onto my street.

Several days ago, the neighbor to my left rented his guest apartment to an older gentleman. When we pulled up to the house, we found him chasing Ollie around my front yard.

I parked and jumped out of the car. "Ollie, Ollie. Come here, boy." How had he gotten from the back fenced yard to the front? I didn't want the man to get hurt.

Ollie ran to me and sat, panting and drooling. I grabbed his collar.

The man approached, laughing, arms spread wide. "That's the most fun I've had in a long time." His teeth gleamed white against his ebony skin.

"I'm so sorry he escaped. I thought I latched the gate." I frowned at the dog and shook my finger. "Bad dog."

The man hung his head. "Don't scold the dog. I let him out. He sounded so unhappy."

Ginny sat by Ollie and stroked his fur. "You're not a bad doggie." She hugged him and frowned at me.

"No, you're right, Ginny. Sorry, Ollie." I patted his head. He wagged his tail and drooled—his version of forgiveness. I glanced at the man. "Why did you let him out?"

"He looked sad. I'm Shrimp, by the way. Your neighbor for the summer." He stuck out his hand.

Ginny giggled. "Shrimp's a funny name." She peered up at him. "You're awful tall to be a shrimp."

More lessons in manners were needed for this summer, apparently.

I shook his hand. "Kat. And this funny girl is Ginny. And you met Ollie. But what do you mean that he looked sad?"

"He was baying. I came outside, and he bayed at me. I've never seen a dog that wasn't a beagle do that. But he's no beagle." His dark-brown eyes twinkled.

"That's for sure. He usually only does it if someone's in the driveway. I'm sorry he bothered you."

"No bother at all. I enjoyed playing with him. I always had a dog at home." Shrimp ran his palm over his short, graying hair. "Guess I won't anymore, though." He shook his head. "Anyhow, I'll let you go inside. I'm sure the little one here goes to bed soon."

"Yes, we spent the afternoon at the park, so she needs to eat before bed." I waved goodbye to Shrimp as we headed inside. "We'll see you around, I'm sure."

"I look forward to it." He returned my wave and climbed the slight hill between our houses.

Shrimp took to carrying doggie treats in his pocket, making him Ollie's best friend. Most afternoons, the two of them played chase. After a few days, I invited Shrimp to dinner. He had a sad air about him and only offered vague references to his past. My curiosity got the best of me.

"There's water or lemonade to drink, no wine." We sat at the table while the chicken finished cooking, and Ginny took her bath.

"Water's fine. No wine ever for me. I'm off that stuff for good." He smiled.

"Oh?" I wanted to ask why, but my mother taught me not to butt into people's business.

He smirked. "I have your number, missy. You've wanted my story for days, I can tell."

Heat crawled up my neck, blotching my face. "I'm sorry. I'm too curious for my own good. Sug says I'm a busybody."

"Sug's your friend I've seen over here?"

"Yes, we've been friends since we were kids. Sixth grade, actually. We spent so much time together that people thought we were sisters." I leaned back in my chair and closed my eyes, remembering. "We even worked at the Cavalier when we were sixteen. People said it was haunted. Sug swears she saw Adolph Coors walking the halls even though he'd died there close to thirty years before."

"Good to have friends like that. Is she married?"

"No." I hesitated. Sug's story wasn't mine to tell. "That wasn't in the cards for her."

"And the man that comes over. Is he your boyfriend?"

I snickered. "No. Mac is at least seven years younger than I am. We're all just friends. He says we're like the sisters he never had. He's been good for Ginny. To have a positive male presence in her life."

Shrimp nodded and glanced around the sunporch. "Nice breeze in here."

I blinked at the sudden subject change. I did love my porch. It remained cool, with a gentle breeze, except during the high heat of summer. And with the house situated as it was, a soft light came through most of the day. Summer evenings like this were perfect.

"I've been here since Becky was a baby." Her early years were some of the hardest I'd gone through. "My husband, Joe, died in Kosovo right after Becky turned one. She and I moved in here to live with my mom. Then, Mom left the house to me when she died of cancer ten years ago. I've been here for twenty-three years. Even when Becky left."

He tilted his head, eyebrow cocked.

Shrimp didn't know my story. "Becky's my daughter. Ginny is my granddaughter."

"I wondered. She seemed, um ..."

"I'd be a little old to have a seven-year-old." I patted the table between us. "After that, don't you owe me a story?"

"You're a sly one. You've welcomed me into your home, so I'll tell you a bit." He stared out at the backyard, where Ollie played. "Once upon a time, I had a house, a wife, and a daughter. I had it all—such a great life. And I gambled it all away. Literally."

I'd never met anyone who gambled to that extent.

"It's an addiction," he continued. "Like alcohol or drugs, or even cigarettes." He gestured to the ashtray. "One reason I don't drink. Addiction is a disease. Did you know that?"

"I read a book on it last summer."

"Why?"

Now we were treading into even harder areas. I sighed. "Becky, Ginny's mom. She started using drugs as a teen. I've only seen her a couple of times in the last nine years. I didn't know anything about Ginny until Becky showed up and dropped her off last summer."

I lifted my hands and dropped them in my lap. "I think Becky still does drugs from things Ginny's said." I drummed my fingers on the table, disgust lacing my words. "Becky left home at sixteen with her druggie boyfriend, Troy. I'm not sure where they've lived or who Ginny's father is. My daughter never hangs around long enough for me to ask questions."

Shrimp nodded. "I understand." He fiddled with his napkin, then stared at me. "Kat, God sent me here for you. I'm not sure why. But I feel it deep inside. Do you believe in miracles?"

I made a noncommittal noise and pushed back from the table to check on dinner. I wasn't interested in him and his miracles. His statement offended me. If I were being honest, I'd admit that dipping into my feelings and memories about Becky just plain hurt. A soul-deep kind of pain.

After we finished dinner, I said Ginny needed to get ready for bed. Shrimp's disappointed expression didn't faze me.

Why would he think God sent him to me? I prayed and believed in God. But the idea that God sent Shrimp to me was ludicrous. If God were going to answer my prayers, He would've fixed Becky long ago. And Joe would still be alive. God didn't seem inclined to answer those prayers. How could a stranger like Shrimp figure into that? And what did miracles have to do with any of it?

Chapter 9

Early the following day, I woke Ginny, fed the dog, and put him out back while she dressed. We were going to Jamestown. In a stern voice, I told Ollie to be a good, quiet doggie. Then I crossed my fingers that he would obey.

The night before, I'd asked Mac to check on Ollie while we were gone. I didn't want him to be a problem, and I sure didn't want to ask Shrimp for help. I needed a break from my new neighbor.

As Ginny munched on her breakfast muffin in the back seat, I told her about what we would see that day. I reminded her of our trip to Cape Henry Lighthouse the previous summer.

"The lighthouse marked the southern entrance of the Chesapeake Bay, near where the English settlers first stopped before they settled in Jamestown. Jamestown became the first permanent English settlement in North America." I checked my rearview mirror to see if she was paying attention. "We'll watch a movie about the area. Then we can go outside and see replicas of the ships and a Native American village."

"What's a replica, Grandma?" She spit out muffin crumbs as she talked.

"Swallow before you speak, please. A replica is like a model. You'll like them."

She swallowed and slurped from her water bottle. "Will there be 'Merican Indians at the village?"

"Well, no. Not real ones. And we call them Native Americans. People dress in period costumes, like what they used to wear back in the 1600s."

"You still have your clothes from then?" She took another bite of her muffin.

I laughed when I spotted her mischievous expression in my rearview mirror. "Girl, you're funny."

Ginny wiggled through the movie about Jamestown, but she loved the outdoor village and the forge.

She ran to a cannon. "Look, Grandma. It's real." She posed for a picture and then hurried to check out the old fort. Before we left, we stopped at the gift shop. She found a coloring book about the Native Americans from Virginia. The reproductions of the dreamcatchers fascinated her, and she wanted to make one when we got home.

We got home after dark. We'd started the day early. Ginny was sound asleep now. After unbuckling her, getting her into a nightgown, and tucking her into bed, I brought Ollie in and fed him. He crunched on his chow while I called Mac to thank him for watching the dog.

"I hope he behaved for you," I said.

"Of course. We took a short walk, but the pavement was hot, and I didn't want his paws to burn. When we got back, I turned on your outside shower so he could cool off."

"I bet he loved that."

"He did, crazy thing. He danced in the spray. He's a good dog, Kat, just a bit overzealous." Mac chuckled.

"That's for sure. He's like a bull in a China shop. Thanks again for watching him."

"No problem. The mail came, so I stuck it on the table. Something in there from Tennessee." His words ended in a question.

"I haven't even looked." I walked to the porch table and found a large mailer postmarked Memphis. "Well, would you look at that?"

I tore open the mailer and shook the contents out onto the table. Becky had sent copies of Ginny's birth certificate and pictures of her as a baby and a toddler. I pressed my hand to my chest.

"What is it?" Mac asked.

"Becky. She sent me some pictures of Ginny when she was little." Tears trickled down my cheeks. I sniffled and wiped my nose. "These are amazing. I'm so glad she sent them."

"Wonder what sparked that?"

"No idea. You never know with her." I yawned. "I'm going to go get some sleep, Mac. Thanks again. I'll have you over for dinner soon. Sound good?"

"Sounds great. Your spaghetti's the best, hint, hint."

"You got it. I'll call tomorrow, and we'll plan a good evening. Night."

I hung up and wandered into the front room, snuggling down in our reading chair and flipping through the pictures. Some of these needed a frame and a place on my dresser. My granddaughter was a beautiful baby.

About a week before my birthday, my phone rang. "Have you seen the news?" Sugar asked.

"No, what's up?" I propped my cell between my shoulder and chin and flipped on the television. "What station?"

"The local news, channel three."

The weatherman discussed a tropical system brewing in the Atlantic. I put my phone on speaker and scrolled to the weather app.

My mom liked to tell the story about the Ash Wednesday Storm of 1962 that slammed Virginia Beach. The storm lasted three days and killed forty people. The water reached nine feet in Norfolk, and close to seven feet in Virginia Beach. She said they rode out the storm sitting on the staircase. Even though it was so close to the beach, Mom's house wasn't severely damaged or destroyed, although they had to replace flooring and several shingles. She always called it a miracle.

Tropical storms and hurricanes impacted the coast and beach every few years, but the house hadn't suffered significant damage since the Ash Wednesday Storm.

At the end of the weatherman's forecast, Sug tutted, "This one looks bad. We need to watch it."

"I think so. They're saying it will intensify quickly. Hurricane Dianna. Great, just great. Wonder if they'll cancel the fireworks."

"Your Fourth of July birthday fireworks are never canceled. It's not bad until Jim Cantore shows up." Sug snickered. "What's on the birthday menu this year?"

"No crab, even though Ginny ate it before with no problem. But I don't want to take any chances, and she hasn't been to the allergist yet. Plus, no coconut and no fruit." Although Ginny told me she ate bananas at home.

"Yeah, we don't want a repeat trip to the emergency room. I'll make you a lemon cake with chocolate frosting. How does that sound?"

"Amazing and delicious." My stomach growled at the thought of it.

"You going to invite Shrimp?" Curiosity laced her words.

I'd quit asking him for dinner even though he still played with Ollie. I couldn't decide how much I wanted him in my life. Still, how could I not invite him to my birthday dinner?

"I guess so. I'll tell him next time he's over to play with the dog." I scribbled a sticky note so I wouldn't forget.

"It's so funny that he loves that dog so much."

"He feels an affinity with Ollie, I think. Shrimp seems so mild-mannered though."

"I think he has a huge story. Lots of mystery there," she said.

"Yeah, maybe so." I didn't want to talk about Shrimp. His words continued to come back to me—a miracle. God sent him to me. That sounded pretentious. So far this summer, I'd hardly thought about Becky and her drug use. Sometimes Ginny made odd comments, but I wouldn't let that threaten my summertime bubble with her. Why challenge that? What did Shrimp know about my life?

I avoided drama, and he seemed determined to bring it to me. Becky created enough of it as a teenager. I wasn't willing to jump back into it. God may have sent Shrimp, but I still wondered why God would speak through him. Couldn't He just write something on the wall?

"I'll ask Mac to grill," I said.

"Sounds good. Let me know if I need to bring anything else."

The system developed into a tropical storm, and on the morning of my birthday, it intensified into Hurricane Dianna. It gathered strength off the southern coast of Florida. The current track showed it would meander up the East Coast, gaining intensity. But my birthday dinner and the fireworks were still on.

Ginny helped decorate the backyard. Her pigtails, wrapped in patriotic ribbons, fluttered in the breeze.

Shrimp arrived in Hawaiian shorts, a button-down Madras shirt, and a straw boater. He carried a bouquet of beautiful yellow and white flowers tied with a yellow bow. "Happy birthday, dear Kat."

"Oh, thank you, they're beautiful." I kissed his weathered cheek. Guilt flushed through me again. I'd locked him out of my life, and he knew why. I vowed to be a better neighbor and friend. Anything to escape from that niggling of my conscience.

Mac showed up in time to grill chicken. I made a huge bowl of potato salad along with plenty of corn on the cob. Sugar, dressed in a red, white, and blue sundress, arrived with a birthday cake and a tub of Neapolitan ice cream.

Mac and Shrimp worked the grill and chatted, while Ginny played in the yard with Ollie. Sug pulled me to the side.

"I'm glad you invited him." She gestured to Shrimp.

"Me too. I'm going to try harder."

She patted my back. "You're a good friend. Cut yourself some slack. Sometimes, even if we know we have things to work on,"—she cocked an eyebrow—"we aren't ready."

"You're so subtle." She always told me the truth, even if I didn't want to hear it.

We ate, then found a spot on the beach to watch the fireworks. Shrimp sat in a low beach chair, and the rest of us vied for a seat on an old blanket. Watching Ginny's face during the display, the best I'd seen in years, made me smile. She oohed and awed after each explosion. The finale erupted in a blinding rush of light and sound – red, gold, and blue bursting across the sky. We watched in awe until the last of it faded into smoke.

Ginny jumped up and down. "That was great, Grandma." Her grin covered her face.

The next morning, I began tracking Hurricane Dianna as she strengthened and sped closer to the Virginia coast. Jim Cantore arrived in town, and he and our local weather forecasters predicted a hit by

Wednesday, warning residents along the coastline to prepare for the storm.

Ginny helped me move the front porch and back patio furniture into the garage. In high winds, they could become a hazard. My house sat low, and I worried about flooding. The hill Shrimp's cozy rental sat on protected him from floodwaters. I envied that.

Mac came over Monday afternoon and helped me cover the first-floor windows with big sheets of plywood. Ginny handed us nails. After we finished, we walked around to the backyard to see what else needed to be done.

"I can't move the picnic table, but I think it will be okay." He tapped it with his foot. "When Sug gets here tomorrow, we'll check back through the house to see if we missed anything."

"You're going to stay here too?"

"If that's okay with y'all. I'd rather be here." He pretended to shiver and wrapped his arms around himself. "I get scared being all alone."

Ginny giggled and scrunched up her nose. "You're silly, Mr. Mac."

After he left, Ginny and I made a trip to Harris Teeter. The shelves were picked over, but I managed to score some canned food and water bottles. I also found easy-to-prepare dry goods. When we'd put everything away, I made sure we had plenty of candles, matches, and a good can opener. Then, I cleaned and filled the bathtub.

"Why are you doing that, Grandma?" Ginny sat on the side of the tub, watching the water flow.

"If we lose water, we can use this to flush the toilet." I found a bucket and showed her what I meant. "We can even brush our teeth and rinse our mouths with it. I wouldn't drink it, though."

She made a face and clamped her hand over her mouth. "I'll use a bottle of water." She spoke through her fingers.

"Good idea." I hugged her and kissed her cheek.

Tuesday afternoon, Sug arrived with various totes filled with clothes, shoes, and her paint supplies. That evening, Mac hurried in between rain bands and stashed his things in Ginny's room. Ginny and Sug would stay in my room with me.

I prepared a quick dinner of chicken salad sandwiches. We ate in front of the TV, keeping an eye on the weather report.

"Hurricanes have a mind of their own." Mac tipped his chin, speaking in a silly voice. "You never know when one might change overnight—speed up, slow down, turn. Just like a woman."

"You want to sleep in the garage with Ollie?" I collected our dirty dishes.

"Pfft. That dog's not sleeping in the garage. We all know that." Sug chuckled.

Ollie sensed the incoming storm and the change in barometric pressure. He stayed quiet and right by my side. Ginny hung close, too, picking up on my stress and busyness. I tried to reassure her, but she followed me everywhere.

That night, Ginny, Sug, and Ollie stayed in my room while Mac snoozed in the spare bed in Ginny's room. I don't think any of us slept much. Each creak and groan set me on edge as the storm moved in.

Early Wednesday morning, I started a large pot of coffee. After that finished brewing, I poured it into a carafe and started a second pot. I snagged a hot cup for myself and stirred in some sugar. If we lost power, cold coffee was better than no coffee at all.

"Save me some." Sug yawned as she entered the kitchen, her short hair sticking out every which way.

I gestured at her head. "You need a comb or hairbrush."

"Caffeine first. That grandkid of yours kicked me all night."

"You should have had Ollie on your side. I'm not sure what he ate last night, but whew." I waved my hand in front of my nose.

"He can sleep with Mac tonight," she said.

A sharp crack of thunder and a flash of lightning made us both jump. A hard downpour beat against the windows.

Mac shuffled into the kitchen. "Here come the stronger rain bands." He scooted behind me to reach for the coffee pot. "You might want to make more of this."

"You get a new roommate tonight." Sugar patted his back. "Maybe two. Ginny kicked me, and Kat said Ollie stunk up her side of the room. It'll be fun."

"Ha-ha." He ruffled her hair. "Leave your hairbrush at home?"

She swatted at him.

"You'll both get sent home if you don't settle down," I warned.

Ollie trotted into the kitchen looking as if he'd like some coffee too. He went out back between bands of rain and sniffed at the wind and the debris in the yard.

"Have you checked the news?" Sug headed for the living room and turned on my television.

I perched on the edge of the sofa. "I checked my weather app several times during the night, but it wasn't working very well."

The lights flickered twice. I turned the television back on and scrolled to the local news.

"Hurricane Dianna sped up overnight." The weatherman stared into the camera. "Folks, be prepared. This one looks bad."

Chapter 10

Sugar and I stared at each other. "What else can we do?" she asked.

"We've prepped the house as much as possible. We'll have to wait and see," I said.

"And pray," she added.

Mac entered the room and plopped into my oversized reading chair. He stretched and yawned. "Ginny still sleeping?"

"At least someone is." Sug was grumpy on a good morning. This would be a fun day.

Ollie scratched and whined at the back door. I used that as an excuse to leave the room. I hurried him into the garage and let him shake the water out of his fur. Then I fluffed him as dry as possible with a towel. His crazy fur took the bad hair prize over Sug's.

When Ollie and I returned, Ginny sat curled up on the couch next to Sug. I snuggled down beside her. According to the weatherman, the hurricane was right over us.

"I'm surprised the power's still on." Another snap of lightning followed Sugar's statement. The lights flickered again.

Ginny scrambled onto my lap. "I don't like this, Grandma."

I smoothed back her hair and kissed her forehead. "I know, honey. Let's find you some breakfast, okay?" She hadn't experienced a hurricane before. I was more concerned than afraid, but I knew better than to ignore this storm.

She ate her cereal at the coffee table while we kept an eye on the weather. We didn't need to since it howled, stormed, creaked, and crackled outside. Later that morning, the eye arrived. We huddled together on the front porch.

Ginny stayed glued to my side. "It's so quiet." She peered up at the sky. "It's over?"

"No, it's just taking a break," Mac said. "There will be more."

"Hey, neighbors." Shrimp stood on the hill separating our yards.

"Hi, Shrimp. How are you?" I waved.

He picked his way down the hill and walked to the bottom of the steps up to my front porch. "I think you should come to stay at my place." He nodded toward the end of the street. "I'm afraid the water will be coming this way soon."

"Grandma?" Ginny's voice trembled.

"It's okay, honey." He didn't mean to scare her, but he made a good point. "We can head up our stairs to the second floor if necessary."

"Please, Kat." His face creased with concern. "Get your things together and come over now. Ollie can come too."

The dog, sniffing the air, heard his name and barked.

Mac nudged me. "It sounds like a good idea."

Sug nodded.

That settled it. I was being stubborn for no reason. I couldn't take a chance with my friends or Ginny. We gathered some basics, I stuffed extra food into a paper bag, and Ollie trotted behind our procession to Shrimp's.

We topped the hill, and a strange noise caught my attention. As I turned, water breached the top of the stairs by the parking lot. The surf pulled back, but the storm surge was on its way.

Shrimp was right—we needed to head for higher ground.

I stood on the hill outside Shrimp's apartment and watched the water inch up the street toward my house. The eye passed, and the pounding rain drove me inside. We lit candles when the electricity went out. Having the windows covered and no power left us all unsettled, but the candles created a cozy setting. My goal was to keep Ginny entertained and distracted.

Shelves lined one wall in the living area of Shrimp's place, a former garage converted into a studio apartment. Mac found several board games and pulled them down to play with Ginny.

"Sounds like the storm is turning east," Shrimp said late in the afternoon. He owned a battery-powered radio and turned it on every couple of hours throughout the day for weather updates.

"Thank God," I said. "That will keep the beach from getting more eroded."

Mac turned from the game he and Ginny were playing. "Your house will be safer too."

"Like I said, thank God."

Ollie dragged me outside a few times to do his business. I could see the water had stopped breaching the stairs. Back inside, Ollie rubbed his wet, stinky, furry body up and down anyone or anything near him. It wasn't long before Shrimp's abode smelled like a damp, unwashed dog. Ginny held her nose most of the afternoon.

Finally, by early evening, when the stench overpowered us, we were able to go outside. Water stood in my yard, but it wasn't as bad as I feared. From my higher vantage point at Shrimp's, I saw bare spots on my roof where shingles had blown off, but I still had a roof. At least on the side I could see.

I had to get inside, check things out, and see the other side—the one facing the ocean.

We tromped down the hill together. I unlocked the front door and automatically flipped the light switch. It might be days before the power came back on. Shrimp, bringing up the rear, carried a large flashlight. Inside, with the windows still boarded up, it was dark, humid, and musty. Shrimp checked the ceiling downstairs for water damage.

When I looked in my room, the true power of the storm hit me. Sometime during the hurricane, a tree between my house and the property next door slammed into the roof hard enough that the limbs pierced through. Rain poured in, and the waterlogged carpet squelched under my feet. My dresser and chest of drawers looked ruined.

Ginny had been exploring with Ollie. At my gasp, she came running. "Oh, Grandma. I'm so sorry." Her shoes squished into the carpet as she grabbed Joe's picture off my nightstand. "Look, Grandpa Joe is still okay."

I took the picture from her and hugged her hard. "As long as you, Ollie, and my friends are safe, everything is all right. Nothing in here can't be fixed or replaced." We had a lot of cleanup work to do. But what I told her resonated deep inside me. Family and friends were what mattered.

Mac and I headed upstairs to check for more damage. One of the side windows had a long crack, probably from a branch during the height of the storm. He taped it from the inside. I put a towel on the floor in case it rained more before I could get it fixed.

"You know, it's strange." He finished taping the window and stood.

"What?" I pushed the towel in place and checked his work.

He stepped back, hands on his hips. "Has Becky checked on you or Ginny? Did she call at all this week?"

I hadn't thought about Becky. My focus had been on Ginny and the house. "No."

His nostrils flared. "I'm so mad at her I could spit. She has no idea what an amazing kid she has. She couldn't even call to see if Ginny was okay? I don't understand her." A muscle in his jaw twitched. "And you. She can't even check on her mom?"

His anger caught me off guard. What he said made complete sense. There wasn't a good reason for Becky's disinterest, but it wasn't anything new to me. She'd been an absentee daughter for years. I didn't expect that to change.

Expectations are just premeditated resentments. I'd read that in the book about addiction. I had a lot of experience with resentment.

And expectations.

"I know, Mac. And while it doesn't make sense, she's been this way for years. But I do understand how you feel. When she first left, I spent a long time wishing she would at least call." I toed the towel closer to the baseboard. "At first, I just wanted to know she was alive. She was only sixteen when she ran off with her no-good boyfriend. But then I got mad. Really mad. I'm glad she didn't contact me for a while. It wouldn't have gone well. I would have taken out my anger on her."

"Don't you think she needs to know how you feel?" He shook his head. "Why don't you get a chance to say anything?"

I couldn't stop the wry chuckle that popped out. "I've wondered the same things. It's so frustrating. I've written her letters and then thrown them away. Even when she shows up, I have no chance to express how I feel." I shook my head. "The one time I tried, she used Ginny as blackmail. I'm sure she doesn't care."

"How do you deal with that?" he asked.

"I don't have a choice. It is what it is."

"Well, it stinks." He picked up the roll of tape he'd used for the window and headed for the stairs. "If she does show up, you need to tell her."

I followed him. "Trust me. I have a list of things to say to that girl."

We removed the boards covering the windows and opened up the house. July at the beach was a bad time to be without air conditioning. Most nights, we went to bed early, exhausted from the heat and hard work.

I emptied my refrigerator and freezer and called my insurance company about the roof damage. Mac and Sug helped me pull up my bedroom carpet. After we dragged the ruined furniture and soggy carpet to the curb for the garbage truck, I looked at the other houses on my road. They'd also sustained damage. The trash piles were a common sight after hurricanes or heavy storms. Cleanup could take weeks or even months.

One day, we walked over to Sug's to help her. We passed three places where most of the roofs were missing. It still surprised me that the storm surge hadn't entered my home. I knew that it could have been so much worse.

Sug's place was a small, solid brick house she inherited from her daddy. Her wrap-around front porch typically held sparkling white rockers, but she'd taken them inside for the hurricane. We helped her bag twigs and small limbs in her yard and set them all at the curb. I swept the porch, and Ginny helped Sug drag the rockers back out. We sat and cooled off with glasses of iced lemonade.

"Have you been working on anything new?" I asked.

Sug nodded and set her drink on the glass-topped coffee table. "Yes, it's a painting I just started. It's called *Storm's Coming*. Come on in, and I'll show you."

Her spare bedroom held her paintings, canvases, brushes, and other supplies. Several local boutique stores carried her drawings, paintings, and notecards. She also took commissions from tourists throughout the year.

We examined her newest creation. "You're looking from my house up toward the beach?" I asked.

"Yes. The idea came to me during the hurricane."

I touched the edge of the canvas. "You have such an eye for this. It's going to be beautiful."

"Thank you. By the way, have you heard from Mac? I still don't have phone service, and I haven't charged my cell."

"He came by yesterday. He had one broken window but nothing else. He wanted to enjoy a few days of guy time. Being with so many females overwhelmed him. I offered to send Ollie to keep him company, but he said no thanks to the stinky dog."

"Totally agree." She waved her hand in front of her nose. "That was one smelly animal."

Everyone in my area waited for the power to be restored. I hung my damp clothes wherever I could find space. When they dried, I stuffed what would fit into Ginny's dresser and closet and put the rest upstairs until I chose new furniture.

Two weeks after the storm, Ginny followed me out back to the picnic table. I'd decided to let her decorate her room. Maybe she could come back during the holidays. Who knew with Becky, but it couldn't hurt to dream.

I plopped my notebook and a pen on top of the table. "I need new carpet for my bedroom and some furniture. What would you like to do in your room?"

She clapped and bounced on her seat. "Oh, I never got to decorate my room before." A worried expression crossed her face. "I don't have any money, Grandma."

Her head tilt reminded me of Ollie when I asked if he wanted a treat. "I'll pay for it, honey. We can paint, too, if you want. Would you like to buy some pictures for the walls?"

She spent a long time planning her room, drawing picture after picture until she had it exactly how she wanted. When the power came on at the end of the week, we pulled the furniture to the middle of the room and painted the walls a soft, creamy pink. At the store, I bought new bedspreads in a floral pattern. Keeping the dog's fur in mind, we chose a tan and cream shag carpet for both of our bedrooms.

In late July, we drove to Norfolk to select bedroom furniture. I liked the lighter-colored wood for my dresser and nightstand. Ginny decided on an ivory dresser and nightstand that would be perfect for her room. After I arranged delivery, we stopped at the boardwalk on the way home for ice cream.

Ginny nudged me and pointed. "Grandma, look. Mr. Shrimp is out there."

He stood on the sidewalk outside the ice cream shop. He shuffled toward the door, his boater sitting cockeyed on his head, a strange expression on his face. Concern rippled through me. I'd been so busy since the hurricane that I hadn't thought to check on him. It dawned on me that he hadn't been over to play with Ollie either.

The bell above the door jingled as he came inside.

"Hey, Mr. Shrimp," Ginny called to him and waved. "Come sit with us."

He lifted his hand in greeting, tottering his way over. I stood to hug him. He was sweating hard and wheezing.

I helped him sit and squatted beside him. "You okay?"

He looked at me with a vacant expression. "I'm all right."

I passed him a few napkins to wipe the sweat off his face. He stared at them. I took them back and blotted his forehead and cheeks.

"Thank you." His breathing eased, and the sweating stopped, but something was wrong.

I handed him a glass of ice water. "Did you walk all this way for ice cream?"

"No. I went to the grocery store." He blinked. "Where's my car?"

I winced. The grocery store was several blocks away. "Where did you park?"

He gestured toward the street. "Right out there."

"Do you have your keys?" Had he driven in this confused state?

He patted his pockets until his keys rattled. He pulled them out and handed them to me. "Can you help me get home?"

Shrimp cooled off and perked up a bit in the few minutes it took us to drive to his place. I pulled into his driveway and helped him inside his apartment. Then I called Sug to see about getting Shrimp's car back.

After we did that, I pocketed his keys so he couldn't drive until he was better. It had been a long day. Ginny and I headed to bed.

Chapter 11

Before the sun came up the next day, a loud knock startled me awake. I hurried to the front door, hoping to get there before the noise woke Ginny.

I opened the door to find my daughter about to knock again. "Becky?" I rubbed my eyes. It was way too early for her to pick up Ginny.

"Hi, Mom." She stepped inside and shoved the door shut. "It's already getting hot out there."

I blinked. The person before me looked like Becky and sounded like her, but she was different. She looked healthy, with clean hair and bright, shiny eyes with normal pupils. Her skin was clear, and her face had filled out.

"You look good, Beck."

She hugged me hard and leaned back with a broad smile. "I did it, Mom. I went to rehab. It took this time." She spun around. "I'm clean."

Her excitement infected me. I grabbed her in another hug, longer this time. "I'm so glad." *Thank you, God.*

"Where's Ginny? I got up extra early to get here and see her." Becky rubbed her hands together.

"You can stay a while?" I wasn't sure how to read her.

"I'd love to. If that's okay with you, I mean."

She looked like my old Becky. My hand trembled as I reached out and tucked a strand of hair behind her ear. "Sure. You're welcome anytime. Come on in, and I'll make coffee." After starting it, I ran to get dressed.

It crossed my mind that she hadn't asked about the hurricane. She must have heard news reports. Maybe she'd been in rehab this whole time. "I'm not going to worry about that," I told myself.

Ginny padded down the hall as Becky and I were drinking coffee out on the sunporch. I winked at my daughter and raised a finger to my lips.

"Hey, Ginny, come on out here. I'm having coffee with someone you know."

"Can I get some cereal?" Her words trailed off when she reached the doorway. "Oh, hi, Mama." She hugged Becky. When she turned to me, her forehead wrinkled, and her eyes were full of caution. "I can't go home. My furniture hasn't come yet."

I reached out and pulled her to me. She might be seven, but she could still curl up in my lap. I brushed her hair back and held her face. "Your mom wants to stay with us before you go home." I kissed her forehead and whispered in her ear, "She's doing well, sweetie."

She studied her mother. Her body relaxed. Her mouth tipped up. "You look good, Mama."

Becky blinked back tears. She opened her arms. Ginny left my lap to climb into hers, leaning into her embrace.

I held my breath. I did not want my granddaughter to be hurt. And while Becky looked clean, would it last? I was only the grandmother and needed to maintain a certain relationship with her to make sure Ginny could stay in my life.

I fixed breakfast while Ginny showed Becky her bedroom and told her about the hurricane.

As they returned to the kitchen, Ginny chattered away, "... and we stayed at Mr. Shrimp's."

"Who is Mr. Shrimp?" Becky asked me.

I gestured toward the neighbor's house. "He's renting the garage apartment next door. Nice guy."

"Is he now?" Her tone was teasing. "How nice is he, Mom?"

I handed her two plates and gestured to the sunporch, where the overhead fan spun lazily.

"He's like seventy-five or something, funny girl." That reminded me of how he'd been the night before. "I do need to check on him after we eat. He had some kind of weird spell yesterday."

"What do you mean?"

I told her that we'd seen him at the ice cream shop and how he'd acted.

"Maybe he had a stroke or seizure or something." Becky tapped her chin. "I worked in home health once and heard of symptoms like that."

Home health? Who would hire an addict for home health? I mentally batted away the questions. "Can you go over with me?" No matter what, she might have experience that could help my friend.

After cleaning up the breakfast dishes, we climbed the hill to Shrimp's. I knocked on the front door. I had his keys, but I hesitated to barge in. After knocking again, I fished his keys from my pocket. My stomach churned. Did something else happen to him overnight?

What if I left him last night, and he had a stroke or seizure, as Becky said? "Wait out here, Ginny. Just till your mom and I check on Mr. Shrimp."

She huffed and crossed her arms but didn't argue.

I unlocked the door and peered inside. The lights were off. The room was warm—too warm—like the air conditioning conked out. I flipped the light switch. On the other side of the one-room apartment, Shrimp lay on his side in his bed. He didn't move.

"Is he dead?" Becky stayed by the door, rubbing her arms.

I ran to his side. He was sweating, his breathing ragged. I shook him gently. "Shrimp? Can you hear me?"

He moaned and blinked. He tried to lift his arm, but only his fingers moved.

"Becky, go call for an ambulance." I turned to Shrimp. "Hang in there. We're going to get you help."

Becky stayed home with Ginny while I rode in the ambulance with Shrimp. I tried to answer the questions the EMTs threw at me, but I didn't know Shrimp well enough to help.

I tapped one of the EMTs on the shoulder. "Is he going to be okay?"

"We'll do everything we can, ma'am. Are you family?"

"No, just a neighbor." I'd already filled him in on Shrimp's odd behavior the night before. "I met him this summer."

"You're a good friend." He patted my hand.

His reassurance fell flat. My irritation with Shrimp had festered. Now, he was in trouble and maybe in pain, and I had done nothing. A true friend would have known more about him and been able to answer their questions.

After a long afternoon at the emergency room, a nurse wheeled Shrimp into a room for the night. They served him dinner, and I helped him cut his mystery meat. The doctors and nurses came in and out, mentioning things like TIA and stroke. So far, their tests ruled out any cardiac problems. I called home and told Becky I was staying overnight.

After I got off the phone, I asked Shrimp, "Have you had anything like this before?" I passed him a napkin and pointed to his chin. He wiped awkwardly with his left hand while his right one hung uselessly.

He shook his head slowly. "No, never before. Did I see you yesterday? Were you and Ginny eating ice cream?" His brows furrowed.

His confusion broke my heart. After explaining we'd seen him at the ice cream shop, he finished his dinner, most of which went untouched. I helped him get comfortable in his hospital bed and then curled up in the nearby recliner.

His eyes were just about closed when he reached out. "Thank you."

I took his hand. "You're welcome. Get some rest now."

Another day at the hospital and a battery of tests left him diagnosed with a minor stroke. He had lost some use of his right arm and hand, but his speech and ability to walk passed the doctors' poking and prodding with flying colors. While he signed the discharge papers, I asked Sug to pick us up.

When she pulled up in his driveway, I stepped out of the car and inhaled deeply, trying to remove the hospital smell from my nostrils. The sky distracted me with its oranges, pinks, and purples.

"Fresh air." I opened Shrimp's door. "Come on now. Let's get you inside before it gets dark."

He stopped and inhaled like I had. His mouth tipped up on the left side. "We look like that dog of yours."

I chuckled. "Yep."

Sugar and I helped him inside. Mac had tinkered with the window air conditioner to get it running again. Shrimp sighed in relief. Once he was settled, Sug and I headed to my house, my mind racing with thoughts on what to make for dinner.

First, I wanted a shower and a good cup of coffee. I opened the front door. The smell of spaghetti hit me, and I grinned. I hadn't been gone long, but I worried about Becky staying with Ginny overnight. Looked like my fears were unfounded.

I enjoyed my hot shower and hot coffee in that order. Sug visited with Becky and Ginny. After we ate, the four of us took some food to Shrimp. We found him sitting at the table, drinking coffee. "Hi, ladies."

Ginny ran and hugged him. "I'm so glad you're back. We brought you psghetti."

He held her tightly with his left arm. "Yum. It'll be better than that hospital food."

"Becky made it. It's very good." I gestured to her. "Shrimp, this is my daughter."

She stuck out her hand, and he clasped it with his good hand. "Becky." He beamed. "I'm glad to meet you. I think we have a lot in common."

I gritted my teeth. My daughter had gone to rehab and was clean. I didn't want him bringing up addiction now. What if he said something that triggered her, and she fell back into drugs?

Shrimp winked at me, a knowing expression on his face. "We both love your mom and Ginny."

Becky and Ginny returned to Tennessee the day after our bedroom furniture was delivered. I holed up in the house and cried. Ollie joined me, his head and tail drooping as he followed me around. He went back to standing outside Ginny's room at night, waiting for her to appear. I wished I could explain to him that she would be back.

Becky hinted they might make it for Christmas. I was so proud of my daughter for fighting for her health. She was a different mom when she was sober. I missed Ginny deeply. Like the summer before, I couldn't imagine life without her, and now she was gone again.

Every day, I fought the black hole. It wouldn't win this time. I went back to my counselor and took Ollie for walks on the beach.

I constantly wondered whether Becky would stay clean and tried to shove the thought away, just like when I wondered why she hadn't asked about the hurricane. It took almost as much energy not to think about those things as it would to deal with them. Almost.

The days between August and December wouldn't go any faster. I made sure Shrimp took his medications and drove him to doctor appointments. Sug kept telling me I didn't need to hover, but guilt ate at me. I tried to be the friend he thought I was—the friend I wanted to be.

One fall afternoon, as I drove him to one of his appointments, Shrimp told me more about his gambling addiction.

"I went through every bit of cash I could get my hands on." He shook his head slowly. "Think I would've gambled away our house if I could have." He stared at his hands, his shoulders slumped.

I steered the car into the doctor's parking lot and pulled into a handicapped spot. "What changed you? Did you just pull yourself out of it?"

"It was God, Kat. All God."

I frowned. How could God do all of that?

He shifted in his seat. "Addiction took everything I had. My wife, my daughter, my joy." His last words were whispered. Pain flashed across his face.

"And then what? A miracle?" I tried to keep the snark from my words.

His lips twitched. "Something like that. Addiction is a disease. God healed me, but I had to do my part too. Still do."

That made sense to me. He had never mentioned how God sent him to me after that one time, but I'd learned a lot from him. I didn't want addiction to suck the joy and happiness from my life, or for it to control me. The anger that held me hostage for so long needed to go. Now that

Becky was clean, I figured everything would be okay. I could relax and enjoy life.

Shrimp extended his rental through the end of the year while he recuperated. He joined Sug, Mac, and me for Thanksgiving dinner. At the end of our feast, he clinked his glass with a fork.

"I have something to say." He stood and raised his glass of sparkling water in my direction. "Here's to our host and friend."

We all toasted each other. I started to say thank you, but he continued. "She's a good friend. I hope you both take good care of her."

"Wait, what?" Mac shook his head.

Shrimp sat. "It's time for me to go."

Sug patted his arm. "Shrimp, why?"

I couldn't say anything. All that time with him, and he made plans without telling me.

He blotted his mouth with his napkin and laid it back on his lap. "I need to head home. I have some amends to make."

"Shrimp." I wanted to say he couldn't leave, but how could I make him stay? "What's going on? Where is home? Why do you need to head back now?"

He narrowed his eyes. "Do you remember what I said shortly after we met?"

Of course, I did. He said God sent him to me and asked if I believed in miracles. I still hadn't seen any miracles or evidence that God sent Shrimp for a reason. Except Becky was clean.

Did those have any connection?

"Yes."

He raised his eyebrows in that knowing manner he had. "It made you mad."

I wrinkled my nose and nodded.

He gripped my hand. "I still believe what I said, Kat. But now I think I have to go."

This man was full of mystery, and I didn't understand. But our friendship had grown over the last few months. I refused to be mad at a frail old man and his fanciful ideas. I squeezed his hand gently and let go.

"When do you need to leave?" I asked.

Chapter 12

Shrimp didn't elaborate on why he had to leave. My curiosity grew, but I didn't know what else to do besides nag him. And he wasn't one to be pestered. He gave me an address in North Carolina so I could keep in touch with him. Two weeks after he left, I sent him a Christmas card and then waited. I missed my friend.

School let out in mid-December. On my first free day, I took down the Christmas decorations from the upstairs storage room. My artificial tree had shed so much that it looked bald, like the one Charlie Brown attempted to save. I swept up the needles and put them and the tree in the trash. My ornaments looked just as bad.

I pulled a lined jacket over my sweater and drove down Atlantic Avenue. When I got to the store, I decided to go all out for Christmas. Ginny and Becky might be here. A picture formed in my mind of what the house could look like. I'd decorate every room, and Christmas would be perfect—a Norman Rockwell kind of holiday.

The department store shelves, full of tinsel, jingle bells, ornaments, and candles, were basically empty when I left. I added two different nativity sets—one for the living room and one for Ginny. I wanted to use it to share with her the true meaning of Christmas.

My next stop—Harris Teeter. I bought the biggest, greenest, sweetest-smelling Christmas tree I could find, but it wouldn't fit in my car. I'd forgotten my cell, so I drove home and called Mac.

"Can I use your truck?"

"Sure. Should I ask what for?" he asked.

He laughed at my dilemma. A female voice spoke in the background. My antennae went up. "Do you have company?"

He cleared his throat. "Um, yes?"

"Yes, you do, or you're not sure?" I couldn't help teasing him. He never said much about the women he dated. None had stuck around long, and he'd not introduced any of them to Sug or me.

"Yeah, I do. You can meet her when you come for the truck."

My curiosity soared. He had a friend who was a girl or a girlfriend. I wanted to investigate this woman. I called Sug, who jumped at the chance to come along.

When Mac opened the door and saw both of us, his eyebrow twitched. I just grinned, and Sug batted her eyes at him.

"We're here for the pickup." I nudged him out of the way and headed inside, Sug on my heels.

As I rounded the corner into his living room, I stopped dead in my tracks. A young woman in her early twenties sat on the couch. She had Mac's pale complexion and lots of freckles.

Mac stood next to her with his hand on her shoulder. "Sierra, meet two of my best friends, Kat and Sugar. Ladies, this is my daughter, Sierra."

Daughter? When did Mac get a daughter? Words escaped me.

Sug remembered her manners first, extending her hand to shake Sierra's and welcoming her. She elbowed me.

"Daughter?" I squeaked out. How long had Mac known about her?

"She means, 'Hi.'" Sug translated for me.

"Yes, hi." I shook my head and raised an eyebrow. "Mac? Can you get your keys to the truck? They're in the kitchen, right?"

He trailed behind me into the other room. "Yes, no, and I don't know." He slumped onto a kitchen chair.

"What?"

"Yes, she's my daughter. No, I didn't know about her. And I don't have any idea how long she'll be here." He raised his palms in a questioning manner.

I leaned against a counter. "Wow, this is huge."

"Tell me about it." He rubbed the back of his neck. "I opened the door today to take out the trash, and there she was, about to knock. She said she'd been aware of me since the beginning of the year, but I had no idea she existed." His voice softened. "You understand I would've been part of her life if I'd been told, right?"

"Yes, of course. I've seen how protective you are of Ginny and how good you are with her. Have you two talked much?"

"She's been here about an hour. She's nineteen, and she moved here to go to ODU."

"Old Dominion is a good university. Must be a smart kid." My words made him smile. "You have to admit she looks like you."

"Yep." He grimaced. "I remember her mom. I was a stupid kid. That's no excuse, though." He drummed his fingers on the table. "What do I do now?"

I shook my head. "I'm no parenting expert. Has she said what she wants?"

"Just to meet me, get to know me."

I nodded toward the living room. "Let's go back in there and find out more then."

Sierra seemed like a nice kid, determined to form a relationship with her father. She agreed to come to my house and help with the decorating. Mac drove me to pick up the tree, and Sug and Sierra took my car to my place. When we arrived, dragging the tree through the front door, Sierra had already won over Ollie.

I tipped my chin her way. "Ollie's a good judge of character."

"Yes, she seems very nice, but I'm not sure I'll let Ollie's opinion sway me. If you feed him, he loves you."

"Hmm, reminds me of some people I know."

Mac kneeled. "Ha-ha. Hold the tree steady here while I secure it in the base." He twisted the screws snugly against the tree stump, muttering to himself.

I'd forgotten how poky and sticky real trees were, but the house smelled like the holidays. And memories. Sug and Sierra toted the decorations in from my car and spread them out on the coffee table.

Sug unwrapped a strand of snowflake-shaped light bulbs. "Did you leave anything for the rest of us?"

I laughed. "Maybe a few things." She continued to unfold the strand. "I thought it said ten feet, and it would be pretty on the mantel."

Mac picked up the box. "That's one hundred feet." He pointed to the number on the cover. "That would go around most of your living room."

"It would look great on the front of the house," Sierra piped up. "Do you have a ladder? I can help hang them."

Sug and I looked at Mac.

Hands on his hips, he hung his head. "I know, I know. I'll run home and get the ladder."

The three of us women burst into laughter. When he left, we opened the rest of the decorations. Sierra set up a nativity on the chest in the corner. I took Ginny's into her bedroom. I wanted to let her arrange the pieces as I told her the story about Jesus's birth.

Sug followed me. "Are they coming?"

"I sure hope so." The room looked so pretty, the way Ginny had decorated it. The paint, bedspreads, and curtains were sweet and little-girlish. She'd left her *Harry the Dirty Dog* book on her nightstand. I touched the cover. I had my heart set on them being here for Christmas.

Ollie wasn't sure about the tree, but he settled down after being poked in the nose a few times. Mac brought the ladder, and he and Sierra hung the lights out front before the sun went down. Inside, Sug and I hung the ornaments and tinsel on the tree. When we all finished, I ordered two large pizzas, and we sat on the sofa, enjoying the twinkling lights and decorations.

Days went by without a word from Shrimp or Becky. I sent a Christmas card to her and Ginny, writing, "Hope to see you soon!" just in case Becky had forgotten. Ollie distracted me by sniffing the tree and whining when he got poked. Tinsel would get stuck in his fur, and I'd tie it around his collar for a festive look. I baked pumpkin bread from my mother's favorite recipe and froze some mini loaves for my friends.

Five days before Christmas, Sug called me. "We're going to have a Christmas party."

"I don't feel like partying." I was a grump, and I didn't care. I convinced myself that Becky and Ginny weren't coming. But Sug kept nagging me. I gave in to stop her.

"We'll have the party at your place. You have more room." She paused. "I'm thinking we can do it two days from now."

"No one will come on that short notice." Plus, I'd have to clean. Dirty dishes were piled in the kitchen sink, and the trash can overflowed with garbage.

Sug talked over me. "I'll be in charge of everything. You can plan the food."

"Aren't you the food lady?"

"I'll bring something, don't worry. But you can do party stuff like those little wienies, barbecue sauce, and meatballs. Maybe some finger sandwiches."

I caved. "Fine."

The following two days were spent cleaning and cooking. Ollie helped me taste test. When I asked how many people were coming, Sug gave a vague answer. On the day of the party, she came over and helped set out the food. At seven o'clock sharp, Mac and Sierra knocked. They entered carrying a fruitcake and a big box of my favorite saltwater taffy.

Sierra presented the orange and chocolate taffies. "Dad said you liked these?"

I hugged her. "Yes, thank you." This sweet girl had worked her way into our lives in just two weeks. I turned to her dad. "Fruitcake, Mac?"

He gave a toothy smile. "Yep, it's a tradition." He reached for a piece of my taffy.

"Mitts off, mister." I held the box behind me. "Buy your own candy."

Sug went to her car, brought in a beautiful carrot cake, and a platter of finger foods. I set the fruitcake and other snacks on the table, but I stuck the taffy in my room. As I pulled my bedroom door closed, two small arms encircled me.

"Hi, Grandma."

I looked down, and there was my Ginny, home for Christmas. All the worries, all the discouragement, fell away. I hugged her, tears filling my eyes.

"Mama's here too," she lisped.

I leaned down for a closer look. "You lost a tooth." We high-fived.

"Yep." She stuck her tongue through the space and giggled. "I didn't think it'd ever come out. And look." She opened her mouth wide and wiggled the tooth beside the missing one. "It's loose too."

"It sure is. What did your friends at school say?"

"It just fell out yesterday. I'm gonna keep wiggling this other one so they'll both be gone when school starts." She tugged me behind her to the living room.

I found Becky and hugged her. "I'm so glad you're here." She still looked healthy. I turned to Sug. "You knew about this, I take it?"

Her face lit up like the Cheshire cat. "I've been staying away to keep from telling you." She opened the front door and peered out the storm door. "Just waiting on two more people."

"Who else is coming?" I sat on the couch with Ginny snuggled beside me. My favorite people were here. My heart swelled with happiness.

"Here they are." Sug opened the storm door wide, and in walked Shrimp, dressed in a warm hat and a gray wool overcoat. Beside him, a woman with deep brown skin and glistening dark eyes had her arm tucked through his.

"Ho, ho, ho, everyone! This is my ex-wife, Beverly."

Leave it to Shrimp to introduce her that way. But I was thrilled. All of my family and friends were with me. My Christmas was complete.

Sug and Mac carried more food inside. Turkey and stuffing, macaroni and cheese, sweet potato casserole, and rolls warmed in the kitchen.

At the same time, cookies and pecan and pumpkin pies sat on the side table, adding to the delicious aromas. I placed the finger food in the middle of the table on the sunporch and lit two fat red candles. White lights twinkled in the garland above the windows. With the candles lit, the room became a festive place to eat.

Before we filled our plates, Shrimp volunteered to ask the blessing. We stood in a circle holding hands, Becky on one side of me and Ginny on the other.

"Heavenly Father, thank You for this day and this time to gather together. Thank You for restoring families."

I squeezed Becky's and Ginny's hands. Mac stood beside Sierra, a great reminder of forgiveness and second chances. I closed my eyes.

Shrimp sniffled, and a quick peek showed tears trickling down his cheeks. "Christmas is special because You sent Your Son, dear Lord. You sent us grace and light, forgiveness, and the chance to be whole. Oh, how You love us. Amen." He wiped his face with a handkerchief. "Wait." He bowed his head again. "Thank You for the food."

I worked my way to his side and nudged his shoulder. "Can't wait to hear more about Beverly."

"It's quite the story." He watched his ex-wife, love gleaming in his eyes.

Shrimp had introduced her as his former wife, and my investigating skills were in full force. I sat next to the older woman. "Beverly, I'm so glad you're here."

"I'm glad too. I've heard lots about you and your family." She took a bite of the turkey. "This is wonderful. Did you cook it?"

Sug coughed. "She makes great spaghetti, but she never makes the turkey." She raised her eyebrows in question. "Can I tell the story?"

I rolled my eyes. "I think you have to now."

Beverly chuckled.

"Every year, we hear this story." I winked.

"Well, it begins with a turkey in the oven and ends with the turkey under the table." Sug's eyes twinkled as she told the tale.

We laughed through the meal, telling stories and sharing our lives, but I didn't learn more about Shrimp and Beverly. After we'd eaten and cleaned up, everyone filled their dessert plates and headed for the living room. I turned off the overhead light and turned on the lamps by the couch. Ginny plugged in the Christmas tree lights. She sat with me in our reading chair and munched on a cookie.

"Grandma,"—she said, spraying cookie crumbs on me—"I'm so glad I'm here with you."

I kissed her on the head. "Me, too." Becky sat with Shrimp on the loveseat, their heads close together, deep in conversation. It warmed me to see them talking. "I'm happy your mom stayed too."

"Mama wanted to come, but she wasn't sure you'd want her here. Then Ms. Sug called." Ginny swiped the crumbs from her mouth. "Mama's been trying hard." She looked at me and touched my cheek. "I told her you pray for her at night."

I blinked rapidly. "Yes, for you both. Every night."

She hugged me as best she could in our crowded chair. "I love you, Grandma."

I snuggled her closer. "I love you too, pumpkin."

Ginny fell asleep on my lap, and Mac carried her to her bed. The conversation turned serious after that.

Chapter 13

Shrimp stood up and walked to Beverly, resting his left hand on her shoulder. "I'd like to tell you why I left so fast after Thanksgiving." He held up his right hand. "After my mini-stroke, this wasn't working well. Kat helped me so much." He nodded to me. "I called Beverly right before Thanksgiving and told her what happened. I also told her I still loved her and wanted to come home."

She patted his hand. "He begged me."

His eyes sparkled. "Yes, I did. I begged." He turned and made eye contact with each of us, one by one. "Some of you know about my gambling problem. No, not a problem. An addiction. I was a gambler through and through, and that addiction made me lose the best woman in the world." He cleared his throat.

"Becky and I were talking tonight, and she knows some of my story. But I wanted you all to hear this part." Shrimp gingerly kneeled beside his ex-wife and took her hand. Looking deep into her eyes, he said, "Beverly, you are the love of my life. I lost everything when I lost you. I was a bad husband and father. You didn't have to forgive me, but you have. I gambled at the racetrack and with the bookies, but most of all, I gambled with my life. And my family." He bowed his head.

Mac passed him a napkin. Shrimp wiped his eyes and nose before he continued. "Beverly, will you do me the honor of being my wife?"

She swiped tears from her cheeks. She leaned forward and kissed him with a loud smack. "Yes." She pulled back and narrowed her eyes at him. "I will marry you. Again." She tipped her head and squinted an eye. "But if you start that mess up, you know what's gonna happen, right?"

He nodded. "Oh, yes, ma'am. I surely do. Yes, I do." He pushed up to stand and pulled her up next to him, his smile covering his face. "Y'all need to wipe those tears. It's time to celebrate."

We clapped and hollered, "Woo hoo!" I found some sparkling white grape juice I'd set aside for New Year's, and we toasted the happy couple.

"If I'd known about this, I would've baked a cake." Sug shook her finger at Shrimp. "You sneaky man."

Shrimp chuckled. "I wasn't positive she'd say yes."

Becky approached and gave Shrimp a huge hug. I wondered about their discussion, but it wasn't my business.

I linked my arm through Becky's. "Thanks for coming, honey."

She squeezed my arm and lay her head on my shoulder. "I love you, Mom."

The peace that passes understanding, the one Paul talks about in Philippians, enveloped me. Healing was happening, and I liked it.

Becky and Ginny left before New Year's. Becky had to return to her job as a receptionist at a real estate agent's office, while Ginny started back to school in early January.

For several years, Becky brought Ginny each June, and they came again at Christmas. Ginny grew taller, and Becky stayed clean. She beat her demons. I was proud of her for choosing sobriety and doing the hard work.

Shrimp and Beverly sent Christmas cards, promising they'd come to visit soon. Shrimp had said God sent him. I believed now that somehow, someway, his presence and his own deliverance from addiction helped Becky. I didn't understand it, but I accepted it as true.

On my fifty-fourth birthday, Becky called me in the morning to wish me a happy birthday. After lunch, Ginny and I walked to Sug's for my party. Ginny skipped most of the way there. I envied her youthful enthusiasm. At ten years old, she often reminded me of an overgrown puppy—all arms and legs and lots of energy. Way more than I had.

She turned around and skipped backward. "Know what I got you, Grandma?"

"No idea. What did you get?" I panted, feeling like I was sucking air through a tiny straw. We arrived at Sug's. She stood on her front porch, holding a black kitten.

Ginny turned around and ran up to Sug, giving her a quick hug and grabbing the kitten.

I trudged up the porch steps. Maybe I'd just turned fifty-four, but my legs were so heavy, my heart pounded, and sweat dripped off my chin. I tried not to wheeze. "Hey."

Sugar hugged me, tipped her head, and looked me up and down. "Are you okay?"

"Here, Grandma." Ginny shoved the kitten at me. "We found you a kitty cat. What do you think?"

I waved the kitten away and grabbed Sug's shoulder. "I don't feel so good." Heaviness weighed on my chest while nausea rolled through my stomach.

"Ginny, go inside and find Mr. Mac. Tell him I need him." Sug said. She grabbed me around my waist.

The porch door slammed shut.

"Sug, I think I need an ambulance." The next thing I knew, I was lying on her porch. She fanned me with a magazine.

"Help is coming. Mac called 911." Her eyes welled with tears.

"Where's Ginny?" I whispered.

Her sweet face appeared in my line of vision. Her forehead creased, and her lips downturned. She stuck her hands on her hips. "This is not the way you celebrate your birthday, Grandma."

"I know, sweetie. You be good for Ms. Sug, okay?" Sirens sounded. "I need to see a doctor."

Mac and Sierra came and stood with Ginny. Sierra wrapped her arms around my sweet girl. "We'll take good care of her, Ms. Kat. Ms. Sug can go with you."

"Thank you." The little black kitten purred and pawed my face, rubbing its head against my cheek. I looked at Ginny. "Come up with a good name, okay?"

Once they admitted me overnight, I sent Sug home. Wires were taped to my chest, and machines surrounded my bed. The nurse came into my room with medication for what the doctor diagnosed as angina.

"It wasn't a heart attack?" I patted my chest.

"No." She adjusted my IV line.

"What's angina?"

She patted my foot and headed for the door. "The doctor ordered more tests to be done in the morning. I'm sure he'll come see you."

"Wait." I raised my hand as she shut the door to my room behind her. "I have more questions." I slumped back onto my pillow. "Ugh. I'm sure he'll come see you," I said in a mocking tone. "Hurry up and wait is more like it."

I burrowed down in my bed, attempting to get comfortable. Before Sug left, she'd ratted me out about my smoking, which I rarely did anymore. The nurse gave me a two-minute lecture on the dangers of smoking.

Like I didn't know.

But, if it meant I'd get out of the hospital and not return, I'd do it.

Ginny called the following day. My breakfast—pale, pasty oatmeal, and watery black coffee that tasted worse than it looked—sat in front of me.

"Hey, Grandma." Her voice cheered me.

"Hi, pumpkin. I'm so glad you called. Guess what I'm eating?"

"I want to know when you're coming home," she said.

"As soon as they tell me, I'll call, okay?" I didn't want to scare her. "I'm feeling much better, and the doctor and nurses are taking good care of me."

Ginny's heavy sigh came through the phone. "I miss you."

"I miss you, too, honey. I'll be home as soon as I can. Are you staying at Mr. Mac's?"

"Yes, they said I can stay with them until you get home." She paused and inhaled. "Grandma ... are you going to die? Do I have to go back to Mama's?" Her words rushed out.

I closed my eyes. "I think I'm okay, Ginny. I really do. They gave me medicine, and I feel much better. But if you need to call your mom and return to Tennessee, you can. I'll understand."

"I don't want to," she whimpered. "I just don't want to be in the way."

"You're not in the way, honey. You're fine at Mr. Mac's, and you can be with me when I come home. Okay?"

Between sniffles, she said, "It's just that Mama sometimes tells me I'm in the way. I don't want that, Grandma. I want to help you."

The pain in her voice broke me. "I promise, Ginny, you make me happy, and I love when you're with me." I gritted my teeth. How could Becky have told her that?

"Okay." She blew her nose loudly.

"Plus," I reminded her, "we have a kitten to name."

She giggled.

"Can I talk to Mr. Mac, please?"

Ginny went in search of Mac while I took deep breaths to calm down. The machine beside me showed my heart rate increasing. Anger at Becky for what she told Ginny bubbled up. I didn't understand my daughter.

When he came on the line, I said, "Hey, Mac. Is Ginny by you?"

"Yep."

"Could you send her to look for something? I need to talk to you."

He asked Ginny to get his soda, then returned to the line. "What's up?"

I repeated what Becky told Ginny. "I don't want her to feel she's in the way. The nurse implied that I'll be out of here in a couple of days. I want Ginny with me when I get home. Is she okay staying with you until then?"

"Of course, she is. Sierra is taking a few classes this summer, but I'm home when she's not, so it's no problem for Ginny to stay here."

"Thank you. I appreciate it. I'll call Becky once I'm home and tell her what's happened, but I don't want to send Ginny back yet." I forced myself to unclench my fists.

"Gotcha. It's all good with me."

"Thank you, Mac. I appreciate you." I lay my head back on the pillow and attempted to relax. The heart rate machine slowly dropped to a better level. My friends were the best, and I thanked God for them.

Angina and heart attacks are different—something I did not know before. Angina was the chest pain I'd experienced. My heart wasn't getting enough blood. My symptoms felt like a heart attack, but the doctor said the tests showed no damage. He informed me that I had to throw out my cigarettes and take my medication. I also needed to reduce my stress levels.

The first two were no problem. That last one? Easier said than done.

The day they released me, Mac and Ginny picked me up. I shifted into the back seat beside Ginny and buckled my seat belt. "Let's go home." I couldn't wait to sleep in my own bed.

Ginny watched me, her big brown eyes filled with worry, before leaning over to hug me. "Hi, Grandma."

I squeezed her tight. "You won't hurt me, honey. I promise." I brushed her hair back and planted a kiss on her forehead. "Where's that tiny black kitten?"

"She's waiting at home."

I patted Mac's shoulder. "Let's go home. We have a kitten to name."

Seeing my house eased my tension. There was nowhere else I'd rather be. I'd pitch my cigarettes and walk every day. And eat right, and cut out stress.

When we went inside, the kitten meowed furiously, winding between my legs before running into the kitchen. I held onto Ginny's shoulders to keep from tripping.

"Red sounds like a good name." Ginny looked up at me. "What do you think?"

"Red? How about Blackie? She is black."

"No." She pursed her lips and frowned. "I like the name Red for her."

The kitten's name stuck. Red was a tiny terror, quickly putting Ollie in his place. He whimpered whenever she entered the room. Her favorite activity was trapping him on the porch. She sat at the doorway between the porch and the kitchen, and Ollie cried until he bayed. She didn't even flinch.

Her antics tickled us. She liked to sleep in my bed, soothing me with her purrs. Ollie slept beside Ginny's bed but stayed alert in case the kitten approached.

One evening, a few days after I got home, Sugar, Mac, and Sierra showed up with a birthday cake, ice cream, and balloons.

"We never got to celebrate." Sug cut me a tiny slice of cake.

I held out my plate. "Ice cream, please."

She gave me the stink eye. "Yeah, no." She pushed the plate back to me.

"I'm not a baby. Ice cream is fine." I huffed.

Ginny giggled. "You're pouting, Grandma." She took a big bite of cake, followed by a spoonful of vanilla ice cream. She pointed at me with her spoon. "You have to eat carefully, remember?"

"How can I forget? I did throw my cigarettes away." I puffed out my chest, my chin high.

Mac patted my head as he sat, his plate full of cake and ice cream. "We are proud of you. But we're not going to enable you, Kat."

I took a bite of my cake. "Yum, Sug. You outdid yourself. Red velvet is my favorite. Feel free to leave the leftovers here."

She pointed to Sierra.

"You made it?" I asked her.

"I did. I'm glad you like it, Ms. Kat." Her cheeks flushed with pride.

"Well, your dad didn't teach you to bake. Everyone knows he can't cook."

He pressed a hand to his chest and dropped his head, pretending to cry. "Kat, you're so mean."

"Grandma, you hurt Mr. Mac's feelings." Ginny patted his back. He grabbed her in a bear hug while she squirmed and giggled. "Help me, Grandma!"

Ollie joined in the fray and barked and danced around us. Red stood at the entrance to the porch and meowed.

No one noticed when I cut myself another small slice of cake. Baby steps.

Chapter 14

Quitting smoking wasn't as easy as I imagined it would be. It turned out that cigarettes were my go-to for stress. I found myself reaching for one, sometimes even when I wasn't stressed. It was a habit I'd cut way back on, but I couldn't seem to shake it.

I didn't understand why.

Becky needed to hear about my hospital visit and angina attack. I dreaded that phone call. She'd been clean for several years, but I was afraid of what would happen when she heard about my health. Shrimp had mentioned expectations being premeditated resentments. That rang true for me.

I still didn't fully trust her. I thought everything would be fine when she stopped using drugs. My life would be normal and easy. She would behave as I wanted and expected. I envisioned sanity, but was that too much to ask? My underlying fear hadn't gone away.

On the Sunday after I got home from the hospital, I sat at the sunporch table, my cell phone sitting in front of me. My hands itched for a cigarette. If I could only hold one...

Red jumped on my lap, purring, kneading, and circling until she found a comfortable position. I stroked her soft fur, comforted by her warmth.

When I dialed Becky's number, an annoying tone sounded, and a recording said, "This number has been disconnected."

I frowned, hung up, and called again, but I got the same recording. She called me on my birthday. It had only been a week since then. Maybe she hadn't paid her bill—no reason to think the worst.

I watched Ginny through the windows as she played with Ollie in the backyard. Would I ever feel grounded? I wanted to get to the point where my stomach didn't roll when I pictured what Becky might be doing. My imagination tormented me.

I pushed back from the table. I'd try her again tomorrow. The doctor advised reducing stress. Having an addict for a daughter didn't make it very easy.

Becky's number continued to ring funny, followed by the same recording. I felt better, so I chose to ignore the situation. I intended to enjoy the rest of the summer with my granddaughter. It wouldn't be long before Becky came for Ginny. I would tell her then.

We went to the beach early each morning, and Ginny made sure we took a short walk on cooler evenings. She kept a close eye on everything I did and ate and worried so much about me. I wanted her to be a little girl, the ten-year-old she was.

One morning, after the beach, I told her we were going to the taffy shop and amusement park. She could enjoy the taffy and cotton candy. I'd be careful with the sweets. Having fun was good for stress.

When I told her my plans, she narrowed her eyes. "Are you sure that's safe, Grandma?"

I put my hands on my hips. "Virginia Morgan Johnson, I'm the grown-up here. It'll be fine. We can have fun. I've been very good. I promise to take care of myself." I crossed my heart. "Plus, it's not so hot today. We need to take advantage of that."

"You're silly, Grandma. I'll change. You change too." She ran toward her room, then slid to a stop and squinted. "Don't forget to tell me if you get tired."

I saluted. "Yes, ma'am. I won't forget. Promise."

We stopped at the taffy shop. Over Ginny's protests, I bought myself my favorite flavors. I ate a piece of each and stuffed the rest into my purse. We drove to the amusement park and watched families having fun on the bumper cars and kiddie roller coaster, which Ginny deemed too dangerous for me. She okayed the Ferris wheel. I snuck another piece of taffy while waiting in line.

"What's that in your mouth?" She glared.

I used my tongue to pry the taffy off my tooth. "Just one more piece. It's all right, honey. I'm being very careful."

She cocked an eyebrow, and I grabbed her in a hug. "I love you, sweet girl. Don't worry so much."

I suspected Ginny was worried that something would happen and that she'd have to return to her mom early. Ten-year-olds should have a fun, carefree childhood. Not be shuttled back and forth between a recovering addict parent and a grandmother. Or worry about either of them.

Which brought me back to Becky. Where was she, and what was she doing? Why didn't her phone work?

After a slow ride on the Ferris wheel and cotton candy for Ginny, we returned to my car. A flyer was tucked into my windshield wiper. I took it off and shoved it into my purse.

We ate a simple dinner of grilled cheese sandwiches and tomato soup. After my hospital stay, Sug filled my freezer with quick meals, but we needed to get back to our old routine. Ginny helped me clean up the dishes and ran off to take a bath. The flyer, sticking out of my purse, caught my eye. I pulled it out and read the front—*Do you love someone who uses drugs?*

I sat on the couch to read the pamphlet. The inside information revealed a new program launching in the beach area, specifically designed for the family and friends of addicts. The back displayed the date and time of the first meeting, along with a contact number. Ginny was still in the bathroom, so I called it.

"Hello," answered a man.

"Hi—" I wasn't sure what to say.

"Are you calling about the flyer?" His voice was gentle.

"Yes, yes, I am. This is for family members of addicts?"

"Yes, ma'am, it is. We have our first meeting tomorrow." He rattled off the location's address. "Do you have other questions?"

"Well, my granddaughter lives with me right now. Is it all right if she comes? She's ten."

The man hesitated. "That's hard. It might be overwhelming for her. But there's a room across the hall where she could wait. She'd be close by. Would that work?"

I could ask Sug or Mac to watch Ginny, but I didn't want to tell anyone about attending this family group meeting until I figured out if it could help me and maybe Ginny.

"That would be okay. I'll have her bring a book to read. She won't be any trouble."

"I look forward to seeing you tomorrow," he said.

I hung up and nodded to myself. This was a good thing, maybe even a God thing. I could meet some other people like me who had an addict in their lives. Maybe they would tell me how to fix Becky.

I wouldn't have gone if the meeting hadn't been the next night. Just thinking about it knotted my stomach. I couldn't eat supper, but at least Ginny thought I was being careful. While she grabbed a book, I slipped outside and lit a cigarette I'd found buried in the back of my desk. A few puffs, and the shakes eased, and my stomach calmed. Back inside, Ginny shot me the stink eye. I didn't say a word.

We pulled up to a church near Seaside Elementary. I unbuckled and got out. The sun was setting in its spectacular colors of oranges and pinks, and a soft breeze wafted the scent of saltwater to me. I steeled myself. *I can do this.* I could learn more about addiction and how to help Becky.

Ginny tipped her head back and looked at the tall white steeple on top of the old brick building. "Wow, that thing goes up and up. So, churches with the tallest pointy things get to talk to God more?"

"That pointy thing is called a steeple, and no, that's not how it works. Let's go find where we meet." I gestured toward the back seat. "Grab your book. They said you can read while you wait for me."

We entered the church through the front door and found the vestibule empty. When I opened the church doors, I spotted an elderly man straightening items on a table at the front of the room.

"Hello?" I spoke in a low voice so as not to startle him.

He held onto the table as he turned toward us. "Hi there, how can I help you?"

"I'm looking for the group for addicts. I mean, families." I rubbed the back of my neck and coughed. "The family group, I mean." This was hard. And embarrassing.

He shuffled down the aisle, shoulders stooped as if the weight of the world bowed him low.

"Yes, dear. We're very excited about this new group." He spotted Ginny, and his face brightened. He held out his hand to her. "I'm Reverend Carson."

She shook his hand. "I'm Ginny. Why's the pointy thing, the steeple, so high? Grandma says that's not how you get closer to God."

His eyes lit up. "No, but it doesn't hurt." He turned to me, his lips tipped up in a grin. "Let me show you where you need to be."

He led us through a side door and down a long hall, his steps slow and halting. We turned left and saw several classrooms. Two doors stood open—a sign pointed to the meeting room.

"Thank you so much." I gestured to the door of the opposite room. "They said Ginny could wait over there."

"She's welcome to assist me, if you don't mind." He tipped his head. "She could be a big help. I have flowers to put out for this Sunday's service." He held up his hands, showing me his knotted joints and bent fingers. "These hands and my feet don't work as well as they used to."

Ginny tugged on my shirt. "Can I, Grandma? It'll be fun."

I didn't know Reverend Carson, but everything in me said he was good. A gentle, kind person. "Yes, that'll be okay." I turned toward the classroom. "I'll see you in an hour?"

"I'll bring her back here. Before, if we get the flowers all set up." He patted my arm. "We'll be right here in the building. Don't worry."

I took a deep breath and squared my shoulders. Nodding once, I forced myself to enter the room and slip into a chair.

The meeting started at seven on the dot. There were three leaders—one man and two women—and the man, Todd, explained that they were facilitators and that we would soon take turns leading. I wasn't sure about that. I just wanted to know what to do so Becky would act right.

I was about to ask when I'd learn that when he said, "Let's take a moment of silence. And then we'll say the Serenity Prayer." One of the women passed out copies of the Prayer so we could each read it.

I'd heard the Serenity Prayer—something about God and change. I didn't need to change. I wasn't the problem, but I mumbled along with the group. "God, grant me the serenity to accept the things I cannot change, courage to change the things I can, and the wisdom to know the difference."

Serenity. I couldn't remember the last time I had serenity. I pictured Mother Teresa or the former Queen of England. Regal women who beat the odds and sat quietly with their hands folded just so and their feet tucked genteelly under them.

Mother Teresa would probably argue with me about that.

"Tonight, we'll dissect this prayer. I think we can learn a lot from it. It gives us a good base for this group." Todd read the first word, "God," then looked at us. "God is who you count on—the being, a higher power if you will, who you know is bigger than you. Our program teaches us to be open to people of all faiths, but I am a Christian. I won't beat you over the head with that. Just want you to be aware of where I stand." He sat back in his seat. "If anyone has something to share, you can do that. We set a limit of just a few minutes per person so everyone can contribute. There's no requirement to say anything. And you don't have to explain your religious or spiritual beliefs."

I glanced around the circle. There were only three other people besides the three leaders, and one of them was me. My butterflies stood ready, on full alert. I wasn't planning to say anything. I dropped my head to avoid eye contact.

Several uncomfortable seconds passed before someone cleared his throat. A deep voice said, "I guess I'll go. My wife forced me to come. Our son is an addict."

The man who spoke had his arm around the lady sitting next to him. I was the only one here who didn't know anyone. How fun.

He shifted in his chair, leaned forward, and dropped his head in his hands. "God—" He choked back a sob, cleared his throat again, and wiped his eyes. "God has been very distant. I, we, have no idea what to do." He held his hands out to Todd. "Can you help us?"

With a nod, Todd said, "I want to. We all want help." He gestured to the rest of the group. "That's what we're here for. To stand by each other."

One of the female leaders spoke. "My name is Maggie. What's your name?"

Todd barked a laugh. "Oops, guess we should've started with that."

A giggle popped out of me. I clapped my hands over my mouth.

Maggie tipped her chin at me. "What's your name?"

"Kat."

"Hi, Kat, I'm glad you're here." Her gentle expression sank deep into my soul. Strength and understanding passed between us in that single look.

"My name is Roger," said the man who had spoken. "This is my wife, Samantha."

She gave a little wave.

"You know who I am." Todd patted his chest. He pointed to the other leader. "This is my sister, Tamara. Our mom is an addict."

Line by line, our small group worked its way through the Serenity Prayer. I fished a pen out of my purse to make notes on the paper. At the end of the meeting, we held hands and said the Lord's Prayer. Maggie pulled me in for a hug.

"I hope to see you next week." She gave me an extra squeeze. "Please come back."

I wanted to ask her what to do about Becky, but Ginny ran through the doorway and grabbed me around the waist.

"Grandma, guess what?" She tugged on my arm. "I helped Rev real good."

"Really well?" I hugged her. "And you call him Rev now?"

"Yep." She pulled a lollipop from her pocket. "He gave me this." She unwrapped the candy and shoved it in her mouth. "He said his whole name was too much to say, so I can call him Rev."

Maggie nodded. "Everyone here calls him that."

"Well, okay, then." I turned to Ginny. "Did you thank him?"

"Course." She swirled her lollipop and took it out with a sloppy slurp. "We comin' back next week? He said I could help him again."

Words from the meeting echoed in my ears. "Yes, I think we will."

Chapter 15

What I learned that night stayed with me over the weekend. Taking the Serenity Prayer apart, piece by piece, helped me understand it better. Just starting with the word "God" stopped me in my tracks.

I knew God. I was a Christian and believed in Jesus. But my prayers were rote, and I had let life come before my relationship with Him. What Roger said—that God felt distant—resonated deep inside me. But maybe I was the problem. Relationships were important to me, even more so since Ginny came into my life.

As hard as I worked to maintain a closeness to her, I wanted to do the same with God. I craved serenity, and deep down, I believed God would help me find it.

Maggie pointed out that the first part of the prayer asked for serenity to accept the things I cannot change. On Saturday evening, while Ginny bathed, I got a pen and paper and sat at the table on the sunporch. The sun inched lower in the late summer sky, and the soft glow filtered through the windows.

On the paper, I wrote "What I cannot change" and "What I can change" and drew a vertical line between them. I chewed on the end of my pen. Some things I couldn't change. Like external things. Todd asked us to think about our relationships as we read the Serenity Prayer.

I wrote Becky's name under "what I cannot change" and laid my pen down. Was it true? That it wasn't my job to change my daughter? Maybe that's why I couldn't find ways to help her.

In case I had it wrong, I added her name to the other column. Maybe there were things I could change about Becky. Todd and Maggie didn't know everything.

I stared at the two columns until Ginny walked in. She stood next to me and tapped the paper. "Whatcha doing, Grandma?"

I wrapped one arm around her and held her tight to my side. She smelled like coconut shampoo. "Trying to figure some things out." I sniffled.

She put her finger under my chin and lifted my head. She looked deep into my eyes and used the pads of her thumbs to wipe my tears. "You're smart, Grandma. You'll figure it out. You don't need to cry."

This young girl was mothering me. She, who didn't have much of a role model in her own mother, was a natural nurturer. She wrapped her arms around me and held me while I cried.

She passed me a napkin to blow my nose.

Ginny picked up the piece of paper. "Why do you have my mama's name on this twice?"

"It's part of what we discussed at last week's meeting." I blew my nose again with a loud honk.

"What'd y'all talk about?" she asked.

Ginny was ten, but an old ten. She'd seen things I would never know about. "We talked about what you can change and what you can't. It's called the Serenity Prayer." I recited it for her.

She nodded, a thoughtful expression on her face. "I think I get that. God is big. He can move mountains. That's what Rev said. But we can't. Grandma, He's the only one who can make things different." She spun around and skipped into the kitchen. "I'm going to pick a book to read, okay?"

"That sounds good. Give me a minute, and I'll meet you in the big chair." I laid my list on the table and circled Becky's name on both sides. Underneath that, I wrote "WISDOM" in capital letters. That's what I needed. Wisdom.

My daughter was somewhere between what I could and couldn't change. God was big, as Rev told Ginny. I wanted to put Becky in His hands to figure this out. He could change her for sure. I hoped He'd get to work soon.

My phone rang Sunday afternoon while I was baking chocolate chip cookies. I wiped my hands on the dish towel and rushed to answer it.

"Kat, it's Maggie. From the meeting on Thursday?"

"Yes, hi, Maggie." I peeked into the kitchen to make sure I'd set the oven timer.

"Listen, Kat, I hate to do this, but I have a situation, and I'm hoping you can help me."

"What is it?" I sat at the table.

"Well, VBS is this week. You know, Vacation Bible School. And I remembered you mentioned you were a teacher. Our first-grade assistant went into labor last night, and I'm in a pickle." She chuckled.

"She didn't know she was having a baby?"

Maggie laughed again. "We just thought she had longer. Anyhow, is there any way I can twist your arm and get you to help us out? When I learned about it, you were the first person to come to mind. And Ginny can participate too. Our program goes through fifth grade."

This would be a great opportunity to get Ginny to church. I hadn't been involved in a church family for a long time, and all she knew about God was what I'd told her through the last few years. With nothing planned for the upcoming week, this seemed timely.

"Sure, I could do that."

"Oh, thank you. I cannot tell you how much this means to me. Can you come in by 8:00 a.m.? We start at nine, so I'll have a chance to show you what to do."

My oven timer beeped. "Yes, we'll see you then. I have to go before my cookies burn, but see you tomorrow. And Maggie, thanks for asking me."

The following day, I woke up extra early, fed Ollie, put him out back, fed Red, and scooped her litter pan.

We arrived at the church just before eight. Ginny bounced in her seat. She'd never been to VBS. I was excited too. Years had passed since I'd helped with it.

Maggie stood outside when we parked, and she waved at us. "Hi Kat, thank you so much for helping me out." Maggie turned to Ginny. "Let me introduce you to Ms. Sammie. She'll be your teacher."

I followed them to Ginny's classroom. It was decorated with an underwater theme. Ginny's teacher got her all checked in.

"Who am I working with?" I asked when we left Ginny's room.

Maggie linked her arm through mine. "You're with me." She tugged me down the hall.

Inside her classroom, sea creatures hung from the ceiling, and posters decorated the walls. Maggie showed me the curriculum we would use and told me what she needed from me. I taught third graders, so helping with this first grade class wouldn't be overly challenging.

The week flew by. Maggie and I grew closer, and the other leaders and assistants welcomed me and doted on Ginny. She bloomed under the love and attention.

Each afternoon, Ginny told me what she'd learned that day. Then, she taught Red the stories and Bible memory verses.

She sat the cat in her lap and stared into her eyes. "Who is a God like you, who pardons sin and forgives the transgression of the remnant of his inheritance? You do not stay angry forever but delight to show mercy. Micah seven, verses eighteen and nineteen."

Red wasn't a very attentive pupil, but Ginny didn't give up.

On our last day, all the kids got ice pops as they left. Rev talked with them before VBS ended and reminded them how much God loved them, just as they were.

Ginny studied her popsicle as we drove home. "Grandma?"

"Yes, honey."

"Rev said Jesus loves us."

"That's right."

She swirled her popsicle in her mouth and pulled it out. "Does He love my mom?"

I pulled into my driveway, parked, and turned around. "Of course He does."

She frowned. "But she's done drugs. That's bad."

"Well, they're not good for her or anyone." I thought for a minute. "What did Rev say?"

She pointed at me with her dripping frosty treat. "Jesus loves us just as we are, and God delights to show mercy."

I handed her a napkin from my purse. "He told you the truth, Ginny. I don't understand it all, but Jesus loves your mom."

August arrived, and I held my breath waiting for Becky to show up. It always startled me when she came without any warning. I hadn't heard from her since my birthday, and I'd stopped trying to call.

A few days into the month, she pulled up in a different vehicle, one in much better shape than her old four-door. I met her in the driveway and hugged her before patting the blue two-door Ford's hood. "This is a big improvement from your old rust bucket."

She ran her hand over the hood. "It's a good little car." She moved away from me, biting her lip and scratching her arm.

I wanted to explain about my angina and hospitalization, but she seemed ... different. I didn't know what it was, but there was something I couldn't put my finger on. A brittle air I hadn't seen in a long time. And she was jumpy, skittish.

"Everything okay?"

"Sure. I'm just tired." Becky headed to the front porch. "Where's Ginny?"

I followed her inside and called for Ginny. "I think she's playing with the kitten."

"Kitten?"

"Yes, she and Sug got me a kitten for my birthday. Feisty thing."

Ginny ran into the room, holding Red against her chest. The kitten pushed with her front paws, trying to wriggle free.

"Hi, Mama." She shoved the cat at Becky. "Meet Red."

Becky patted the kitten on the head. "Red?" She raised an eyebrow and looked at me. "Did you name it?"

"Oh, no. That would be your daughter. Ginny, put her down. She looks tired of being held."

Red bolted from the room as soon as her paws touched the ground. Ginny hugged Becky and pulled her toward the sunporch. "You gotta see Ollie too, Mom."

I fixed glasses of sweet tea while Becky patted Ollie. We bathed him the day before, so his fur was white and soft. I joined them on the porch and gestured to the dog. "He likes to lie on the floor in here because it's cool."

"I'm sure." Becky sipped her tea. "Ginny, can you get your things packed?"

"You can't stay the night?" I asked.

Ginny stuck out her bottom lip. "Last time you spent the night."

"Not this time." She pulled a cigarette from her purse and looked around the table. "Where's your ashtray and lighter?"

"I had to quit smoking." No way to soften this news.

"Grandma had a heart thingy." Ginny stood next to me and leaned against my arm. "She stayed at the hospital on her birthday. I think that stinks."

Becky rubbed her forehead. "You had a heart attack?" Her voice ended on a shrill note.

"No, no, an angina attack. It's different."

Becky crossed her arms, eyes narrowed. "Why didn't you call me, Mom? You should've told me. I could've come and gotten Ginny."

I sat back and mimicked her position, my arms crossed. "I did call you. Lots of times. Your number is disconnected. Ginny was fine. My friends took care of her until I got home." I kept my chin high. Her number being disconnected was not my fault.

She flipped her hand. "Oh, yeah. That's true. They messed up the bill again."

I couldn't help the grunt that came out. That excuse didn't ring true. I'd gone to three family group meetings and learned more about addiction each time. They talked about how I had to adjust my thoughts about it and how to deal with my addict. I wasn't the one with the problem, so I couldn't figure out why I had to change. I still hadn't gotten a chance to ask how to fix Becky. She'd been clean for a few years, but from what I'd learned, an addict was always an addict.

They also said addiction was a disease. That's what Shrimp told me too. I was still trying to wrap my mind around the concept. I understood that diabetes and high blood pressure were diseases. They affected the body in so many ways and required medication. How was an addiction like that?

"You don't believe me?" Becky shook her head and smirked. She tipped her chin at Ginny. "Go get your stuff. We need to go."

Ginny ran off to her room, tears running down her cheeks.

I put my hand on Becky's arm. "Don't leave mad." Inside my mind, I scolded myself, *Ask her for the truth.*

She shook my hand off and stood. "I'm not mad, Mom." She rolled her eyes.

I followed her outside, and Ginny came out with her bags stuffed full. Her eyes widened when she spotted the car.

"Where's our car?"

"This is a friend's."

She hadn't told me that. I helped Ginny put her things in the seat and hugged her tight.

"I grabbed that book we were reading, Grandma."

I brushed her hair off her forehead and kissed her. "Good. Let me know if you like it." I shaded my eyes and looked at Becky. "Tell me when you get home?"

"Sure." She shrugged. "If I can." She got in the car and shut her door.

That had to be enough. I pulled Ginny in for another hug. "I love you, sweetie."

"I love you too, Grandma. Tell Red goodbye. I couldn't find her." A tear rolled down her cheek. "I'll see you soon."

I swallowed the lump in my throat and shut the car door, blinking hard. I waved until I couldn't see them anymore. Another summer down. I wasn't sure I'd see them at Christmas this year.

Chapter 16

Ollie and I shuffled back inside, the screen door slapping shut behind us. I wasn't sure what just happened. Becky came in like a whirlwind and upended my life yet again. My world wobbled. I feared it might tip completely this time.

Why hadn't I confronted Becky? I kept telling myself it was to protect Ginny, but really, if I wanted that, I would have a face-to-face meeting with Becky, even if she screamed and ranted and walked out.

I'd become a peacekeeper, and I hated it.

I picked up the things Ginny left behind and put them in her room, smoothed her bedspread, hung up some clothes, and carried her dirty clothes out to the washing machine. After returning her laundry basket to her closet, I sat on her bed. Ollie stood in the doorway, staring at me.

I opened my arms. "Come here, boy." Ollie hugged me in his unique doggy way while I cried into his fur.

The family group met that night. I'd attended for almost a month and learned more about addiction and about myself. I forced myself to get ready. My new friends would help me, even when I didn't feel like going anywhere.

Todd opened with prayer, and then he turned to Maggie. "I've led since we started the group, but Maggie asked to facilitate tonight's meeting."

She passed out a handout. "Tonight, we're going to talk about acceptance. Accepting that we cannot change our addict." She looked at the paper she held. Her hands shook, and when she glanced up, she blinked away tears. "If you've ever noticed, I haven't talked about my addict." She held my gaze. "That's because I'm the addict."

"What?" She never told me that. I served the whole week at VBS with her, and she never said or indicated anything like this. Her demeanor and life were so different from what I'd experienced with Becky. It hurt that my new friend kept this from me. "Why are you here?"

She tipped her head. "When Todd and Tamara discussed starting this group, they knew my history. They asked me to step in and speak from the other side. The side about recovery." She leaned toward me and touched my hand. "Kat, I didn't mean to hide this from you. But I think I can help you guys understand your addicts and how they think a little better."

I took a minute to digest what she'd said. It made sense. It also spoke to the input she'd given in past meetings. I assumed she understood from years of living with an addict. In reality, her knowledge of addiction came from living it.

I waved my paper in the air. "Well, let's start learning."

She smiled gratefully. "Okay. Tonight, we're going to look at accepting three things. First, our addicts as they are. Then, the craziness addiction has brought into our lives. And last, the fact that we can not change our addicts."

Roger propped his elbows on his knees. "One of the hardest things for me is accepting my son as he is. How do I separate how much I love him from how much I think he's messing up his life?"

Maggie's expression softened. "Great question. I know from my end that when my family detached, it made a difference. My addiction belonged to me. It had nothing to do with my parents or how they raised me. Does that make sense?"

"Sort of." He shook his head. "Sometimes it's all so confusing. I try to do my best." He motioned to his wife. "We both do. But it's hard."

"Maybe this will make more sense." Maggie chewed on her lip before she spoke. "Nothing I chose to do happened because my parents did something. I wasn't reacting to what they did or didn't do."

He nodded slowly. "Okay, I get that."

"Sure, some addicts are raised in that environment and can't break out. But many become addicts because of bad decisions. And because it is a disease." Maggie lifted her hands. "My family detaching made an impact, though. I did react to that."

"Learning to detach is tough," Todd said. "Our mom was so out of control. That's the craziness part Maggie talked about. We'd lived with her addiction for many years, and it was so bad. It took until I left home before I could really detach."

"Me too. It's tough to live with an addict," Tamara said.

I understood that. When Becky was a teen, her drug problems were minimal at first. They snuck up on me. I often thought all teens went through that phase. I'd been learning that for some people, drugs capture them and hold them hostage. Drugs change their brains, and they don't think like other people.

I raised my hand. "So, you've told us that addiction is a disease, and I have to accept Becky as she is. I can't change her. So, where does that leave me?"

Todd grimaced. "It seems like a lose-lose situation, I know. Tamara and I have studied this a lot and attended several conferences about addiction to understand it better. Talking with Maggie helped too. In future group meetings, we want to help us all learn to deal with our addict."

"We, you, can't change your addict. You can't. You'll have to trust me on that one," Maggie added. "There are studies you can look up on your own. But it's true."

I crossed my arms, unwilling to accept everything Maggie said. If I could find out what to do about Becky, I'd tell her, and she'd stop the craziness. Finally. I might not be able to change her, but if she knew what to do, she could make those changes.

Maggie ended with a prayer and then assigned us homework. "This week, write down the things you like doing and what you want to do but haven't because of your addict's behavior. Bring that with you next week."

I had my list ready for the next meeting. Besides teaching, which I loved, I enjoyed helping at VBS and spending time with Ginny. I had to think back to when Becky lived at home to find things I wanted to do but hadn't.

Maggie started the meeting with the Serenity Prayer. Then, she asked, "Does everyone have their lists?"

We all nodded.

"Let's go around the group, and each person can share two things they want to do but haven't because of their addict."

Todd spoke up. "I'll go first." He read from his list, his hands shaking. "I wish I could've invited friends over when I was a kid. But I never knew if my mom would be sober."

Tamara nodded and patted his leg.

"Anything you want to do now but haven't because of your mom?" Maggie asked.

"I'll have to think about that." He laid his paper in his lap. "I focused on back when I was a kid."

"That's fine." Maggie looked around the circle. "Who wants to go next?"

"I will." I held my paper out so I could read it. "Okay, I spent a lot of time on this. I haven't lived with Becky since she was sixteen. At that time, I didn't feel like I could leave the house without wondering what I'd come home to. I worried about what she would or wouldn't do, you know? I'm still afraid to leave in case Becky shows up with Ginny." I lowered my hand. "I haven't gotten very far, that's for sure."

Now that I was in Ginny's life, I lived with the same anxieties as when Becky was a teen. What if Becky showed up —the norm for her—and dropped Ginny off or came to pick her up? I never felt prepared.

"Peace is what I want. And not just keeping the peace at all costs," I said.

Everyone agreed.

"That's probably something all parents, siblings, and children of addicts want. Peace and serenity, like we talked about in our first meeting," Todd said.

Serenity would be lovely, I thought.

Roger went next. "I'd like to buy a new car. We've spent so much money on our son—bailing him out of jail, paying for rehab—that we have nothing left over. A car may seem silly, but it's what I came up with." He leaned back in his seat. "And peace sounds pretty good to me."

"Me too," Samantha said. Roger's wife, usually quiet in meetings, added, "I'd like to go back to college and take a vacation without worrying."

"A vacation. Can you imagine? I'm going to add that to my list." Tamara scribbled on her paper. "I'm like Todd in that I thought more about when I was a child and how my mom's addiction affected us at home. Now that I don't live with her, I'd like to call her and have a real conversation. One with depth, you know?"

Boy, could I relate to Tamara's words. Talking to Becky was like walking through a minefield. The only conversations we'd had in the last few years that were relatively normal were the few times she'd been to my house after rehab. The last time she came for Ginny, we didn't have a productive discussion.

Maggie's nose wrinkled. "Communication with an addict is tough. My mom would tell you she never got anywhere trying to talk to me when I was in active addiction. Addicts have an answer and an excuse for everything you say to them." She pointed to each of us. "Recheck your lists. Think about the things you wrote. Are they material things like Roger's car or Samantha's vacation? Or are they relationship issues? Or a bit of both?"

"I think mine is a bit of both. Because Becky ran away before I experienced much of her addiction, I never had the money issue that Roger and Samantha have had, but not knowing when or if I'd hear from her kept me from doing things," I said. "And it took a toll on my health."

Tamara raised her hand. "Mine is a combination too." Todd, Roger, and Samantha nodded in agreement.

"So this week's homework is to think of ways to achieve what you want. Brainstorm. And dream." Maggie waved her hand. "Dreaming at this point is hard, I'm sure. But allow yourself to picture the life you want. Include good conversations, peace, and serenity if you want them. Take some time with this. Bring your answers to next week's meeting."

I worked on my classroom, preparing it for the start of the school year. While I created a new bulletin board, I considered the homework Maggie assigned. Dreaming was hard, just like she said.

The day before our next family group meeting, Mac rapped his knuckles on my classroom door.

"Hey, Mac, how's your classroom going?" I rearranged books in the reading area.

"I'm not making any big changes this year. If it's not broke, you know." He paused. "Guess what?"

I cocked an eyebrow.

"Come on, Kat. Guess."

"You're dyeing your hair blue."

"Funny woman." He pushed away from the door frame. "Sierra has a boyfriend."

I stood and brushed my hair from my face. "Really? That's great. Have you met him?"

Mac pursed his lips. "I have."

"You don't seem very happy."

"He's a good bit older than Sierra. Eleven years older." His eyebrows shot up.

"Well, that's a big difference. Is he nice? Is he good to her?"

"I guess." Mac ran his hand through his hair. "He's coming to dinner tonight. Can you and Sug come too?"

"I think that's a great idea. I'll call Sug when I get home and let you know if she can come."

Mac clapped his hands. "Great, thanks." He turned to go. "See you tonight around six. And Kat, thanks. I'm interested to hear what you think about Troy."

Mac left, but Sierra's boyfriend's name stuck with me. No way it could be Becky's Troy. Sierra wouldn't fall for some druggie. I shook my head and got back to work on my room.

I stopped at Sug's a little before six. We walked to Mac's under a soft, colorful, late summer sky. I hadn't had much time with my friend lately, and I missed her.

"Got your classroom set up?" she asked.

"Almost. I like the theme I've chosen this year, so I'm excited. We're going to focus a lot on reading classics. *Charlotte's Web*, *Charlie and the Chocolate Factory*, and *The Mouse and the Motorcycle*. I'll have the kids design book covers of what we're reading and use that for my bulletin board."

"That sounds fun."

"I think it will be. I'm still upset about how Ginny left, but planning my classroom has helped."

She linked her arm through mine. "Still going to your family group meetings?"

"Tomorrow night is the next one. We have homework again this week. We're supposed to brainstorm about what we want to do, be, or somewhere we want to go."

Sug cocked an eyebrow. "How's that going?"

"Tough, actually. I don't think I've let myself dream in a long time." I paused for a moment. "I think I'd want Ginny to live with me if I could have anything. I never thought I'd say that after years of living alone. I don't want to hurt Becky, though, you know?"

"That's a big decision, for sure. Changing the subject, but guess what I'm working on?"

"What?"

"I got a commission to paint a song." She smiled.

"What does that mean?"

"I listen to the song and then paint how I feel." Sug's cheeks grew rosy in the glow of the setting sun. "It's fun. Something I've never done before."

"I'd love to see it when you're finished." I knocked on Mac's front door and turned the knob to enter.

The door swung open, and I came face-to-face with Troy. Becky's Troy.

Chapter 17

He held up his hands and backed away from the door. I gritted my teeth. "Hello, Troy."

Sierra came to the door, slipping her arm around his waist. "What's going on? Come on in, Kat, Sugar." She gestured for us to enter. "I'm glad you could come to dinner."

Mac walked down the hallway. "Come on in, y'all. Why is everyone standing in the doorway?"

"You need to ask him." I jabbed my finger in Troy's direction.

Mac frowned. "Kat?"

I turned to Sugar. "Becky's Troy."

She gasped and covered her mouth.

"I ... I don't understand." Sierra glanced between her boyfriend and me. Troy backed further into the house.

Mac blinked. "Becky's Troy?" He turned and glared at Sierra's boyfriend. "What are you doing here?" His words came out in a growl.

Sierra grabbed her dad's arm. "What's going on? We're dating. You already knew that. You said he could come for dinner. Why are you all acting like this?"

"Ask him." I ground out the words.

"Troy?" Her voice broke.

He shook his head and held up his hands again. "Look, I used to date her daughter. That's all."

Mac, Sug, and I stood together, facing the couple.

"That's all, Sierra. I swear." He dropped his hands. "She's just mad because her daughter ran away when we were dating."

I wanted to punch him, to hurt him as badly as he'd hurt me. Years of frustration and anger boiled inside, and a pinching feeling filled my chest.

"She did not run away." The words came out deep and husky. "You promised her you'd build her a house in Florida. You gave her drugs. She was sixteen, Troy. Sixteen." I ended with a moan. Tears streamed down my cheeks. I swiped them off and gestured to Sierra. "You need to stay away from him. He's toxic. He ruined my daughter."

Sierra's face paled. "Is that true?"

"You heard what I said, Sierra." Troy raked his hands through his hair. "Becky ran away—simple as that." Disgust lined his face. "She basically forced her to."

I stepped back, stunned. How could he say that? "That's not true. I can't stay here, Mac. I'm sorry. Sierra, you have a decision to make." I looked at Sugar. "Are you coming with me or staying?"

She joined me on the front doorstep and linked her arm through mine. "I'm coming with you. Come on, Kat. Let's go to my house. You can't stress your heart like this."

I followed her to the road. My head alternated between feeling like it would explode and feeling as if it would fall off—like one of those wobbly-headed dolls. I clenched my fists. "Can you believe this? I could've punched that boy."

"He's a man now, Kat," she said softly.

We turned onto her street. Her place beckoned with its wide, wrap-around porch and white wooden rocking chairs. I tromped up the front steps and plopped onto one.

"He may be a man, but he's still Troy."

"I know." Sug slowed my rocker. "Be careful, or you'll rock clear off the porch."

Huffing out a breath, I stopped. "I don't know what to do. When Troy and Becky first ran off, I could've pressed charges because she was underage. I searched for her for a few years but never found any trace. Do you think there are statutes of limitations?"

"I have no idea, but I'm going to make us sandwiches. You stay here and cool off. I'll be right back." She leaned over and looked me in the eyes. "You have to calm down, Kat. This stress and anger are not good for you."

No, they weren't good for me, but still, I stood and paced the porch, grumbling to myself. I sat, dropping my head in my hands. What in the world should I do?

I didn't hear Mac until he cleared his throat. Lifting my head, I said, "Hi. I'm sorry I ruined your dinner party." He deserved an apology. He hadn't done anything wrong.

"I came over because Sierra and Troy need to 'talk.'" He made air quote marks. "I don't want to be part of that." He stomped up onto the porch and settled into another rocker. He shook his head. "I cannot believe this."

"Me neither."

Sug came out with two peanut butter and jelly sandwiches, saw Mac, and handed him one and me the other. "I'll be right back." She brought us each a glass of lemonade and joined us with her sandwich and drink. "Where were we?"

I licked peanut butter off my lip. "There's nothing like a PB&J."

"It's better than what we were having at my house." Mac sipped his lemonade and smacked his lips. "Grilled chicken, fresh asparagus, new potatoes, French bread." He bit into his sandwich. "Give me a PB&J any day."

Sug and I both groaned.

"Don't tease us." I wiped my mouth with my napkin and sipped my drink. "Let's just sit here and not solve any problems. Not talk about Troy at all. Can we do that?"

So that's what my friends and I did. We relaxed, drank our lemonade, and enjoyed the evening breeze until it was time to head home. We didn't talk about anything important. We didn't solve any problems. We just relaxed. My head cleared, my hands stopped shaking, and the pinching in my chest eased.

When darkness shrouded us, I stood to go home. "Thanks, you guys. You're the best." I would have to deal with Troy, but after waiting twelve years, another day or two wouldn't make a difference.

Using the list-making tools I'd learned from Sug and Maggie, I wrote my thoughts and did my family group homework.

Maggie stressed that accepting our addicts as they were, realizing the craziness addiction brought into our lives, and acknowledging that we couldn't change our addicts were all things I could work on and through.

On my list, I put the headers "Dreams" and "Acceptance." Underneath "Dreams," I added peace and serenity, as Maggie suggested. I also put "vacation," like Samantha.

Looking at "Acceptance" was different. I didn't know how to accept Becky as an addict or if I could change her or influence her to change. That column got a big question mark. I wanted to learn more, but why did I have to accept it without a choice? It seemed so passive.

I'd had enough of that.

That made me think of Troy again. *How dare he accuse me of being the reason Becky left?*

I had stuffed him in the back corner of my mind all day. As the family group meeting approached, he consumed my thoughts. I wrote a separate header on my list of "Troy" so I could talk about him at the meeting. Maybe they could offer some input on how to handle him and provide insight into what he'd said.

Maggie led again, and before we dove into the subject, I asked if I could share something.

She waved her hand. "Sure, go ahead."

I took a deep breath. "So I ran into the guy who started my daughter on drugs, and that she ran away with years ago. It's thrown me for a loop. I'm not sure what to do or what to avoid doing. Just seeing him made me furious." I paused. "And he said I forced Becky to leave. To run away." My voice cracked.

Maggie raised her eyebrows. "That's a tough situation. Will you see him again?"

"He's dating my friend's daughter. I told her what he did and that she needed to stay away from him. Plus, what he said is not true. I didn't make her leave." I crossed my arms and slumped in my chair.

"What do you think will happen?" Roger asked.

I made a face. "No idea."

Samantha leaned forward. "Is he your granddaughter's father?"

My stomach rolled. "Oh, my goodness. I hadn't even thought of that." I sat up straight, one hand over my mouth and one on my stomach. *What if she was right?*

"I'm so sorry, Kat." Samantha crouched by my chair and patted my thigh. "I assumed you wondered who her father was."

I swallowed against the nausea. "It's okay. Not your fault. I wondered about it when Ginny first came, but she didn't know. I've never asked Becky. What do I do with this? Do I ask him? Do I even want to know?"

Todd cocked an eyebrow. "That, we can't tell you. We try never to tell people what to do. But we can help you talk through it. You'll figure it out. Just might take some time."

Maggie piped up, "I think this falls under what we discussed last week—acceptance. Why don't you take out your homework? Before we look at that, we'll talk more about it. One thing that helps is to accept the present, where you are right now, and where your addict is. Not physically, but emotionally and mentally. Find out who you are at this point in time." She nodded. "That'll be your homework for next week, by the way."

Roger raised his hand. "What if you don't know where your addict is? Our son left again two days ago. We have no idea where he went or who he's with. And Kat has the same problem with her daughter."

"Let's think about the Serenity Prayer we discussed at our first meeting. Who and what can you control?" Maggie looked at each of us.

"Ourselves," we all droned.

"That wasn't very enthusiastic." Maggie chuckled.

Tamara's lip curled. "It's hard to be enthusiastic when you can't do anything about your addict's life or problems."

"True." Maggie held her palm out to Tamara. "And?"

"And I suppose if I cannot change my mom, I have to accept her where she is and for who she is," she said.

"Yes." Maggie pumped her fist. "You got it."

My shoulders slumped. "Oh, Maggie, you make this sound so easy. But it isn't. If I accept Becky for who and what she is, where does that leave me?"

"It leaves you free, Kat. Free."

I can't say my whole life changed that night, but I left the family group meeting thinking differently. *If* I accepted Becky the way she was, I could dream about my own life. And could live life without waiting for the other shoe to drop.

Could I do that? I would have to trust someone to do it, right? God? Becky? Myself? Trust didn't come easily—too many reasons not to believe in or depend on someone.

Ugh. As much as I wanted to live a full life, picturing it and making it happen still felt out of reach. Hope dangled before me, but something kept pulling it out of my grasp.

The next day, I worked at the school. Mac stopped by my classroom.

"How ya doing?" He leaned against the door frame.

"I'm okay. Come on in."

"I wasn't sure if you'd want to see me," he said.

"I'm not mad at you. I'm mad at myself." I chose a decorative border to add to the wall in my room.

He perched on the corner of my desk and crossed his arms. "How so?"

"I don't think I ever really dealt with my feelings about Troy. I focused more on Becky." I set the border on my desk. "But seeing him? It brought up a lot of anger. I think some of that anger is more toward Becky than him. Does that make sense?"

Mac stood and hugged me. "You're learning a lot about yourself, Kat."

I stepped back. "I have a potential problem, though. What if Troy is Ginny's father?"

He sat back down. "Oh boy, I never thought about that. Ginny's been 'ours' for so many years."

"Yep, four years since her first summer with me. Sug and I talked about who her daddy might be back then, but I just never thought about it after that. Last night at my meeting, someone asked me if Troy could be Ginny's biological father, which got me wondering."

"Yeah. Would it change anything? To know, I mean?"

I inhaled and blew it out. "If Becky returns, do I tell her he's here and ask if he's the father? Would he want to be part of Ginny's life? Would I want him in her life?" I shuddered. "That's a huge consideration. Does he deserve to know her after all this time?"

"That's something you need to pray about. I don't think there's any easy answer." He put his hands on his hips. "I know how I felt finding out about Sierra after nineteen years. I wish I'd known sooner."

"But you're a good guy."

"Her mom didn't know that. I missed out because of someone else's choice." He shook his head. "It's not a simple question, and there's no simple answer."

I turned back to the border. "Nope, I don't think so either. Hey, while you're here ..." I gestured to the ladder. "You'll do a great job. I'll hand you what you need."

"I'm going to quit stopping by your room." He held his hand out for the border. "Every time I do, you put me to work."

I invited Mac and Sugar over for dinner that weekend. School started the next week, and I'd be busy with the beginning of the school year. Sugar brought salad, and Mac contributed a big jug of lemonade. As usual, I made spaghetti.

Sugar helped set the table while Mac poured our drinks. I set out the salad bowls before serving our food. When I sat down, Ollie curled up by my feet.

"Did you tell Sugar what you asked me about Troy?" Mac asked.

Sugar twirled her fork in her noodles. "What's up, Kat?"

"I'm wondering if Troy might be Ginny's father."

She slurped her noodles so hard one flew up and smacked her in the cheek, leaving red sauce on her face. "What?"

I handed her a napkin. "It's a possibility. Becky left at sixteen and had Ginny at eighteen. She's never said who Ginny's father is, and I never asked."

Sug wiped her face. "Ginny's never said either." She stared at her spaghetti, stirring it round and round. "What does Troy seem like, Mac? Did you talk to him the other night?"

"We hadn't made it past saying hello when y'all showed up. He'd left by the time I returned from your house that night, and Sierra has made herself scarce for the last few days. I don't think she's happy with me for siding with you two."

"It's an ethical thing, I think." I held up my hands like scales. "If he's Ginny's father—and we don't know that for sure—does he deserve to be in her life? Also, doesn't Ginny deserve to know her father?" I took a bite of my salad. Speaking around a tomato, I said, "And, I hate to bring this up, but is Becky even aware who Ginny's father is?"

Sug raised an eyebrow. "True."

"Too much to decide tonight. Mac said I need to pray about it and keep doing that until I have an answer."

"Good idea." She looked under the table. "By the way, where is Red?"

"She's sleeping on Ginny's bed. She figured out this big guy,"—I nudged Ollie with my foot—"loved the room, and she took it over. Anything to keep him on his toes."

"Poor Ollie."

Hearing his name, he wagged his tail and gave a soft woof. Sug pinched a piece of bread off and fed it to him.

"Yeah, poor Ollie." I laughed. "You're just going to make his love handles bigger."

Chapter 18

The new school year began, and I stayed busy learning my students' names and establishing class rules. When the temperatures turned chilly, Ollie stayed inside while I worked. I worried that Red plagued him, but I couldn't do anything about it.

My cell rang on a Friday night in late September as I washed my dinner dishes. I wiped my hands and answered.

"Hi, Grandma, it's me."

My girl's voice filled me with warmth. "Ginny, I'm so glad you called. How are you?" I sat at the table.

"I'm good. I'm in fifth grade now."

"Yes, I know. You'll be in middle school soon."

She giggled. "Mama said I could call you on Friday nights."

I wanted to shout for joy but settled for a happy dance in my chair. "That sounds wonderful."

Her sigh was heavy. "I miss you, Grandma."

"I miss you too, honey. Did you ever finish that book you took?"

"I did. I'm reading *The Black Stallion* at school now."

"That's a great book," I said.

We talked about horses until Becky told her to hang up.

"I have to get off the phone now. But I'll call next Friday, okay?" she asked.

"Yes, I can't wait to talk to you again, Ginny. Have a good week at school. I love you."

"I love you, too."

I hung up the phone and wiped happy tears off my cheeks. I could get used to talking to her every week. I looked up. "Thank you for this, God."

A couple of weeks later, as I debated what to have for dinner, my phone rang.

"Grandma." Ginny's voice shook, and she sniffled. "Grandma, Mama didn't come to get me."

Ginny had called me on several Friday evenings so far, but this was a Wednesday. I looked at the clock on the stove. Ginny and Becky were in the Central Time Zone, and it was after five my time. Usually, Becky got off in time to pick up Ginny when school ended, so she didn't have to ride the bus.

"Are you at school? Your mom didn't pick you up when school let out?"

"I'm at school." I could hear someone speaking in the background. "Hang on, Grandma. Mrs. Patterson wants to talk to you."

When she came on the line, she introduced herself and said, "I believe we spoke a few years ago."

"Yes, Mrs. Patterson, we did. What's going on? Ginny said Becky didn't come to pick her up. I don't understand why you called me?"

"Mrs. Johnson, Ginny asked to call you from the school phone. Her mother always picks her up at three-thirty on her way home from work. It's after four now, and Ms. Johnson hasn't shown up."

I sat on the couch. "I don't mean to sound like I don't care, but I don't understand why you called me. I live in Virginia. I'm not sure what I can do."

"Ginny insisted she call. You see, your daughter has been routine in her schedule for so long. Ginny is very concerned, and frankly, so am I after what she's told me."

"What did she tell you?"

Mrs. Patterson cleared her throat. "Ginny said her mom has a new boyfriend."

"I didn't know about that."

"She said we may be able to get him on the phone. Apparently, he hangs around at their house while Ginny's mother works." She paused. "Those are Ginny's words."

"Will you do that, please? Try to contact him and let me know what you find out. Thank you for calling. I'm worried too."

Mrs. Patterson promised to call back. I paced the kitchen. Becky had been clean for so long. What had she done?

Guilt filled me when I immediately suspected Becky of using drugs again. I thought she'd beaten drugs when she went to rehab. Maybe I was jumping to conclusions. Maybe she had car troubles or worked late. But this past summer, she seemed so off. Brittle. And different.

I hadn't heard about the new boyfriend. Ginny hadn't mentioned her mom having anyone in her life.

I sat at the table out on the sunporch with the phone beside me and bowed my head to pray. After praying for Becky's safety and Ginny's well-being, I asked for guidance for myself. Depending on what I learned today, I had decisions to make, and they wouldn't be simple ones.

My phone rang, and I jumped. My hands shook when I answered. "Yes? Did he tell you anything? Did you find Becky?"

"Mrs. Johnson, we called your daughter's place to get hold of the boyfriend, but no one answered."

I tapped my fingers on the table. "Is there a neighbor or friend that Ginny can ask to check on Becky and see if she's home?"

"I'll try that and get back to you."

I waited again, pacing between my kitchen and living room. Sitting wasn't helping me calm down. My phone rang.

"Ginny had a neighbor's phone number, so I called." Mrs. Patterson hesitated. "The neighbor went to the apartment and knocked. The door was unlocked. She went in ..."

Sweat trickled down my back. "What did she find?" My hand hurt from gripping the phone. I lowered myself to the floor in the kitchen. Ollie lay next to me, his head in my lap, his warmth offering comfort.

Mrs. Patterson cleared her throat. "Ms. Johnson seems to have left. The neighbor said her car was in the driveway, but her closet was empty, and her purse wasn't there. It looks like she's gone."

I leaned back against the oven. Gone? What did that mean? Would Becky desert Ginny? That thought brought me up short. Yes, she would. She'd done it four years before when she left Ginny with me. But why would she abandon Ginny at school?

"May I speak with my granddaughter?" I strained to keep my tone calm and even.

"Of course."

"Hi, Grandma." Ginny sniffled. "Mama left me, Grandma."

I waited until she stopped crying. "Can you answer a few questions for me?"

In a small voice, she said, "Yes."

"When did your mom's new boyfriend show up?"

"She brought him home Saturday night, I think. He was there Sunday morning when I got up." She blew her nose.

That made sense. Ginny hadn't mentioned him in our recent phone conversation. Today was Wednesday, so this boyfriend had been there for several days.

"And he didn't go to work or anything? How did your mom seem this week? You can tell me the truth, honey."

In a rush of words, she filled me in. "I wanted to call you, Grandma. He just hung around all day. And he stunk. I think Mama's using again. I can tell. I remember what she acted like before she got clean. I even told her I knew." Ginny paused and sniffled. "She told me I didn't know what I was talking about. She said she was fine and yelled at me for asking. But she's not fine. I think that guy gave her drugs." Her voice cracked. "And now she's left me."

My heart broke for my granddaughter and my daughter. I had no idea where Becky could be, but one thing I knew—I had to get to Ginny. I did some quick calculations.

"I'll leave now and come get you. Is there someone you can stay with tonight? I'll be there tomorrow, sweetie."

"I ... I don't know."

"Let me talk to Mrs. Patterson, honey."

The principal helped me arrange for Ginny to spend the night at a friend's house. The following two days were a break for their school system, so Ginny wouldn't be at school when I arrived in Memphis. I'd swing by the friend's place to get her.

I talked to Ginny briefly and gave her an idea of when I'd arrive. Sug said she'd watch Ollie, feed him, and take care of Red. And then I called my principal, who volunteered to arrange a substitute for the rest of the week.

Then I packed what I'd need for a few days. I would pick up my granddaughter and bring her back to live with me. Becky's actions spoke volumes. It would take more than an apology from her to fix this.

I drove six hours that night. Exhaustion crept in, but anger forced me on. The need to reach Ginny and wrap my arms around her was overpowering. Imaginary conversations with Becky kept my mind busy. I didn't understand my daughter. How could she go back to drugs? How could she throw away the last several years of sobriety?

What in the world was she thinking?

And why would she—*how could she*—desert her daughter?

What I'd learned in the family group meetings swirled in my mind. I thought I'd accepted Becky for who and what she was, but when she hurt Ginny, that took things to another level. Ginny was innocent in all this.

When Becky first returned after eight years, I pushed my issues and feelings aside because of Ginny. I don't think I ever dealt with all of that stored-up anger, and now rage tried to consume me.

Over and over in my mind, I cried—how could she leave my sweet girl?

I stayed overnight in Bristol, Virginia, and left for Memphis in the pre-dawn hours. Mrs. Patterson had given me the address where Ginny waited. I arrived shortly after lunch.

I knocked on the door and took a moment to survey the yard and neighborhood while I waited. An older neighborhood; most yards were unkempt, though this one looked clean, with baskets of flowers lining the brick front porch.

After waiting several minutes, I knocked again. My heart raced. Where could Ginny be? My imagination went into overdrive, and my skin crawled.

I looked to the side of the house. A driveway with weeds growing through the cracks led to a rusty chain-link fence. I followed it to the open gate leading to the backyard. I pushed it wider and ventured into the yard.

Ginny sat on a swing in a rusty metal swing set. She pushed herself in slow circles, head down, eyes closed.

"Ginny?" I spoke softly as I approached her.

She looked up. Her lips trembled—*my dear, sweet girl.* I reached for her and pulled her into a hug. She leaned against me and sobbed.

After she calmed down, I tilted her chin to look into her eyes. I thumbed tears from her cheeks. "I'm here, honey. I'm here." I glanced around the yard. "Where is your friend?"

She stepped back. "They went to the store, so they left me here to wait for you. They've been gone for a while."

I grunted. It wasn't her fault that these friends deserted her. It wasn't her fault that her mom abandoned her. I clenched my fists, opened them slowly, and relaxed my shoulders. Ginny didn't need to deal with my anger on top of her own pain.

"Let's get your things." I followed her to the back door. The inside was tidy, like the outside, but I couldn't understand why they left Ginny here alone. It didn't make sense. What if I'd been delayed?

"That everything?" I asked as Ginny grabbed her backpack.

"Uh-huh."

I found a scrap of paper and scribbled a note for the friend and her mother. "Let's go." We went out the back door, pulled it shut, and she followed me to the car. "Where is your apartment?" We needed to pack more of her clothes and things.

Ginny rubbed her eyes. "I don't want to go there, Grandma. I'm tired. I don't want to go home."

"I know, sweetie, but we have to get some more things for you. I don't know how long you'll be staying with me in Virginia. And we can check to see if your mom left a way to contact her."

I wanted to investigate and see what I could find. Maybe something happened to Becky, and she hadn't wanted to leave. I worried that this new boyfriend forced her to go somewhere without her consent.

Ginny gave me directions to her apartment. I pulled into the parking lot and locked the car, noticing how rundown the complex appeared.

A thin woman in a tattered pink robe and house shoes stood on one of the ground-floor porches. "Whatcha doin' here, girl?" She pointed to Ginny. "Your mama's got a new boyfriend, don't he?" She cackled.

Her screeching made my teeth hurt. *Be polite*, I told myself. "Did you see Becky leave?"

"Nah, but I saw her with that fella. He shacked up there all week." Disgust laced her words.

I cringed. "Well, thank you for checking and for letting me know." I waved and nudged Ginny inside, closing and locking the door behind me.

"She's nosy like that, Grandma. Mama said we have to ignore her."

I'd ignore her, even though I was thankful she'd checked out the place. I looked around, walked through the tiny kitchen, and searched the papers on the dining table for a note. All I found was a stack of unpaid bills.

It looked like Becky just packed up and ran off. Ginny showed me Becky's room, and while I checked the dresser, she opened her mom's closet. Becky's clothes were gone. Ginny plopped on the bed and shook her head. "What is wrong with my mom?"

What should I tell her? Becky was a grown woman. Still, I had learned enough about addiction to know that when an addict used, they didn't think like sober people.

I tried to explain some of that to Ginny, but it overwhelmed her. Finally, I sat beside my granddaughter and put my arm around her. She leaned into me.

"Here's what we're going to do, sweetie. We'll leave a note for your mom on the table. You go pack your clothes and anything else you need. Don't forget books and your toothbrush. And then," I brushed a strand of hair off her face, "you will come live with me."

We drove home slower than I'd traveled to Memphis. Ginny relaxed and cheered up a little. We talked about the mountains in East Tennessee and Virginia. As we drew closer to home, I made a mental list of things to do.

I would enroll Ginny at Seaside Elementary. Gardenview Elementary could send her school records. Depending on what happened, I might have to hire an attorney.

No way would I give Ginny back to Becky without a fight.

Chapter 19

The drive, a quick turnaround with so many emotions—up, down, and sideways—took the starch out of me. A week-long nap might fix me up, but there were so many things to take care of. We had the weekend to make sure Ginny had the clothes and school supplies she needed. After texting her future teacher, we hit the mall with her supply list in hand.

"Some of this you can bring through the year. We need to buy more clothes today too." I scanned my list.

Ginny ran her fingers along a rack of shirts. "I have clothes, Grandma."

"I know you do, honey, but ..." How could I explain that her torn and stained jeans weren't what the Seaside Elementary kids wore? We didn't require uniforms, but the students wore nicer clothes.

"Let's keep what you have for playing after school, okay?" I held up some jeans and grabbed a pink top from another rack. "What do you think of this?"

Ginny made a face. "How about I pick out my own shirts?"

Okay, then. Pink wasn't her color anymore. I forgot she was in fifth grade now. I raised my hands. "Sure. Pick out five or six tops, and I'll grab some jeans and pants."

It took a while, but Ginny found enough mix-and-match clothes to satisfy me. She tried on the pants and jeans and even found a cute skirt.

We left the mall and headed back toward the beach to pick up school supplies.

My blood pressure shot up whenever I thought about Becky abandoning my granddaughter. I took deep breaths and blew them out, then rolled my neck from side to side. I craved a cigarette now more than ever before.

Ginny probably wondered who this crazy woman was that she'd gotten stuck with.

At the local Walmart, Ginny led the way to the school supplies. "What do I need first?" She fingered a cute cheetah print backpack. "Is this too much?"

"I think cheetah is popular right now."

"No, I mean, you know, money. Is it too expensive?" She scuffed her shoe on the floor.

"Oh, honey, no. It's fine." I plucked the backpack from her hands and set it in the cart. "There." I checked that item off my list with a flourish. I handed her the scrap of paper. "Here, see if we need anything else."

Her grin made me flush with warmth. I'd be happy if I could put that smile on her face every day.

"It's not on there, but I think I'll need a lunchbox," she said.

"True. I don't have anything that isn't pretty old." We looked through the picked-over selection. "Maybe I'll buy a new one, too."

"You should, Grandma. You need to treat yourself."

Sweet girl, don't change. "You're good to me, kiddo." I hugged her.

She grabbed a tan lunchbox to match her backpack, and I chose a dark blue one.

We added pencils, notebooks, and a calculator before checking out. As I stowed our bags in the trunk of my car, Mac called my name.

"Hey, guys." He stopped next to us, a questioning expression on his face. "Ginny, why are you here?"

"She's going to live with me and attend school here." I raised my eyebrows, attempting to send him nonverbal clues.

"Okay. That's great." He turned to her. "I'm glad you're here. How's your mom?"

"Ginny, get in the car." I handed her the keys. "You can turn on the air conditioner."

We watched as Ginny did what I asked, then I turned to Mac. "Ginny called me last week. Her mom ran off again. Left her at school. I drove to Memphis and picked her up. We got in late Friday night. I didn't have a chance to call you before I left." I shook my head. "Becky abandoned her."

His body tensed. "What? I'm so sorry, Kat. I didn't know why you weren't at school the last few days. I'm sorry I asked Ginny." He rolled his eyes. "That poor kid."

I grabbed his arm. "Look, Mac, don't say anything to Sierra, please. I still haven't decided what to do about Troy, and I haven't had time to think about it. I'm not ready for Ginny to hear anything about him."

Mac looked over my shoulder. "Too late." He gestured with his chin.

I turned to find Sierra walking toward us. "Hi, Sierra." I glanced at Ginny in the car, not missing how her face lit up when she saw Mac's daughter.

Sierra nodded but said nothing. It seemed she still held a grudge over what I'd told her about Troy.

I opened my car door. "Well, we need to go." Ginny said something, but I shut the door before she could talk to Sierra.

"I wanted to tell Ms. Sierra hi." Ginny crossed her arms, her lip jutted out in a pout.

"They were on their way somewhere." Not a lie. They had to be going somewhere. "We'll see them later. Let's take your things home, and you can get ready for school tomorrow. We can take the tags off and pack your backpack." I rubbed my chest. I'd had little pangs since leaving on Wednesday to get Ginny. I couldn't have heart problems. I didn't have time for that. Another deep breath and hard exhale.

I walked Ginny into her classroom the next day. I worried about her adjustment to so many changes in such a short time. Being the new kid in class was tough. I spoke with her teacher before I left and asked her to let me know if she noticed any trouble. That Friday afternoon, she walked Ginny to my classroom.

She leaned against the doorframe as Ginny put the books back on the shelves in my reading corner. She'd taken up that task each day after she got out of class.

"She's doing great, Kat," her teacher, Mrs. Swanson, said.

"I'm so glad. This will be a day-by-day process. I don't know if or when I'll hear from her mom."

Mrs. Swanson nodded. "Well, I will do what I can to help her. She's very sweet."

"I think so." I grinned. "I hoped Mr. Thomas would talk with her." Mr. Thomas, our school counselor, handled incoming students. "Maybe he can help her with this transition. Becky will have to make some big improvements for me to let her return to Memphis."

Mrs. Swanson pushed off the doorframe. "Do you have custody of her?"

I crossed my arms. "No, not legally. But her mom deserted her. That has to count for something."

"I suggest you find a good family attorney. I think you need one. I don't know anyone to recommend, but you can ask around."

Mrs. Swanson waved goodbye to Ginny and headed down the hall. She was right. I needed a good lawyer. How did I find one?

That weekend, I wrote out several questions for an attorney. I had missed the family group meeting the last two Thursdays, but I hoped someone in the group would have a contact they'd recommend. That way, I'd be prepared if Becky showed up.

Sugar came by Sunday afternoon. When she and Ginny walked to the beach, I scrounged around in my desk. One last cigarette had rolled to the back. I pulled it out and studied it for a long time. Here was the solution to my anxiety, my fears. I remembered the relief I used to feel at that first puff. My shoulders would relax, my stomach would stop churning. My heart ...

"What are you doing?" I scolded myself. I tore the cigarette into tiny pieces and flushed it down the toilet, then I picked up my cell phone and called Maggie. I told her why I had missed the meetings.

"I need to tell you something else." My hands trembled.

"What's going on?" she asked.

I cleared my throat and told her about the cigarette. When I finished, I waited for her judgment and scorn.

She let out a gasp. "Way to go. You did it!"

"Did what? You're not mad?"

"Kat, come on. What have you learned all of these months? Even if you'd smoked that cigarette, I'd still love you. Even. If." She emphasized the words.

"Thank you." I wiped tears from my cheeks. I filled her in on what happened with Becky, and then I asked about attorneys.

"I can check around," she said. "I've never needed a lawyer. My parents used one a few times for things I'd done, but I didn't."

"Okay, thanks, Maggie. I need to get some kind of custody of Ginny. And I have to figure something out about Troy."

"That's true. Is he still around, dating your friend's daughter?"

My stomach rolled and burned. "I'm not sure, but I think so."

"Let me find a lawyer's name for you. I'll get back to you as soon as possible, okay?"

"Thanks, Maggie." I hung up the phone and wandered through the house, straightening things and thinking. I wanted Ginny to stay with me. But would the courts see things my way? How many rights did a grandparent have?

I sat on the sofa, my chest tight and heavy. Making a cardiology appointment was next on my list.

The screen door banged shut when Ginny and Sug returned, startling me awake. I sat up slowly and rubbed my eyes, realizing the sun had set. "You guys were gone a while."

"We took a long walk, Grandma." Ginny sat beside me. "I found some shells." She opened her hand to show me a handful of small coquina clam shells. "These are my favorites."

I looked through them. "I love those colors. There's a glass jar in the kitchen. You can put them in it. Go wash them off in the bathroom, and I'll find the jar." I headed to the kitchen. "Oh, Ginny, plug the sink, or they'll wash down the drain," I called.

"I will, Grandma."

Sug followed me into the kitchen. "You okay, Kat? Your color is off."

"I've had some pain." I tapped my chest. I didn't want to complain, but Sug needed to know.

She leaned against the counter. "How long has it been since you saw your cardiologist?"

I squatted to check under the sink. "I missed my last appointment. But I made a note to call tomorrow to get in to see him." I handed her the glass jar and stood. "I promise I'll make an appointment on my lunch break."

Sug waved me to the living room. "You go sit down. I'll make a quick supper for the three of us. I want you to rest."

I hugged her and sat on the couch. I leaned my head back and closed my eyes, consciously relaxing. *Deep breaths in and out.* I recited the Serenity Prayer to myself, and some of my stress began to ease. I couldn't allow myself to get sick. Ginny needed me.

My cardiologist couldn't see me for another month. But when I explained my symptoms and told the receptionist about the stress I'd been under, they fit me in on Wednesday. I arranged for a substitute and asked Mac to take Ginny home after school, hoping Sierra wouldn't be there. I wasn't ready for her or Troy to see Ginny, but I had no choice. Sug was busy finishing a painting, and I didn't want to bother her.

Dr. Thompson entered the room and frowned. "Why are you here? I'm not supposed to see you yet." He flipped through his notes. "Wait. You missed an appointment, didn't you?"

"Yes." I told him how I'd been feeling. "The nurse worked me in."

"Let's see how your heart sounds." He removed his stethoscope, plugged the ends into his ears, and pressed the cold part onto my skin.

I yelped.

He patted my shoulder. "Sorry, dear." He listened, then stood up, stuffing the stethoscope into his coat pocket. "Are you taking your medication?"

"Yes."

He pulled a seat up in front of me. "Tell me how your stress is. I remember you had your granddaughter with you before, and that was a difficult situation."

"She's with me full-time now." I told him what happened with Becky. He pursed his lips. "This stress isn't good for you, Kat."

"I know, but what can I do?" Tears filled my eyes. This had become a brutal and endless cycle.

"Now, now, don't cry." Dr. Thompson patted my knee. "Let's try a couple of things."

He wrote on his prescription pad and handed it to me. "This medication helps with anxiety. It works well in combination with the one you're on for depression. It would also be beneficial to walk daily. Short walks, especially if it's hot out. That can help with your stress level too."

I wiped my cheeks with the back of my hand and took the prescription from him. "When do I need to come back?"

"Let's give it a month. But Kat," he narrowed his eyes, "call 911 at any signs of pain or shortness of breath. You don't need to wait."

I assured him I'd follow his directions, then I filled my prescription and headed home.

School hadn't let out yet, so I took a short nap. How could I be only fifty-four and have heart problems? My dad had never been in the picture, and I didn't know if he had any cardiac conditions. With no way to know, I put it out of my mind. As the cardiologist said, the best course of action was to take my medications and walk daily.

And cut back on stress.

The shrill ring of the house phone woke me. I hurried to the kitchen to answer it.

"Hello." My voice was scratchy from sleep, so I cleared it and said hello again.

"Hi, Grandma," Ginny said. "Are you okay?"

"Hi, pumpkin. Yes, I'm fine. Just fell asleep." I stifled a yawn.

"Mr. Mac wanted me to ask if you want to come for dinner."

I looked through the windows on the sunporch. It was growing darker. "Sure, that sounds good. Will you tell him I'll be there in a bit?" I stretched.

Ginny yelled my answer to Mac. I heard his deep voice talking to her. "He said that's fine. And to tell you Sierra isn't here."

"Okay, see you in a bit." I hung up and inhaled. With a deep exhale, I rolled my neck and shoulders, twisting them side to side, thankful I wouldn't have to face Sierra. I still needed to get that number from Maggie for an attorney, but right now, I wanted to focus on my health and Ginny.

One step at a time. That's the best I could do.

Chapter 20

Rev's face lit up when he saw Ginny at the next family group meeting. He hugged her, and she stayed to help him while I headed to the classroom. Maggie pulled me aside and handed me a piece of paper.

"I asked some friends for a good lawyer, and this is who they all suggested. She does family law and should be able to help you."

"Thanks, Maggie. I appreciate it." I tucked the paper into my purse as we took our seats.

Todd led us in prayer and announced, "Tonight, we have a special speaker." He looked at Maggie. "Do you want to introduce her?"

Maggie nodded, her whole body radiating joy. "My mom is here to speak to us tonight." She clapped and bounced in her chair like a little girl. "I'm so excited for you all to meet her and hear how she dealt with my addiction."

We'd never had a speaker before. Now I'd hear from a mom of an addicted daughter. She would offer insight I could relate to. Maybe she could tell me how to change Becky. I pulled a notebook and pen from my purse.

Maggie introduced her mother, and Nora stepped up to a tabletop podium.

"Hi, everyone." She waved. "I'm so glad to be here with you tonight. Several years ago, I was in the same boat you are now. Desperate, confused, angry, alone. I didn't know what to do to help my daughter, but

I thought someone could tell me what to do. I knew I could fix Maggie if I had the right words." She paused. "Do you hear what I just said? Everything was about me. Everything I thought about, or wanted to learn about, involved *me* fixing Maggie."

Nora pursed her lips. "But here's the thing. There's nothing I could do or say to make her quit using drugs. Nothing."

Ugh. That's not what I want to hear.

Maggie nodded and gave her mom a thumbs-up.

"I've learned through the years that I had to let her go. Give her up and let her do her own thing," Nora said.

I frowned. How could I do that? I tried, but Becky still ruled my world. Look at what just happened—she'd deserted Ginny. Again. Everything Becky did caused ripples, sometimes really big ones, in my life.

Nora grimaced. "I know exactly what you're thinking. Maggie told me you had been talking about enabling recently. As you've learned, enabling is when you do anything for the addict that she can do for herself. How many of you have given your addict money, loaned them your car, or done the footwork to line up a lawyer and all that required?" She waited before adding, "No judgment here."

Everyone nodded or raised a hand. I'd learned that addicts seemed to have a universal "script." They did the same kinds of things and used the same types of excuses. And they had manipulation down to a fine art.

"That is enabling, and it's tough to stop." Nora gripped the podium. "If your addict is your child, you have to break that pattern of being the parent. Because, as parents, we want to do things for our children. We want to pick them up, kiss the boo-boo, and send them on their way. But addiction doesn't work like that."

Nora tipped her chin at Maggie. "How many times did I bail you out of jail?"

I gasped and stared. Maggie had been in jail?

She held up one hand with her five fingers spread wide.

Nora looked at each one of us. "Five times. Five. Times." Her eyes welled up with tears, and her voice trembled. "Never in a million years did I imagine my child would be in jail once, let alone five times." She swiped at the tears on her cheeks. She looked at Maggie again. "How many times were you in jail?"

Maggie made a face. "Six."

"You see, I had to make a decision. That first time, yep, I bailed her out in a heartbeat. How could my baby have done what they said? No way was she guilty. She even told me that herself." Nora chuckled. "Y'all may have heard that too—'It wasn't me, Mom.'"

I barked a laugh. I'd heard that for sure, even if Becky hadn't called me from jail. Nothing was ever her fault.

Nora raised her eyebrows. "Daughter?"

I nodded.

She continued. "Second time she called me? I bailed her out. The third time, I thought, Hmmm, how does she keep doing this? Why do the police have it in for her? But still, I provided that bail money. By the fifth time, I was furious." She shook her head, leaned forward, and whispered, "But I still paid."

Nora rocked back on her heels. "That sixth time when Maggie called. I didn't go. I didn't help. It hurt so bad, but she would keep getting in trouble if I kept fixing her problems." She banged her fist on the podium. "I. Could. Not. Fix. Her."

She pointed at her daughter. "And that's what it took. I decided not to be in charge of her life anymore. And when she called, I told her that. Oh, the words she said." Her lips twitched. "Well, I won't repeat them."

"Please don't, Mom." Maggie covered her face. "Under the influence, addicts will say all kinds of things they'd never say sober."

Nora nodded. "It took a while before Maggie truly believed me. She cooled her heels in jail. She was mad when she got out. She came by the house and yelled at me. I kept the door locked and wouldn't let her in. Finally, I told her I would call the police if she didn't leave. I guess she didn't want to get hauled back to jail, so she left. It was two years before I saw or heard from her again."

"Two years?" I shook my head.

"Yes. It sounds awful, and it was."

I understood what that wait was like. I'd waited eight years to hear from Becky.

"I didn't do anything during that time except pray for her. I didn't search for her. I laid her down, and I couldn't pick her up again. I didn't have it in me. It never did any good before, so why would it now?" Nora's brow furrowed. "What is that famous saying by Einstein? 'Insanity is doing the same thing over and over again and expecting different results.' That was my life—insane. And I was tired of it. So, I quit."

Roger raised his hand. "Can I ask a question?"

"Sure."

"What isn't enabling? It's hard for my wife and me to figure that out."

"Great question. Enabling is doing something for them that they can do on their own. Offering unasked-for advice, trying to control their life, directing them by telling them what they *need* to do." She looked at Todd. "Do you tell the people in this group what to do?"

"No," he said. "We can share our own experiences and what worked for us. But we don't tell people what to do."

"Pretty much the same with the addict," she said to Roger. "You don't have to solve your addict's problems. They created them. They can solve them."

Roger sat back and folded his arms. "It's not that easy."

"No, it's not." Compassion shone in her eyes, and her voice softened. "None of this is easy. Don't misunderstand me." She waved a hand in Maggie's direction. "When I said that's what it took? For me to quit saving Maggie? I mean, that's what it took for me to begin to save myself."

She leaned forward. "What happened with Maggie won't happen every time just because you stop enabling. I'm not going to lie to you and tell you that it will. There's no magic solution to addiction."

She made eye contact with each one of us. "Each of you has an addict that you love. Each of you has enabled. And each of you can stop. But that's not a guarantee that your addict will come around." She banged her fist on the podium again. "Oh, how I wish they all would. But people, why you're really here is for *you*—what you need to do for you, what kind of life you can have, free of stress and worry and full of peace and serenity." She held up her hands. "Freedom. That's what you can have. With or without your addict."

I kept hearing that word—freedom. Being free from stress and worry sounded wonderful, but as Nora said, there was no guarantee that Becky would change. I'd made some progress, but I'd backtracked since Becky deserted Ginny.

Somehow, I had to separate the two in my mind and heart. I could love Ginny and be her grandmother, and love Becky and be her mom. But I had to lay my daughter and her problems down. They weren't mine to deal with.

She no longer needed me to actively parent her, and she hadn't for a long time.

Calling the lawyer Maggie recommended and getting custody of Ginny was priority number one. Then we could move on.

Friday afternoon, while Ginny was busy doing her homework, I called the number Maggie gave me. The office was closed, so I left a message asking them to return my call and briefly describing what I needed.

Ginny walked into the kitchen as I hung up. "Who was that?"

I couldn't keep this from her. "I had to call a lawyer."

"Why?"

I put my hands on her shoulders. "Because I need custody of you to keep you here with me."

"You didn't have custody in the summers, did you?"

"No, honey." I tipped up her chin and smoothed her hair back. "But it's different this time. I want you to stay with me, and I can take care of you, and you'll go to school. We can't depend on your mom."

Her eyes filled with tears. "I miss her, though."

I hugged her, rocking back and forth. "I know. I'm so sorry she's done this."

Ginny went to the sunporch and plopped into a chair, setting her chin in her hand. "Do you think she'll come back? Like she usually does?"

"I don't know. If she does, we'll cross that bridge then, okay?" I pulled out the chair beside her and sat. I couldn't tell her that I wouldn't just hand her back to Becky.

"Okay."

I rubbed her arm. "I know you love your mom, honey. You don't have to stop that."

She wiped tears off her cheeks and buried her head in her arms. "I love her, but I'm so mad at her."

"I am too."

Ginny's head popped up, and her mouth dropped open. "You are?"

"I love your mom, but I'm mad at her because she doesn't take the best care of you." Over the past few days, it became clear that I let Becky back into my and Ginny's lives because I couldn't let go of the hope that she would change. I expected it of her, even knowing where expectations had taken me in the past.

I sighed and pulled Ginny close. "She loves you, but the drugs make her act differently. You saw how she acted when she was clean. She's a good mom when she's sober."

Ginny snuggled against me. "I'm so glad I can be with you."

I kissed her cheek. "Me too, honey. Me too."

We spent the weekend at the house, just taking it easy. I tried to rest, but Ginny made sure I walked every day. Our favorite thing was going to the beach at dusk to collect seashells. We already had three glass jars full of them.

On Monday, when we arrived home from school, my cell phone rang. I dug in my purse and clicked "accept."

"Hello, this is Mrs. Edwards from Banks & Banks Law Office. I had a message to call a Kat Johnson?"

"Yes, thank you. I'm Mrs. Johnson." I put my purse on the coffee table and settled on the couch. Ginny sat beside me. "I have some questions."

"Sure, what can I do?" she asked.

I described how Becky left Ginny, and that I went to Tennessee to get her. "I want custody of Ginny, but I'm unsure what to do."

Papers rustled on the other end of the line. "First of all, your granddaughter is a resident of Tennessee, so you'll need a lawyer in that state."

"Oh." My shoulders sagged. "How do I do that?"

"You'll have to go to Tennessee. I can recommend someone. You said the Memphis area?"

"Yes." I rubbed my forehead. I did not want to make that drive back to Memphis.

"I can call you back with a name and number."

"Is there any way I can do this over the phone?" I asked.

"Possibly, however, I recommend going in person to get the process started. Double-check with that lawyer, though."

I was exhausted just thinking about it all.

"I know it's a lot to do, Mrs. Johnson. Time is of the essence." Mrs. Edwards clicked her tongue. "I wouldn't wait if I were you. If the mother turns up, she could claim you kidnapped your granddaughter."

Her scare tactics worked. My heart beat triple time. "Please let me know the name and number of the Tennessee lawyer as soon as you can."

After we hung up, thoughts and questions whirled through my mind. I had no idea what to do next. I'd probably have to go to Tennessee in a few days. I couldn't pull Ginny out of school. She needed a place to stay, and I had to arrange a substitute.

"Grandma, is there anything I can do?"

"Could you bring me paper and a pen?" Red jumped on the couch beside me and curled up, purring loudly. She always knew when I needed comfort.

Ginny handed me what I'd asked for and scooped up the cat, plopping her onto her lap as she nestled beside me. "List time?"

"Yes. The lawyer said I'll need to go to Tennessee. I want you to stay here for school, though, okay? You can't miss any more days."

"Can I stay with Ms. Sug?"

"Yes, I'll ask her." After writing the things I needed to do, including arranging for Mac to care for the animals, I snuggled with Ginny.

I needed the Tennessee lawyer's number and to schedule an appointment. Then I could make the other plans. Mrs. Edwards mentioned getting emergency custody, but most of what she said went over my head. My heart twinged, and I forced myself to relax. I laid the paper and pen on the coffee table and put my feet up beside them.

"Grandma, the sun is setting," Ginny said after a bit. "We need to get in our walk."

She set Red down, and we both stood. "Sounds good to me. Let's take Ollie too."

Chapter 21

Wednesday afternoon, Mrs. Edwards returned my call. As soon as I had the necessary information, I called the lawyer in Memphis that she recommended, but I got their answering machine. At the rate this was going, it would be next year before I got hold of the right person. I wanted to solve this immediately, but it wasn't going my way.

Friday was a school holiday, and I had to work in my classroom. Ginny tagged along, reshelving my books and straightening the chairs.

Mac stopped by just before noon. "You guys want to grab lunch?"

"Yes." Ginny jumped up and hugged him. "I'm hungry, Mr. Mac."

I set my work down, noted what I still needed to do, and picked up my purse. "Where should we go?"

"Have you tried Taste?" he asked.

"Taste what?" Ginny said.

Mac helped her put on a light sweater. "It used to be a wine and cheese shop, but now it has what they call locally sourced food."

"I've heard of it, but I've never been." I fished my keys out of my purse. "Want to ride with us, and we'll drop you back here after?"

"Sure." Mac followed us to the parking lot and climbed into the front passenger seat.

I turned left onto Pacific Avenue, heading toward Fifteenth Street, where we parked in front of a modern-looking white building with both indoor and outdoor seating. Ginny wanted to eat outside at the black wrought-iron tables, so we placed our order at the counter and waited at the table for our food to arrive. A soft breeze brought the ocean scents our way, and I consciously relaxed my shoulders.

Ginny wiggled in her seat. "I can't wait for my sandwich."

"I thought you'd order their PB&J." Mac tugged her hair.

"Nah, I don't like strawberry jelly. Grape's my favorite, right, Grandma?"

"Yes, we buy a new jar every time we go grocery shopping." I winked. "I picked the Princess Anne sandwich. I love avocado and cheese."

"That sounds yummy." Mac rubbed his hands together. "I got the Beach Club like Ginny, but I kept the onions."

Ginny made a face. "Onions are yucky."

I bit my lip. If she only knew how many meals I made that included onion, like her favorite psghetti.

The door to the porch smacked shut, and the waitress approached with our food. She passed out our plates and handed us a stack of napkins. My stomach growled in anticipation.

Mac poked Ginny's arm. "She must know how messy you are."

She took a bite of her sandwich. "Not funny, Mr. Mac." She took another bite. "This is so good. I'm glad I didn't get onions."

While we ate, Mac asked about her costume for the school's fall festival.

"I'm going to be Ollie." She sipped her water.

"How are we going to make you look like Ollie?" I opened my bag of chips and crunched on one. "What if he thinks you're him?"

Mac elbowed Ginny. "I know how you can look like him. Don't shower for a couple of weeks, so your hair is crazy, and then you can hug him all day and rub his stinkiness on you." He wiggled his eyebrows. "Better get started now."

Ginny made a face. "Ollie's not stinky." She tipped her head, eyebrows raised. "I can skip showers, though, Grandma."

"Nope." I winked. "Not doing that. But how will you be Ollie?"

"I need a white wig and a white sweatsuit. You can glue fur on it. Will that work?"

"Sure, that sounds cute. We can paint a doggie nose on you and find some floppy ears." I tapped her nose.

"I can't wait to see you in that costume," Mac said.

I was picking up my sandwich to take another bite when the door thwacked shut again. Looking up, I saw Sierra and Troy heading our way. I dropped my sandwich on the plate and looked at Mac. He covered my hand.

"It's okay. Just relax." His brows furrowed. "I did not invite them."

"Okay," I said. Troy stared at Ginny, and my stomach soured.

Sierra stopped at our table, hugged her dad, and waved to Ginny and me. Ginny hugged her. As she stepped back, Sierra placed her hand on her shoulder. "Ginny, this is my friend, Mr. Troy."

Ginny shook his hand—the one time I wished her manners hadn't improved.

Sierra put her hand on Troy's back. "Mr. Troy knew your mom a long time ago."

My face heated up, and I ground my teeth. Mac nudged my leg with his knee.

"You did?" Ginny tipped her head. "You're a lot older than Ms. Sierra."

Straight from the mouths of babes.

"He was older than your mom too." I bit my lip, wishing I'd kept my mouth shut.

Troy cocked an eyebrow. I stared at both of them, trying to see a resemblance. My granddaughter looked so much like Becky, but I'd never thought about what her father might look like.

"Your grandma's right," Troy said. "I knew your mom a long time ago. Haven't seen her in,"—he tipped his head and pursed his lips—"probably ten, eleven years."

My stomach clenched again, and sweat beaded my forehead. The thought that they followed us to Taste to confront us crossed my mind.

"Gosh, I'm ten." Ginny bounced on her tiptoes. "Did you know me then?"

Troy looked surprised, then narrowed his eyes and glared at me. "No, no, I didn't." His nostrils flared. "It looks like we have some things to talk about."

I shook my head. "I have nothing to say to you." I picked up my purse and touched Ginny's shoulder. "We need to leave."

"I haven't finished eating." She crossed her arms.

I rolled a napkin around her sandwich, grabbed her bag of chips, and stuffed both in my purse. "Let's go, Ginny. Now." My tone left no room for argument. I tipped my head at Mac. "Maybe Sierra can take you back to your car. See you later."

Ginny followed me from the restaurant, glancing back at Troy and Sierra.

We reached the car, got in, and fastened our seatbelts.

"Grandma, why are you mad?"

I wanted to be honest without sharing my suspicions with Ginny. "I don't like Troy, that's all. He wasn't a good influence on your mom." I started the car and backed out of the parking space. We drove by the outdoor seating area. The two of them still sat with Mac, and Troy glared at me as we passed.

Seeing Troy and knowing for certain when he'd last seen Becky made me more determined to contact the lawyer in Tennessee. Ginny holed up in her room, pouting, so I called again. When the answering machine beep sounded, I left another message, emphasizing the urgency of the situation, and hung up. I rubbed my chest and sat in the living room, trying to relax. My chest had been hurting since Troy came to the restaurant.

I didn't have time to be sick.

My cell rang. A wave of dizziness hit when I jumped up to answer. I held onto the kitchen door frame for a few seconds. I answered, took a deep breath, blew it out slowly, and carried the phone into the sunporch so I could sit.

"You okay?" Mac asked.

"Oh, Mac." My voice shook. "I don't know what to think. Did Troy say anything else?"

"He's wondering if he's Ginny's father. He says if Ginny is ten, he probably is."

My chest tightened, and pain radiated into my shoulder and jaw.

"Kat? Are you okay?"

"Mac," I enunciated my words, "can you call 911? I think I'm having a heart attack." I hung up and lay my head on the table.

"Ginny," I called. "Ginny, I need you."

She ran out to the sunporch. "Grandma, are you all right?"

I raised my head and sat up. The pain and tightness eased, but my jaw still hurt, and my stomach churned. "Honey, I'm not feeling well. I asked Mr. Mac to call an ambulance." I hated to scare her. "Will you unlock the front door and put Ollie out back?"

"Yes, Grandma, right now." She rushed to do what I asked and returned to sit by me. She rubbed my back. "Is it your heart?"

"I think so. Will you call Ms. Sug?" I pushed my cell to her and told her the number to dial.

"Ms. Sug, Grandma doesn't feel well, and an ambulance is coming." I heard the sirens and lay my head back down.

The front door flew open. "Kat?" Mac called out.

"In here." I kept my eyes closed and my head down. He touched my back. "Will you tell Sug what's going on?" I waved at the phone. "Ginny called her."

Mac took the phone, and I asked him to take Ginny to Sug's. He let the EMTs in and took Ginny out of the room so they could assess me.

A female EMT leaned over me. "Do you think you can stand?"

I lifted my head. "Maybe? I'm dizzy."

"Slowly. Take your time. We want to get you on a stretcher, but it won't fit in here. We can carry you if you need."

I eased upright, and she reached for my arm. She helped me stand and walked with me into the living room.

Once I was on the stretcher, Ginny came over and smoothed back my hair. "I love you, Grandma. Ms. Sug said she'll come to get me."

I took her hand and kissed it, refusing to let tears fall. "That sounds fun. Maybe she'll let you paint."

The stretcher bumped across the lawn, and I clung to its sides. The female EMT patted my hand. "It's okay," she said. "We've got you."

Mac leaned over me. "I'll stay here till Sug comes, Kat. Don't worry about anything. I'll take care of Ollie and Red."

Thank you, I mouthed. I had no energy to say anything else.

The next few hours were a blur. My cardiologist, Dr. Thompson, ordered multiple tests and admitted me to Princess Anne Hospital that afternoon. It was late in the day when I got to my room. I had no appetite but forced myself to sip some broth the nurse offered. I wouldn't be allowed anything else until more tests were done the next day.

I'd been through this before, and it wasn't fun. Tests were postponed, and in the meantime, my stomach growled. I couldn't sleep, but I forced myself to rest and attempt to relax. Ginny was safe with Sugar, Mac had the animals under control, and there was nothing I could do about Troy at the moment.

I finally dozed off, but nurses were in and out adjusting things and taking my blood pressure. The Serenity Prayer ran through my mind. I focused my thoughts on myself and what I could control. It took some doing, but I stopped thinking about anything outside of my control.

Early the next morning, when breakfast trays were delivered to other rooms, someone knocked and pushed open the door to my room. I turned my head to see Maggie.

"Hey, there. How are you? Sugar called and told me what happened." She pulled the only chair in my room closer to the bed and reached for my hand.

Tears filled my eyes. "Thank you for coming. I've tried so hard not to worry. That's what put me here."

"Was it a heart attack?"

"They haven't said yet." I reached for my cup of ice chips on the side table. She helped me get a spoonful. "I've had angina, but this stress with Troy took its toll."

Maggie listened as I told her about seeing Troy at the restaurant and hearing that he thought he might be Ginny's dad.

"I'm so sorry, Kat. This is a lot of stress. Let me know if I can do anything."

"I will." I rolled my head toward her. "I trust you."

"I'm so glad." She patted my hand. "God brought us together, for sure."

The door pushed open again, and a nurse entered. She picked up my chart and reviewed it, marking notes on it from the machines I was hooked up to. "You ready?" she asked.

I made a face. "Sure."

Maggie stood. "Behave, Kat. The sooner they do these tests, the faster you can come home."

"She's right." The nurse unhooked me from everything and pushed my bed toward the door. Maggie held it open and followed us to the elevators.

"I'll come back later, okay?"

"I'll be here." I shot her a wink. "Maybe you can bring me a burger?"

The nurse snorted. "We'll be searching all your visitors now, Ms. Kat."

We giggled. Maggie waited outside the elevator, and I waved to her as the doors shut.

Lots of hurry-up and waiting went on at the hospital, as usual. When Dr. Thompson came to see me after testing, blood work, monitoring, and more, he said, "Minor heart attack." He laid my chart at the end of my bed.

"I've done what you said to do. I take my meds, go to counseling, walk, and eat well. I quit smoking years ago." I raised my hands. "What else can I do?"

"You told me about your granddaughter staying with you. What's going on with that?"

I filled him in on the latest—the lawyer, having to go to Tennessee to see a lawyer there, Troy, and my concerns that he was Ginny's father.

"Kat, I'm just going to say this." He sat next to me and leaned forward, elbows on his knees. "I think you have two choices regarding this and your health. You can give Ginny up. Or you can find out if Troy is her father and work to establish a healthy relationship with him."

I was shaking my head before he finished his sentence. "I'm not giving Ginny up."

He smiled. "I didn't think you would. But you must take care of yourself. You absolutely must cut back on stress. This is your life we're talking about." He patted my hand. "Think about it—what I said about Troy."

Chapter 22

No way would I give up Ginny. That wouldn't happen. And it couldn't happen with Becky's issues. But could I establish a positive relationship with Troy? I wasn't sure. What I did know was that the stress in my life threatened to kill me, and only I could control that.

On Tuesday afternoon, Mac picked me up and took me home. Ollie greeted me with his typical enthusiastic joy—jumping and tippy-toeing on the floor, wagging his tail, and licking my hand. Red hid until Ollie calmed down, and then she came and curled up in my lap.

Mac tipped his chin at her. "That's good medicine."

"The best." I stroked her shiny black fur, enjoying the little purrs she made. "It's good to be home."

"What did the doctor say you need to do?" He joined me on the couch.

"Cut down on the stress in my life." I rolled my eyes.

"Oh boy." He smirked. "He must not know you very well."

"Ha-ha." I rearranged Red. "He said I either need to give up Ginny or have some sort of relationship with Troy. If he is her father."

"Well, I know you won't let Ginny go."

I shook my head. "Even if I wanted to, which I don't, I couldn't. Becky is not a fit mother."

"True. What's next then?"

I leaned my head back and closed my eyes. "I've gone round and round with this. I still haven't talked to the lawyer in Tennessee. I haven't heard anything from Becky in weeks. I suppose I need to talk to Troy and find out if he's Ginny's father." I opened my eyes and looked at him. "Then, we go from there."

"Sounds like a good plan. Let me know if I can help in any way. Mediate or whatever."

I patted his arm. "Thank you. Where would I be without you all?"

Sugar brought Ginny home before dinnertime and fixed us something to eat. They hovered over me until I told them to stop.

"We just worry about you, Grandma." Ginny munched on her salad.

"You need to rest. Do you have this whole week off?" Sug asked. I had already shared the doctor's advice with them.

"Yes, my substitute can cover for however long I need. If that lawyer ever calls me back, I have to go to Tennessee."

"I don't think so," Sug blurted.

I put down my fork. "I need to do this. Could you drive me? Mac, could Ginny stay with you and go to school? I want to talk to them soon."

"Okay." Mac risked a glance at Sugar.

"Make that appointment, and we'll see what we can do." Sug tapped the table with her index finger. "But we'll do it my way or not at all."

I saluted her.

Sugar enlisted Ginny to help clean up the kitchen and care for the animals. I scooted my chair closer to Mac's and lowered my voice. "If Troy is around Ginny, that's okay. I don't want you to worry about that. I trust you to keep her safe. Just make sure he doesn't say anything to her about being her father. We don't know that's true yet."

"I understand. I'll talk to him before she comes to stay."

I managed to get in touch with a live person in Tennessee the following day. They gave me an appointment for Friday, and Sug and I made plans to leave. When school let out, I called Mac, and Ginny gathered her things to stay at his house until we returned.

When I dropped her off, Ginny rushed to his guest room to put her things away. I gave Mac the hotel's phone number that Sug and I planned to stop at. "Call if you have any problems, please."

He pocketed the number. "You know I will."

Ginny hugged me, and I went home to pack.

Sugar picked me up early the next morning, insisting she would drive the whole way. I tried to argue with her, but she wouldn't give in. "Do you have your compression socks on?"

"Yes, doctor."

"Look, you have to behave. You just had a heart attack," she said.

I crossed my arms and slumped in my seat. "Minor."

"Whatever." She waved her hand. "Rest, relax, sit back."

"Yes, ma'am." I pulled my pillow up beside me and lay my head down. "I'm going to nap right now. I didn't sleep much last night."

She patted my leg. "I know. This is stressful. But we're going to do this together."

The drive seemed to take longer than ever, probably because I was a passenger. I napped, watched the scenery fly by, and complained, but Sugar never let me drive. We stopped for the night in Knoxville. Sug snored while I dozed. We finished the drive on Friday and arrived on time for our three o'clock meeting.

Sug parked in front of the office building. "You ready?"

I showed her my shaking hands. "Not sure. Everything is on the line now."

"Remember what Mrs. Edwards told you. They should grant you emergency custody."

I inhaled and unbuckled. "Let's go in."

Mr. Matthews' receptionist showed us to his office. Our feet sank into the deep, sand-colored carpet, and I admired the mahogany furniture. His desk, twice the size of mine at school, only held a notepad and a pen. Pictures covering the walls showed him with various celebrities, including one with Elvis.

"This guy is going to cost a fortune." I sank into one of two padded armchairs.

Sug grimaced as she sat beside me.

Mr. Matthews entered, and we stood. He was a tall man with a deep tan, sparkling blue eyes, and a smile that revealed his shiny white teeth. He shook our hands, then perched on the edge of his desk, legs crossed at the ankles, and waved us to our seats.

What I wouldn't do for that kind of ease.

"What can I do for you, ladies?"

"Well." My voice trembled, and I cleared my throat. "I need some help. My granddaughter lived in Memphis until recently. Her mother deserted her here. I took her back to live with me in Virginia. I talked to a lawyer there who said I needed a Tennessee lawyer because Ginny was a resident here." I blew out a breath. It sounded convoluted even to me.

Mr. Matthews nodded. "That's true." He went around his desk and sat. He made some notes on a legal pad. "You haven't heard from her mother since?"

I shook my head.

"Is the father in the picture?"

Sug and I exchanged looks. "Well, maybe."

He leaned his elbows on his desk and clasped his hands, eyebrows raised in question.

I briefly told him about Troy. "I'm willing to find out if he's Ginny's father. I want her to be safe and cared for."

"Okay, here's what we'll do for now." He stood and walked toward the door. "I'll file a petition for temporary custody and run it by the judge. He's still in today. I think we can rush this through."

"Okay. What do I do about Troy?"

"Let's take care of custody first. We don't want anything to happen to you or Ginny. Then we'll proceed with the possible father."

For the first time in weeks, I knew I was doing the right thing, the best thing. Ginny would be safe, and that's what mattered the most.

Sug and I waited in Mr. Matthews' office. When he entered with paperwork in his hand, my stomach unclenched for the first time that day.

He handed me the temporary custody petition. "You need to know the judge was hesitant to sign this."

"Why?" Acid rolled up my gut.

"Custody cases aren't cut and dry. Typically, the parent has first rights. You're heading back to Virginia?"

"We need to get some rest," Sug said, pointing her thumb at me. "She just got out of the hospital."

Matthews took a step back, a frown on his handsome face. "Why?"

"Just a minor heart thing." I waved away his concern, but his eyebrows lowered more.

"That might be a problem."

"My health?"

"Yes. This is temporary custody, Mrs. Johnson. You will have to file for permanent custody at some point if you want Ginny to live with you permanently." He shook his head. "And your health might impede that."

I wanted Ginny to be safe and live with me, but my health might prevent that. And my health suffered because of the circumstances Becky created.

Everything came back to Becky.

We checked into our hotel and then headed to Central BBQ on Butler Avenue.

Sug looked at the menu on the wall while we waited to place our order. "Barbeque nachos. Sounds like an oxymoron."

I rolled my eyes. "Maybe to you, but I think it sounds yummy. That's what I'm getting, plus a sweet tea."

"Not exactly heart-healthy."

"I'll order the barbecue chicken nachos, the small size, with cheese on the side."

We sat on barstools in the back room. Across the street was the Lorraine Motel. Cars filled the parking lot.

When the waitress brought my nachos and Sug's ribs, I asked about the motel.

"They've turned it into a civil rights museum." She set down our drinks and retrieved our ticket from her apron pocket. "Y'all need anything else?"

"No thanks," I said. When she left, I pointed across the street. "That's where Martin Luther King Jr. was shot and killed. I'd love to come back and see the museum sometime."

Sug chuckled. "I'm sure. You and history. I'm not surprised you know what the Lorraine Motel is." She winked. "How are those nachos?"

I scooped up a chip full of barbecue and crammed it in my mouth. "Yummy." I pushed my basket toward her. "Want one?"

She pushed the basket back and took a bite of her ribs. She wiped sauce off her mouth. "So, what will you do next?"

"Two things. I need to file a missing person's report on Becky with the police here." I sipped my tea. "And I need to find out if Troy is Ginny's father."

Sug grabbed my arm. "I never even thought about a missing person's report."

"I hadn't either until today. Can we stop by the police station tomorrow morning before we leave?"

"Of course. Mac knows we won't be home until Sunday evening," she said.

After dinner, we drove to Riverside Drive to see the big "M" bridge over the Mississippi River. We sat in the parking lot of the Pyramid—now a Bass Pro Shop—and breathed in the river scent and enjoyed the milder weather before heading for our hotel to get some rest.

In the morning, we headed for the Criminal Justice Center at 201 Poplar. It loomed, its brick walls and razor wire daring me to go inside. My hands shook as I asked to file a missing person's report on Becky.

Three weeks. She'd been gone three weeks. Guilt crashed over me—I'd been so wrapped up in Ginny, too angry at Becky to really think about her. I doubted the police would find her, but at least I'd finally taken a step.

When we stepped outside the building, Sug and I filled our lungs with fresh air.

"Whew. I felt guilty just being in there." She gave a nervous laugh.

"Me too. That's my first time in a police station. Not something I want to do again." I held in a shudder.

As we drove out of downtown Memphis, I looked for Becky. I spotted several homeless people and groups of adults loitering. Was my daughter living on the streets? Did she have friends or anyone to keep an eye on her, provide her with food, or offer her a place to stay? Sug merged onto I-40 and headed east. I couldn't look anymore. Was Becky even alive?

Sug drove late into the evening, and we stopped at the same hotel in Knoxville. While she changed for bed, I called Mac.

After greeting him, I said, "We're in Knoxville and will be home tomorrow afternoon. How's everything going?"

Complete silence on his end.

"Mac, you there?"

He cleared his throat. "Yes, I am."

My stomach rolled. "What's going on? Is Ginny okay?"

"Yes, yes, Ginny is fine." He paused. "It's Becky."

"Becky's nickname is now 'Monkey Wrench,'" I said when Sug came out of the bathroom.

She stopped brushing her hair. "Huh?"

I tipped my chin at the phone. "Just talked to Mac. Becky's back." I plopped onto my bed. "Mac and Ginny went by my house, and Becky was parked out front. She said she'd been sleeping in her car for several days."

"Oh my." Her eyebrows drew together. "What does she want? Where has she been?"

"Mac said she wants Ginny. That she acted like she hadn't abandoned her at school several weeks ago."

Sug set down her brush. "What?" She shook her head. "She makes up her own reality, doesn't she?"

"She does. She's so consistently inconsistent. Whenever I think I have things under control, she comes along and throws a monkey wrench into the mix." I closed my eyes, drawing deep breaths.

"You okay?" She leaned over me.

I opened one eye. "Yep. Just 'relaxing.'" I made air quotes.

"Pros—Becky's alive." Sug, ever the optimist, sighed. "That's the only pro I can come up with."

"Same here." I lay down and turned on my side, tucking my hand under my cheek. "I'm going to take a short nap."

She clicked the bedside lamp off. "You do that. Nothing we can do tonight anyhow."

I slept till morning, waking with a stiff neck. While I showered, I prayed, *Lord, please guide me in this situation. You know what's best for Ginny, and I don't want to get in Your way. I pray for Becky too. I'm not sure how to pray for her, but I lift her to You and trust You with her life.*

We checked out of the hotel after a quick breakfast and several cups of coffee. The fog over the mountains lifted, and the trees were beautiful with their rich fall colors of red, orange, and yellow.

"When I checked out, the lady said this is one of the best times to see the fall foliage," Sug said.

"It's beautiful. I love the beach, but we don't have this kind of fall."

"We could do a road trip up to Shenandoah. Skyline Drive isn't too far away. We might even see some bears." She growled playfully.

"Ginny would love that. I drove Skyline years ago and stayed in Strasburg." I shifted in my seat. "It's a great little town with a lot of Civil War history. They even have a reenactment nearby in Middletown. Maybe we can plan that for next fall."

"That would be fun. Making plans is a good idea."

"If Ginny is still here." I frowned. How quickly I'd forgotten about Becky. "Sug, do you have any idea what I should say to Becky?"

"First, let's see if she's sober. Find out how long she's been living in her car and where she's been. I want to hear her story of why she deserted Ginny. I think we deserve to know that."

"I agree." I stared out my window. "As a mom, I don't think I'll ever truly understand why Becky's done anything she's done."

"I've never been a mom, and I don't understand it."

"I think I'll keep the fact that I have temporary custody to myself until we see what she says." I chewed on the inside of my cheek, wondering how she'd take the news.

"And what she wants."

I nodded. With Becky, odds were she wanted Ginny. But I wasn't letting go so easily—not this time.

Chapter 23

When we arrived at Mac's, he and Ginny were gluing faux fur on a white sweatsuit for Ginny's Ollie costume. I'd forgotten Wednesday was the school's fall festival. Ginny hugged Sug and me, then sat down to continue gluing.

I leaned over her costume. "How much do you have left?"

Ginny squinted one eye. "Maybe half?"

Mac waved at the pieces. "We found the fur and the sweatsuit, but we still need some kind of wig or ears, and we have to make a tail. Plus, makeup for her puppy dog face."

"You guys have been working hard." I ruffled Ginny's hair. "Ready to get your things together?"

Worry filled her eyes. "You know my mom's back?"

"Yes, Mr. Mac told me."

"I don't want to go back with her, Grandma."

"I know, honey." I squeezed her shoulder. "Keep on gluing. We'll head home in a bit."

Mac crooked his finger at me, and I followed him into the kitchen.

I shook my head. "I should be surprised Becky's back, but I'm not. What all did she say?"

He crossed his arms and leaned against a counter. "We stopped to pick up a few things for Ginny and to feed Red and Ollie. Becky was in her car in the driveway, sound asleep."

"When was this?"

"Yesterday morning." Mac shook his head. "When we got there and closed our car doors, she got out of her car. She was drunk. She said she'd been there a few days, but there's no way. You didn't leave until Thursday, and I stopped there Friday after school to take care of the animals."

"Drunk?"

"Yes. She looked rough, and she smelled like alcohol." He grimaced.

"Did she talk to Ginny?"

"She tried to hug her, but Ginny backed up. Becky didn't like that and started cursing." He shook his head. "I'm sorry. I got Ginny inside and locked the door while we took care of what needed to be done. Becky stood in the yard and yelled. When we went back outside, she had passed out in her car again."

My heart broke for my granddaughter. "You did the right thing. Was Becky there today?"

"No, I went to feed Red and change her litter this morning. Ollie stayed here last night, so I put him in your backyard. Her car was gone."

"I got temporary custody of Ginny in Tennessee," I said. "And I filed a missing person report yesterday morning before we left Memphis. I didn't know she was here." Becky, unpredictable at best, couldn't be trusted. Who knew where she'd been or when she'd show up again? My focus had to be on my granddaughter. "Thank you for dealing with all this, Mac. I really appreciate it."

"I enjoy spending time with Ginny. It's like I get to be a parent even though I missed Sierra's growing-up years," he said.

"Speaking of ..."

"Sierra and Troy never came by. At least things are quiet on that front."

I made a face. "For now."

He patted me on the back. "Come on, Eeyore, let's see how the dog costume is coming."

Ginny and I stayed until all the fur was glued on, and Mac fed us dinner. When Sug turned onto my street, I held my breath until I saw that the driveway was empty. I wasn't sure I could confront Becky tonight.

Ginny piped up. "Mom's car wasn't here this morning either."

"That's what Mr. Mac told me. Let's take our things inside and let Ollie in."

Red meowed and circled our ankles, but she hid once the dog came inside. I was glad to be home. I was exhausted.

"I'll pick up Ginny for school tomorrow," Sug said before she left.

"Thank you." I hugged her tightly. "Thank you for everything."

She tapped Ginny on the head. "See you tomorrow morning, kiddo. Let your grandma get some sleep, okay?"

"I will, Ms. Sug."

Morning came early the next day. I'd arranged for my substitute to work all week, knowing I'd need to rest up. Ginny got herself up and ready for school while I packed her lunch. A car pulled into the driveway, and thinking it was Sugar, I called for Ginny.

"Your ride is here." I opened the front door and saw Becky's sedan. Sug pulled in right behind her.

I shut the door and turned. "Ginny." She stood beside me, slipping her arms through her backpack straps. "Your mom just pulled up, and Ms. Sug is behind her. I want you to go straight to Ms. Sug's car, okay?"

Her bottom lip trembled.

I tipped her chin up. "Don't worry. I want to talk to your mom for a bit. But you need to go to school. I'll take care of things with your mom."

A single tear slid down her cheek. I thumbed it away.

"You're not going with her. I promise. I have paperwork from the judge in Tennessee proving you're with me now." I wrapped my arms around her. "I'm sorry this is so hard, sweetie."

She sniffled. "Straight to Ms. Sug's car?"

"Yes, honey. Don't stop for your mom, please."

I walked her out, one hand on her shoulder, my body between Becky's car and Ginny. I kept my eyes trained on Sug. She jumped out and held her back door open until Ginny was safely inside.

"Thanks, Sug. I'll call you later."

She nodded and backed out quickly.

Becky climbed out of her car. Her movements were slow, jerky, and stiff. Her greasy hair lay flat on her head. Her wrinkled clothes were damp and stained, her skin yellow.

I swallowed. Was she in any shape to have an honest conversation? Thoughts of how she acted when she'd been clean flowed through my mind. I remembered her talking to Shrimp just a few Christmases ago and how I forgave her. I didn't know if I even wanted to forgive her this time.

I stopped on the other side of the car. "Hi, Becky."

"Mom." She wobbled around to me, holding onto the car. "Where is Ginny going?"

"To school." I could smell the alcohol seeping from her pores. When did she start drinking? It wasn't even eight in the morning.

She held up her palms. "I wanted to see her." She stomped her foot and lost her balance.

I caught her by the arm. "Let's go inside, honey." I coached her across the lawn and helped her up the front steps, trying not to touch her anywhere else. Ollie greeted her at the front door but backed away from her scent.

She and I maneuvered through the living room until she plopped into a chair on the sunporch. I didn't want her sitting on my couch. I didn't think I'd be able to get the stench out.

"I'm going to make some coffee." In the kitchen, I leaned against the counter and bowed my head. *Lord, what do I say to Becky?*

A sharp snort came from the sunporch. I peeked around the doorway to find Becky, head down on the table, sound asleep.

Well, that answered that question.

I made coffee for myself, and while waiting for her to wake up, I worked on the rest of Ginny's costume.

I created a tail from an old white pillowcase and stuffed it with batting. Using a marker, I drew some Ollie-like markings on it. I was deep into stitching the tail closed when a knock sounded on my front door. Sug pushed the door open and peeked inside.

"Is it safe in here?" she asked.

"Hey, yes, come on in."

She shut the door behind her and looked around the room and into the kitchen. "I waited a bit after dropping Ginny off before I came over. How's it going?"

"Becky passed out at the table. I'm working on Ginny's costume for the fall festival."

She peeked in on Becky. "She's still snoring. What's up with her? She stinks." She pinched her nose.

"I know. She's a mess." I made a face. "I didn't want her sitting on the couch. At least I can clean the table and chair she's sitting on out on the sunporch. I'd open the windows a bit, but I don't want to wake her."

"I don't blame you. Let her sleep. Gives you time to figure out what to say."

"It's just crazy. Working on Ginny's costume is helping, though. Good stress relief." I handed her the headband and material for the dog ears. "Here, you're creative. Make this look like Ollie's ears."

Ollie lifted his head and let out a yip.

I put a finger to my lips. "Shush, Ollie, we want Becky to sleep."

He wagged his tail and laid his head down.

Sug held up the material and took the scissors off the coffee table, expertly cutting out dog ears. She wrapped the headband in some leftover pillowcase material and then attached the ears.

"You're quick." I handed her the marker. "You can make some Ollie markings on them."

Ollie wagged his tail again.

"He's very excited that Ginny will be him for the fall festival," I said.

"I see that." She finished with the marker and put its cap on. "Ta-da!" She held up the headband, and I held the tail beside it. "Ginny's going to be adorable."

"What's she going to look adorable in?" Becky leaned against the doorframe.

I waved the tail at her. "You're awake. We're making Ginny a costume for the school's fall festival."

She stared at me. "Can I have some coffee?"

"Um, sure." I passed her on my way into the kitchen. "When did you shower last?"

"I've been sleeping in my car, Mom." She picked at her nails.

"Hi, Becky." Sug patted her shoulder with two fingers.

"Hey." Becky grabbed the coffee mug I held out and headed for the living room.

I took her by the shoulders and steered her back to the sunporch. "Let's sit in here. There's a nice breeze." I tipped all the windows open and sat at the far end of the table. Sug sat beside me.

Becky frowned. "Do I smell that bad?"

"Yeah, you do." I couldn't stop my snarky answer. "So what's going on? I had to pick Ginny up from Gardenview a few weeks ago."

"Thanks." Becky chewed on a fingernail and spat it out.

Sug looked at me and raised her eyebrows. She put her elbows on the table and held out her hands toward Becky. "Where have you been?"

Becky quit gnawing on her thumb and huffed. "Sleeping in my car. I told y'all."

"Why did you leave Ginny at school?" Pulling teeth would've been faster.

"Well, I knew you'd come to get her, Mom." Becky leaned back and crossed her arms. "Why are you making such a big deal about this?"

Her surly tone grated. My heart pounded in my ears, and adrenaline surged through my body. I don't know what I would've done if Sug hadn't grabbed my arm. I didn't understand Becky's careless attitude. And what did she mean, she knew I'd get Ginny?

I squared my shoulders. Patting Sug's hand on my arm, I whispered, "I'm okay." I looked at Becky. "I want you to leave."

Becky flinched. "What?"

"You heard me." I stood and pointed. "You need to leave. You're not welcome here."

"I need Ginny. I came here for her." She banged her fist on the table.

I shook my head. "Ginny isn't yours to have." I pointed again and stepped toward her. "Leave."

Becky stood. "You can't keep my daughter."

I cocked an eyebrow. "Try me," I growled.

Becky grunted and turned to Sugar. "Ms. Sug? What's going on? My mom has lost her mind."

"Listen to her, Beck." Sug stood beside me.

Becky walked backward into the kitchen, smacked her mug on the counter, and ran to the front door. "I'm leaving, but I'll be back, Mom. I'll be back for Ginny. She's mine." She slammed the door.

I spent the rest of the day on the couch, totally wiped out emotionally and mentally. I couldn't get Becky out of my mind, and I knew that she'd be back, like she said she would.

How could I prevent that from happening?

In the early evening, I called my lawyer in Tennessee. As usual, I had to leave a message. I hoped he'd call back soon. I needed his advice.

Thankfully, I had custody of Ginny. She was my priority. I spruced myself up a bit before she got home. I didn't want her to worry about me or my health. Sug brought her home at dinnertime.

I made a quick supper of soup and salad, and Sug helped set the table. When we sat to eat, Ginny asked, "Grandma, why was Mom here?"

"She wants to take you back to Tennessee."

Her eyes widened, and her spoon hung in mid-air.

"I'm not going to let her. Don't worry," I said, attempting to reassure her.

Sug patted Ginny's back. "Your grandma was a mama bear today. I was proud of you, Kat. You did the right thing."

"It was hard." I pointed my spoon at Ginny. "You're safe with me. Just remember, I have custody of you. That means that legally, you live with me."

She nodded, but her concerned expression lingered. She shouldn't be pulled between her mother and grandmother. It wasn't right.

I drove Ginny to school the next day and came home in time to hear my phone ringing. I dashed to answer it.

"Mrs. Johnson? I was about to hang up."

"Who is this?" I asked.

"Ms. Andrews. I'm Mr. Matthews's paralegal. I had a message to call you."

"Thank you for calling me today. My daughter has come back. She was at my house and wanted Ginny back."

I could hear her shuffling papers.

"Ginny, right. That's your granddaughter?" she asked.

I rolled my eyes. I'd left my patience somewhere back in Tennessee. "Yes."

"I'm just familiarizing myself with your information. Give me a minute."

I tapped my toe and waited.

"All right. So you have temporary custody of Ginny, correct?" she asked.

"Yes." I gritted my teeth. Her saccharine tone hurt my ears.

"And her mother is back in the picture?"

"Mm-hmm."

"Well, that's good, isn't it?" Ms. Andrews' cheerful voice ran through me like nails on a chalkboard. "Shouldn't Ginny be with her mother?"

"No." I opened my mouth and wiggled my jaw. I'd clenched so hard my head hurt. "No," I repeated. "It's not good. Her mother deserted her. Left her at school. And Ginny's lived with me for almost a month."

"Ah ..."

I cut in before she could say another word. "Look, I want to speak to Mr. Matthews." I wasn't waiting on this woman any longer.

"He's in court all day," she said with a curt tone.

"Would you please have him call me as soon as possible?" I raised my voice. "It's essential. I need his advice."

"Yes, I'll tell him." She hung up.

I set my cell on the coffee table, resisting the urge to slam it a few times. *Deep breaths. In and out.* I sat back and groaned. Ollie trotted to me, whining. "It's okay, boy." I scratched his head. "I'm just not in the mood for that woman."

If I'd known then what would happen that afternoon, I would've suffered through dealing with Ms. Andrews.

Chapter 24

I took my place in the school pickup line at 3:15. As each child was released, I pulled forward but didn't see Ginny anywhere. When my turn came, the teacher who helped in the car line approached.

I rolled down my window. "Where's Ginny?"

She shook her head. "I haven't seen her." She looked back at the remaining students. "She's not here."

My stomach rolled. "What do you mean? I'm supposed to pick her up."

The teacher scanned the group of waiting children again. "She's not out here, Kat. You'd better park and check inside. Maybe she's in the office. I haven't seen her." She waved me on.

After parking, I hurried inside the school. I looked through the office window but didn't see my granddaughter. I made a beeline for her classroom to check with her teacher.

"Is Ginny here? I waited in the pickup line, but she's not out there." I leaned on the doorframe, panting.

Mrs. Swanson frowned. "The office paged her to leave class at about one-thirty."

We both looked at the clock. It was three-thirty.

"Who picked her up?" *This isn't happening. Where is Ginny?*

"I don't know, really. They called for her from the office. They didn't say anything specific."

I ran up the hall to the office. Bursting through the door, I yelled, "Who checked Ginny out?"

"Whoa, Kat." Christine, the office secretary, held up her hands. "What's going on?"

I was sweating, and my heart pounded. I propped my elbows on the counter, forcing myself to lower my voice. "Who checked Ginny out? Mrs. Swanson said she was called up here at one-thirty to be checked out." I banged on the counter. "I need to know who took her, Christine."

"I was at lunch then." She stood. "Let me check with Principal Carr."

I wrapped my arms around myself. This couldn't be happening. Did Becky come for her? I couldn't imagine what would make Ginny go with her.

The principal approached. She swung the counter door open and patted my back. "Try to calm down, Kat. We'll figure this out."

Tears filled my eyes. "Do you know who took her?"

"No. Christine was on break at the time, but we're trying to get hold of her fill-in." She steered me to a chair. "Sit. You're pale. I don't need you to pass out."

I sat and lowered my head. "What if Becky took her?" My voice broke.

"Give us time, and we'll find out. Hang on just a minute. I'll be right back." She returned with a bottle of water and handed it to me. "Here, sip this."

I did as she said and leaned my head against the wall, closing my eyes. "Will you see if Mac is still here?" I wanted a friend with me. He could help me find Ginny.

Principal Carr paged him. He arrived in minutes and waited while the principal explained the situation.

He pulled up a chair beside me. I lay my head on his shoulder, thumbing tears away.

"I don't know where she is." I looked up at him. "What if Becky took her?"

"We'll get this figured out. Have you called Sug? To make sure it wasn't her?"

"No." I knew Sug wouldn't do that without telling me.

"Can I use the phone in here?" he asked Christine.

I could hear his brief conversation with Sugar and knew she didn't have Ginny. She'd have no reason to pick her up unless I asked her to.

Mac dropped into his chair. "Do you really think Becky would take her?"

"Yes." I told him what Becky threatened when I ordered her out of my house. It had only been one day. She'd already carried out her threat.

"I don't know, Kat." He shook his head. "It's hard to imagine Becky being strong enough to come here and take Ginny. She hasn't been in her right mind."

"Who else could it have been?"

He leaned forward, elbows on his knees. "What about Troy?"

I was so focused on Becky that Troy hadn't even entered my mind. Could he have checked Ginny out? Would the school allow that?

"Christine, what is the check-out policy? I've never had to do that," I asked.

"We have the list up here for whoever checks a student out," she said.

I blinked. "A list? Where? Why didn't you show me that?" I hurried to the counter, scanning her desk.

She raised her eyebrows. "I forgot. I'm so sorry." She handed me a clipboard, and I scrolled through the check-outs, looking for Ginny's name. It took me several minutes to realize Becky had written Ginny's full first name—Virginia.

I clapped my hand over my mouth and pointed to her name and Becky's scribbled signature. "Mac, look."

Becky did precisely what she said she would. Her words—*I'll be back for Ginny, she's mine*—flashed like a neon sign in my mind.

Becky had Ginny, and I didn't know where they were.

Mac followed me to my house. I searched through Ginny's room. Nothing seemed to be missing. None of this made sense.

Sugar came over, and we sat at the table, brainstorming ideas of where the two might be.

Paper and pencil in hand, Sug said, "Do you think Becky would take her back to Memphis?"

"I think so. Where else would she go?"

"Does she know anyone else here besides us? Write that down, Sug." Mac paused. "Put Troy's name down, for sure. Any friends from her teenage years, Kat?"

"None that I can think of. Anytime Becky has been here, she's just been with us, not gone to see anyone. Plus, she'd been sleeping in her car the past few days. She would have stayed with them if she had a friend here."

"That's true," he said.

"Have you called Troy?" Sug sat, pencil poised above her list.

"I don't know how to get hold of him. Mac, could you call Sierra and ask for his phone number?"

While Mac called his daughter, I chewed on my thumbnail. "Should I file a missing person's report on Ginny?" Tears filled my eyes just thinking of involving the police. This all felt so surreal. Surely Ginny would pop up, and everything would be fine.

"It might be kidnapping, Kat. Let's talk with Troy, and then we can go to the police."

"If I wait too long, though, that gives Becky more time." I choked back a sob.

"I know, but I think she'll head back to Memphis." Sug reached over and squeezed my hand. "I hate to say it, but she's not real smart right now. I think she'll go home."

I shuddered. "I hate the thought of Ginny being in the car with Becky driving. I should call Mr. Matthews in Memphis and see what he has to say. Write that down, Sug. I'll call after Mac gets Troy's number, and we'll check with him."

The setting sun dimmed the room. I flipped the overhead lights on. Mac came back to the sunporch with a slip of paper.

"Here's Troy's cell number." He laid it on the table. "Want me to call him?"

"Let me call my lawyer in Tennessee first, then you can call him." My stomach sank when the paralegal answered. *Please be helpful this time.*

"Hello? Who is this?" Her shrill voice came through the line.

I cleared my throat. "It's Kat Johnson, Ms. Andrews. I spoke with you yesterday."

"Yes."

I closed my eyes. "Is Mr. Matthews in?"

"Let me check." Elevator music filled my ear for several minutes before she came back on the line. "No, he's gone for the day."

"I told you yesterday I needed to speak with him. It was necessary then and imperative now."

"I'll write your name and number down and give it to him. He'll get back to you as soon as he can."

"Ms. Andrews." My teeth ground together. I forced myself to unclench my jaw. "My daughter checked Ginny out of school today and took her. What do I need to do?"

"You have temporary custody of Ginny?" she asked.

At least she remembered that. "Yes."

"Did you also arrange for custody in Virginia?" she asked.

"What?"

Ms. Andrews' groan came through the line. I assumed at this point that she didn't like me any more than I liked her. "You have to have custody in Virginia too. The court there has to uphold your Tennessee temporary custody."

"No one told me that." I sat back and raked my hand through my hair.

"I'm sure Mr. Matthews did. He wouldn't forget something like that." Her snippy tone set my teeth on edge.

I'd had enough. "Okay, well, I haven't done that." My tone mimicked hers. "Right now, Ginny is missing. Her mom took her today."

"Well, that's kidnapping!" she exclaimed.

I laughed. I couldn't help it. I had been through the wringer, and my emotions had gone from the deepest pit and worst thoughts to dealing with this woman. I reminded myself that God would want me to be kind.

I drew in a deep breath. "Ms. Andrews, I agree. Becky has kidnapped Ginny. What should I do?"

"I suppose you need to call the police, Mrs. Johnson. I'll have Mr. Matthews call you soon." She hung up.

I disconnected and rolled my eyes. "Did you guys get the gist of that?"

Mac and Sug nodded, both of them wide-eyed.

"Sug, did Mr. Matthews ever tell me to get temporary custody here in Virginia?"

"No. I remember he asked if we were coming back here, and I mentioned your heart attack. Maybe he meant to?"

"Maybe so, but it hasn't been done. I need to find Ginny. That's the most important thing right now." I pointed to Mac's cell phone. "Try Troy, please."

Troy's phone rang and rang, but no one picked up. Mac called Sierra back and emphasized how important it was for me to speak with Troy. She volunteered to help search for Ginny.

I touched his arm. "She's a sweet girl, Mac."

Ollie barked to go outside. The sun had set, and my stomach growled.

"I'm starving. Want me to make a quick dinner?" I rose and headed for the kitchen.

Sug stopped me. "Let me do that, Kat. Do you have the fixings for spaghetti?"

I nodded.

"You sit." She waved me toward the living room. "You've been under a lot of stress today." Sug motioned to Mac. "Take her in there and make her relax."

Mac saluted her. I scooped Red off the couch and plopped her onto my lap, stroking her fur. Her purring soothed me.

"Mac." I looked at my friend. "Do you think I'm doing the right thing?"

"What do you mean?"

"Is it right for me to try to keep Ginny? She's so young, and I have health problems. Is that the best thing for her?" I lay my head against the back of the couch. "Could Becky be a good mom if she gets clean? If Troy is her father, should he raise her?" I raised my hands. "I want what's best for her."

Mac blinked several times. "I didn't know you were thinking all this. I thought you wanted to raise Ginny. What's up with all the doubts?"

"This is going to sound so selfish. I was thrilled to meet her when Ginny first came here and so sad when she left."

"I remember," he said.

"Finding out I had a granddaughter filled me with so much joy." I hesitated. "Let me ask you this. How much has having Sierra changed your life?"

"In every way," he said. "Good ways. Challenging too."

"Do you ever wish you could return to your 'simple life'?"

He frowned. "No, I love Sierra. I can't imagine my life without her now. Even the tough times, as we've had to get to know each other." He shifted on the couch. "And this stuff with Troy."

"I'm just a bad person, I guess." I shook my head. "I miss the easy days. When it was just me."

Sug came in with a ladle covered in spaghetti sauce, her hand cupped under it. "I've been listening to you two." She gestured to me. "You were alone, Kat. And you made yourself okay with that. You were afraid. You're still afraid." She turned and stomped back to the kitchen.

Mac chuckled. "She doesn't ever hold back."

"No, she doesn't."

Sug hollered from the kitchen, "No, I don't. Someone has to tell her what's going on."

"Where would I be without you two? Here's another question. What about Ginny in all this? She had a rough time adjusting when she was little. She even ran away to Sug's that time. She's still young, only ten. She's being tugged and jerked back and forth between her mom and me. She has to make choices and decisions no child her age should have to."

Mac tapped my knee. "But Becky's been the cause of all of that. You've been the steady one in her life. And Ginny is one strong kid."

His honest words struck me hard. I took good care of my granddaughter. And truthfully, I loved it, even the hard parts. I loved her and couldn't imagine my life without her.

"Thank you. You don't hold back either, do you?"

"No, and I'm glad," Sug said from the kitchen.

We ate supper and discussed what needed to be done to find Ginny. My first stop would be the police in the morning. What Becky had done must be considered kidnapping. Sug volunteered to contact Mr. Matthews. She knew how much his paralegal got under my skin.

"That's a good idea," Mac said. "I'll track down Troy."

Ollie raised his head, woofed, and ran to the front door. When the doorbell rang, he bayed.

"Maybe it's Ginny." I pushed back my chair and rushed to the door. My hopes fell when I spied Sierra and Troy waiting on the front porch.

Sierra opened the storm door. "Hey, Mrs. Kat. Can we come in? We heard about Ginny."

I opened the door wide. "Of course, come in." I hugged Sierra and turned to Troy. "Thank you for coming."

He tipped his head and held out his hand. When I shook it, he said, "Mrs. Kat, I want to apologize for so many things. Now isn't the time for that conversation, but please forgive me. I want to help search for Ginny. Whether or not she's my daughter."

I held onto his hand and pulled him in for a hug. "I forgive you. Please forgive me too." I stepped back. "Y'all come in and sit. We're just finishing dinner."

Sug dished up bowls of spaghetti for them, and we kicked around other ideas about finding Becky and Ginny.

I buttered some bread for each of them. Troy folded his and took a huge bite.

"I was thinking," he said around his food. He chewed and swallowed. "Sorry. I thought I could go to Memphis and look for them. If you don't mind, Mrs. Kat."

"That's a great idea." Sug nodded. "We just got back from there, and Kat doesn't need to make another trip like that. It's too hard on her."

"You guys act like I'm eighty-five." I patted my chest. "I know my heart's not healthy, but I'm not that bad off."

Sierra gripped my hand. "We're just protecting you."

"I know. Thank you, Troy. I would appreciate it if you looked for them in Memphis. I'll make more calls to my lawyer and the one in town here. I still don't know if I need to go to the police," I said.

He nodded. "I'll leave in the morning."

"Can you take off work?" I asked.

"I'm self-employed." He winked. "Didn't think I'd amount to much, did you?" He folded another piece of buttered bread and stuffed it in his mouth.

My face heated up. "You got me. But you have to admit you didn't give me much to go on."

"Yeah, I know." His smile softened his words. "Once we find Ginny and she's back here, you and I can sit down and hash some things out. I want to find out if I'm her father."

"I agree. But we'll put that aside until we get her home. Deal?"

"You got it." He took another bite of his food. "I love spaghetti."

Mac, Sugar, Sierra, and I exchanged looks. "You're in the right place, then."

Chapter 25

Having dinner together and making plans gave us all a brief respite amid the drama Becky had created. But thoughts of Ginny—where she might be and what she might be doing—haunted me. My questions returned and worry and anxiety took over. I couldn't keep my hands from shaking and finally stuffed them under my thighs.

I repeatedly reminded myself of everything I'd learned in my family group and recited the Serenity Prayer. Becky wasn't clean. She wasn't a good mother—at the moment. But could she be? Did I need to work toward keeping her clean and on the right path?

Was that even my responsibility?

Where did acceptance come in? Accepting Becky was one thing, but what she did—taking Ginny—I couldn't accept or approve of that.

Sugar hit the nail on the head when she said I was afraid. I'd lived alone for so many years and made myself okay with that. I lived a quiet life. Boring, even. With Becky back in it, it was drama, all day, every day.

I've never been a fan of drama.

Digging through my old memories of Becky felt like torture. She was easygoing until she turned thirteen, and in those teenage years, a switch flipped, and she became a different person. She began to get into trouble at school, and her grades started to slip.

At fourteen, she got caught shoplifting and had to perform community service. She met Troy while doing her service hours, and the on-again/off-again relationship I couldn't stand began. He fit the typical bad-boy stereotype. If Joe had been alive, he would have chased him off.

But Joe wasn't there. He hadn't been since Becky was a baby. Dead or not, I still blamed him. If he'd stayed, none of this would've happened. My life would've stayed simple. No Juvenile Court, no service hours at the library or animal shelter. No screaming fights. No drugs. No Troy. No runaway daughter. No mess to clean up now.

But then I might not have Ginny.

That realization stole my breath. A punch in the gut. Where would I be without Ginny? How could I live life now without my girl?

After years of wavering between standing strong and overcoming my fears, I finally had to take action. I could no longer sit back. I was strong, thanks to the support of my friends and the new family group. I also had my faith in God.

I'd kept God in a box. One I opened when I couldn't do something. I had all the control. Over Becky. Over God. At least, I thought I did.

Maybe I needed to rethink that.

Wednesday morning, Troy called to tell me he and Sierra were leaving for Memphis. I prayed they'd find Becky and Ginny. I felt sure Becky had headed home. Sugar was tracking down Mr. Matthews, so I left a message for Mrs. Edwards, my lawyer in Virginia Beach, for guidance on contacting the police.

While I waited for return phone calls, I took Ollie for a walk on the beach. The wind made the water choppy. Waves crashed on the shore. As winter closed in, the sea would grow more turbulent. A cold breeze buffeted Ollie, and my hair whipped in all directions. I could taste the salt of the sea spray coating my face.

It made me think of how the ocean changed with the seasons. That was something God created and controlled. If He could do that with the seas, wouldn't He help me with these different seasons of my life?

In places, the surf came up high, exposing more sand and revealing shells and some coins. Ginny would love to gather the seashells for our glass jars. She'd put the coins to good use at the taffy store.

Life eroded at times, but even then, beautiful things were exposed and revealed. God showed some powerful truths to me during my walk.

Ollie tugged me back to the parking lot and down the street to my house. Sug sat on the front porch, rocking in one of the Adirondack rockers. I waved and stomped sand off my feet before tromping up the porch steps. I sat beside her. Ollie collapsed on the deck.

"Hey. Y'all must have had a long walk," she said.

"Good stress relief." I toed Ollie's side. "This old lug loves the beach. I'll have to wipe all the sand out of his paws before we go inside."

"Rinse him off with the shower," Sug said.

Ollie raised his head and woofed in agreement.

"Did you get hold of Mr. Matthews?" I asked her.

Sug grunted. "I got to talk to his dragon lady."

My lips twitched. "That's not nice."

"She's a piece of work, Kat. She wore me out with her back-and-forth. Did you get hold of Mrs. Edwards?"

"I'm waiting for a callback. Her paralegal is nice, but she didn't want to steer me wrong." I ran my fingers through my hair, hoping it would go back in the right direction.

"That's good." She stood. "Let's head inside. I want a drink of water."

I unlocked the front door for her and took Ollie to the side of the house to rinse his paws before we went inside. Red saw the dog coming and hissed, jumping sideways and then hopping up on the table.

I picked her up and vigorously rubbed her fur. "You're a silly feline, you know that?" I kissed her on her soft head and set her in the kitchen, blocking Ollie from going after her. My cell rang, and I jumped.

Sug shook her head. She answered the phone, said, "Just a minute, please," and handed it to me. "Lawyer," she mouthed.

"Hello, Mrs. Edwards?" I said.

"Yes, Mrs. Johnson. I had a message to call you."

I filled her in on the situation and answered her questions the best I could.

Finally, she said, "I think you should go to the police. They will help by contacting Memphis law enforcement and getting everyone looking for Becky and Ginny."

"I'll go do that now." I hung up after thanking her for her help and turned to Sug. "Want to go to the police station with me?"

Sug drove while I worried. We'd just been at 201 Poplar in Memphis trying to locate Becky, and now we were headed to the First Precinct on Princess Anne Road.

"Not a fan of these police stations," I said.

"Quit shaking your hands," she said. "You're making me nervous."

I tucked them under my legs.

"Thank you." She steered into the parking lot and pulled into a spot by the front door. "Let's go see what they can do to find Ginny."

Ginny. Yes, my focus would stay on her. Picturing her sweet face strengthened me. I unbuckled and joined Sug on the sidewalk.

"We're not in trouble, Kat. We're here to help our girl." She tucked her arm in mine.

"I know." I hoped the police felt the same way.

It took a long time and discussions with three different police officers before they finally seemed to understand what had happened. It wasn't kidnapping. It was an abduction. Even though my legal custody of Ginny was for Tennessee and not Virginia, if Becky took her back to Tennessee, she could be picked up for abducting Ginny.

"Will she go to jail?" Sug asked.

"We'll cross that bridge when we get to it." The officer handed some paperwork off to another officer tasked with contacting the Memphis police. He looked at me. "You said the girl's father went to find her?"

"I *think* he's her father." I made a face.

His eyebrows rose. "What?"

I waved my hand. "It's a long story, but I think Troy is Ginny's father. We have no real proof yet. But he volunteered to go search for her and Becky."

He hollered at the man on the phone with Memphis PD. "Tell them this guy,"—he turned to me—"Troy Turner?"

I nodded.

"Tell them he's looking for the lady and the little girl. Grandma says he's a good guy."

I snorted. Who would have thought I'd say Troy was a good guy? People change, that's for sure.

Sug and I were starving by the time we left the police station. We stopped for sandwiches to go and enjoyed them on the sunporch. Ollie sat outside on the back step and drooled while Red circled my ankles.

I kept praying we would hear something from Troy and Sierra soon.

"I guess they won't be in Memphis until tomorrow." I wiped my hands and stood to throw away my trash.

"They'd have to drive fast to make any better time than we did." Sug took the last bite of her sandwich. She opened the back door and clicked her tongue at Ollie. "I saved you a bite, big fellow."

Ollie scrambled inside and gobbled up the piece of turkey meat she handed him. Red hissed and danced backward into the kitchen, back humped like a Halloween cat.

And that's when it hit me. Today was the school's fall festival. Ginny's costume sat on the extra bed in her room, ready for her to wear. She loved the tail and ears we'd made and planned for hours how to do her doggie makeup.

Sug looked up in alarm when I sniffled. Tears trickled down my cheeks. The doorbell rang, and Ollie bayed and took off for the front door. She looked out the window to see trick-or-treaters coming up the street.

"Oh, Kat." She covered her mouth.

"Ginny should have been wearing her Ollie costume today." I wiped my face and blew my nose. The doorbell rang again. I grabbed the dog's collar and dragged him back to the sunporch.

Sug shouted over his barking and baying. "You have candy?"

I pointed to the pantry. Without a word, she got two bags out. I could hear her commenting on the kids' costumes and them thanking her for the candy.

She brought me a mini chocolate bar before the next round of cowboys and princesses. "Thought this might cheer you up."

I shrugged. "Originally, I bought three bags of candy." I unwrapped the chocolate and popped it into my mouth. "But thanks."

Sug and I tag-teamed answering the door. Ollie barked for the first half hour before he gave up and sat at our feet, wagging his tail. Sug snuck him a couple of pieces of peanut butter candy.

I tried to stay busy on Thursday, but every time the phone rang, I jumped. Sug and Mac checked on me, but I didn't hear from Troy or the police. I forced myself to eat lunch out back with Ollie. Then we went on another walk, my cell stuck in my back pocket.

I rehashed all my doubts and worries while we trudged up the beach. What would it take for Becky to be free from addiction? Tonight was a family group meeting, and I knew that's where I had to be.

When Ollie and I got back home, I called Maggie. "Can we meet before family group? Maybe have dinner?"

"I'd love it if you came here," she said. "Come about a quarter till six, and that will give us time to eat and chat. Then, we can walk to the church."

Maggie's place was a cute pale peach-colored beach cottage on Sixteenth Street. The sun had almost set when I pulled into her driveway. I admired the glow it made on the front of the house.

She waited at the front door for me. "Hi, Kat, come on in."

"I love the color of your house."

"Thank you. I painted it last summer." She gestured toward the open living room and kitchen. "Let's eat on the back porch. It's such a pretty evening."

Her small porch faced the Atlantic, and the cool breeze brought enticing sea scents and fresh air. She'd set the table, just big enough for two, with rust-colored placemats, matching cloth napkins, and gold chargers. She spooned chili into heavy, dark green bowls and added a square of cornbread.

"This is so pretty." I admired my surroundings. "When you come to eat at my place, just remember I don't have the decorator gene you do." I told her about Sug's paintings. "You'll have to come over one night when Sug and Mac are there."

"I've heard you talk about Sug, but who is Mac? A boyfriend?" She broke off a bite of her cornbread.

"No, he's considerably younger than Sug and me. He's probably closer to your age." I raised my eyebrows and tipped my head. "Hmm ..."

Maggie giggled. "What are you thinking?"

"I'm just picturing you and Mac together." I wiped my mouth. "You guys would make a cute couple."

She covered her eyes. "We are not in middle school!"

"I'm just teasing you." I patted her hand. "Actually, I wanted to talk to you about something, and I'd like your honest opinion."

"Sure. What's going on?"

I caught her up on what happened with Ginny and Becky, including our visit to the police station and Troy's offer to help.

"He's going to Tennessee?" she asked.

"Yes, he should be there today. I hadn't heard from him before I left home." I patted my purse. "I have my phone, though, just in case."

"That's amazing, Kat. I'm thrilled to hear this."

"You are?" I couldn't imagine why.

"Yes. It shows so much growth on your part." She put down her spoon and wiped her mouth. "You see this house and porch?"

"Yes."

"Remember I was an addict?" Her eyes twinkled.

"Of course." Where was she going with this?

"But I own a house and have a good job." She sat back, arms crossed over her chest.

"You're saying Troy has changed." Now I caught her drift.

"Yep." She took a bite of chili, swallowed, and pointed at me with her spoon. "You've changed too."

Chapter 26

I sat back. *Was that true? Had I changed?* I thought about when Becky first left and all the grieving I'd done. I mourned a relationship with her that honestly hadn't ever been there. At least since she was a young girl. Now, I knew the truth about Becky. Her problems weren't a result of a lack of good parenting on my part. Nor were they because of anything I didn't do.

Her addiction and all that came with it were because of the choices she made—things she chose to do. Or not do. And because addiction is a disease, she couldn't stop once she started. It was all a horrible cycle.

I recognized that I had done things before and hoped God would approve. Now, I made conscious choices to let God lead—another thing I learned from my family group.

"I guess I have changed." I lifted my hands. "So, where do I go from here? Do I trust Becky? Should I ask her to get clean and keep Ginny?"

"You're looking too far into the future. Let's deal with each day as it comes."

I chuckled. "You've said that in meetings before."

Maggie picked up our empty bowls. "Because it's true. We need to focus on what's true." She turned. "And you are projecting expectations onto Becky."

Sometimes the truth seemed elusive, intertwined with God. If I learned more about Him, I would discover more truth. That would guide me in making future decisions and help me keep Him in front of me, not behind.

I could see how what I'd discovered in family group had been building in my life. I learned about serenity and peace and was challenged to dream.

That was tough.

I thought back to what I learned on my beach walk: that God controlled the oceans, the seasons, and even the erosion of the shore.

I followed Maggie inside, carrying our glasses. "Yes, expectations, ugh. I know better." I handed her the glasses. "You asked us to dream, and that's about the future."

"It is." She loaded the dishwasher, turned around, and leaned against the counter. "Dreaming is different from making choices now that you have to stick to days, weeks, or months from now."

"Okay. That makes sense."

Maggie checked her watch. "Let's get going. It's a short walk from here to the church."

It was Roger's turn to lead the meeting. After he opened with a short prayer, he passed out blank sheets of paper and pencils.

"It's getting close to Thanksgiving, so I thought we could talk about thankfulness tonight." He gestured to the paper he held. "Take a few minutes and write five things you're thankful for." He held up a finger. "And don't just list five different people."

The thought had crossed my mind, but that was the easy way out. My list started with my family and my friends. I added my job and then the family group. Finally, I wrote down "addiction."

When it came time to share what we were thankful for, I volunteered to go first.

"My family, obviously." I smirked. "I almost wrote five different names, but I listened to you." I nodded in Roger's direction.

He winked.

"I also put my friends, my job, and this family group because I don't know where I'd be without you all and all I've learned."

Maggie held up four fingers. "That's only four, Kat."

I stared at my list. "This last one is tough. I wouldn't have said I was thankful for it earlier this year." I paused. "The last thing I wrote was that I'm thankful for addiction."

I put my paper on my lap and palmed tears from my cheeks. "Because, without Becky's addiction, I wouldn't be who I am and where I am today. And I don't think I would have Ginny. Maggie says I've changed. I'm starting to realize she's right. And I'm glad about it."

Maggie clapped. Everyone clapped with her, even me.

"Yay for addiction!" Maggie cheered.

"I wouldn't go that far." I laughed. "But yes, yay for healing and growth."

Maggie linked arms with me on the short walk back to her house. "When can I come and eat with you, Sug, and Mac?"

I stopped and stared at her. "Mac needs to be there?"

"Well, it seems like a good idea." She tugged me to continue walking. "Even I need to grow and change."

When I got home, I called Mac and let Ollie out back to do his business.

"Have you heard anything from Troy or Sierra?"

"They got there and told me where they're staying. Sierra said they got held up in traffic on I-40 and didn't arrive until after dark. She wasn't sure whether to go by Becky's tonight or wait for daylight. She wanted to call you, but I told her you'd be at your meeting."

"Thanks. I'm not sure, but going during the daytime is probably better. If Becky took her back to Memphis, they didn't get in until yesterday. What do you think?" Ollie barked at the door, and I let him inside.

"I told them the same thing. You said it's not a great area, and it might be safer when they can see well."

"That's fine. I want everyone to be safe." I paused. "I have peace about all this, Mac. God has shown me so many things in the last few days. When you hear from Sierra again, tell them I'll be home tomorrow, and they can call me. I'll stick close to home and have my cell with me."

After I settled Red and Ollie for the night, I curled up in Ginny's reading chair with my Bible. I'd been praying and saw how God worked in my life. I needed to return to His Word and learn more about Him.

My cell woke me on Friday morning. I rushed to the kitchen, where the device was charging, and answered before the caller hung up.

"Hi, Mrs. Kat," Sierra said. "We're heading over to Becky's now."

"Okay, good. Thank you for letting me know." I pushed the "on" button on my coffee pot. I'd need my morning brew today. "Be careful, Sierra. I'm not sure how Becky will be if she and Ginny are even there. Or how she'll react to seeing Troy."

"I understand. I'll call as soon as I know something." She said goodbye and hung up.

I poured a cup of coffee. Before my first sip, someone knocked on my front door. Ollie trotted out from my room, baying his head off.

The door still stuck, and I had to set my mug down to tug it open. Sugar stood on my porch with her coffee cup.

She raised it. "Figured you could use a friend this morning."

I pushed the door shut behind her, and we headed to the kitchen. "Yes. Sierra just called, and they're going to Becky's. I'm a bit nervous."

"Of course you are." She poured herself some coffee. "Let's go sit on the porch while we wait."

I handed her my mug. "I just jumped out of bed when the phone rang. Let me brush my teeth and fix my hair. I'll be right out."

When I got to the sunporch, I found Sug feeding Ollie pieces of vanilla wafers.

"Breakfast?"

"Yep." She grinned. "First thing I found in the pantry."

"I've got to stay busy while we wait for a call. I'll scramble some eggs and make toast. Sound good?"

Ollie woofed, and Sug nodded.

It was a long day. After breakfast, Sug helped me clean the kitchen. She took Ollie out back and threw a ball for him. I didn't want to take him for a walk and risk missing a call from Sierra in case I didn't have cell coverage.

My mom always said, 'A watched pot never boils.' It seemed like the same held true for phones and phone calls. Sug dragged me out on the front porch to eat lunch. She pocketed my cell to keep me from checking it constantly. Red sat on the armrest of my Adirondack chair and watched the birds. She chattered, chirped at them, and made the strange grinding noise cats make.

Sug put her sandwich on her plate and wiped her mouth. "That's some predatory noise cats make. It's like they're frustrated that they can't catch the bird."

"I'm pretty sure Red could catch a bird. She's Ollie's boss, remember?" I petted the cat's soft fur.

Ollie lay on the other side of Sug, as far from Red as he could be. He thumped his tail and whined.

"It's okay, boy." Sug patted his head. "I'll protect you from the tiny fur-ball."

He lay his head down with a big whole-body groan.

"When will we hear from them?" I picked at the crust on my sandwich. "I keep imagining horrible scenarios with police and guns and poor Ginny being scared. I had peace, but now my imagination is going wild." I patted my chest. "My heart is fluttering."

"It's hard to wait." Sug gathered our empty plates. "Stay out here and relax. You gotta keep that heart healthy." She opened the storm door. "Give your brain a break too. Worrying doesn't help anything."

I leaned back and breathed slowly in and out, forcing myself to relax. Red curled up in my lap and went to sleep, one paw over her eyes.

"I wish I could sleep like that, Ms. Red." I stroked her head. Ollie stood and placed his chin on the arm of my chair. I patted his head, and he drooled. He sensed my concern. His fear of Red wouldn't keep him from my side right now.

In the late afternoon, when the sun was beginning to set, my phone finally rang. It had been so quiet all day that when it rang, Sug and I both yelped.

"Gracious!" Sug clasped her hand to her chest. "Answer it, answer it."

My hands shook as I answered the call and pressed the speaker button. "Hello?"

"Hi, Grandma." Ginny's sweet voice trembled.

Peace flooded my body. "Oh, Ginny, I'm so glad to hear your voice. How are you?" Sug and I exchanged wide grins.

"I'm okay, Grandma." She sniffled. "Ms. Sierra and Mr. Troy are here."

"Yes, they said they'd come to find you."

Sug grabbed my hand.

"I'm sorry I went with my mom." Ginny sniffled again.

"No, honey." I shook my head even though she couldn't see me. "You did nothing wrong—nothing at all. You should be able to trust your mom."

She blew her nose. Voices sounded in the background.

"Can I talk to Mr. Troy, honey?" I asked.

"Yes. Here he is."

"Hello? Kat?" Troy's voice came through the phone.

"Hi, how did everything go?"

"It's been a long day, that's for sure." He blew out a breath. "We found Becky's place. She'd left Ginny here, alone." He cleared his throat. "I didn't call you right away. I'm sorry. We wanted to talk to Ginny, and then Becky came home."

I grimaced, imagining the worst. "How did that go?"

"Ugly at first. Sierra took Ginny outside. Becky yelled at me and accused me of all sorts of things." He paused. "She threatened to take Ginny again if I brought her back to you. She also said she had more rights as a parent than you do as a grandmother."

I couldn't speak for a minute. Images of Becky abducting Ginny another time flashed through my mind. The law would be on her side as a parent. I reminded myself that I had temporary custody.

"She did tell me one more thing." He paused.

"You're Ginny's biological dad." I knew it. I just hadn't fully acknowledged it.

"Yes, I am. Becky confirmed that. We can still do a DNA test, though."

"Troy, I believe you're Ginny's father. I think the test would be a good idea in case we have to take Becky to court."

"What do you mean?"

"It looks like you and I will raise our girl together." The idea of Troy and me working together to raise Ginny popped out of my mouth. I almost wanted to shove the words back in, but they made sense, given all the circumstances. My doctor had put the thought in my head, and I'd pushed it away until now.

My health wasn't the best. I was thankful this last crisis hadn't caused any chest pains or symptoms. I didn't want to take chances. Ginny's care would come first before what I wanted. She needed all of our love to grow and flourish—even Troy's.

And she needed our protection from anything Becky threw at us.

I'd known Troy was her father since that day at Taste. They shared similar features, and Ginny's long legs came from his side. I just didn't want to acknowledge it. Maggie said I'd changed, and over time, I saw the changes in Troy.

There was silence on his end, and then he spoke in a husky voice, "I love that idea. Thank you. I also wanted to let you know that the police arrived during Becky's rant. She was arrested for abducting Ginny."

I wondered what she would do about that. Or if I even needed to be involved. Unfortunately, I'd have to call Mr. Matthews, which meant getting past his paralegal. In the meantime, Troy and Sierra would bring Ginny home.

Sunday afternoon, Sug and I waited outside on my front porch for the three of them. Mac joined us late in the day. I tried not to pace or jiggle my leg. Sug gave me the stink eye when I fidgeted. When Troy pulled into the driveway, we all stood. I hurried down the steps to meet Ginny at the car.

I tugged the car door open and held my arms out to her. "I'm so glad you're safe." I hugged her.

She tipped her head up. "Mom went to jail, Grandma."

I swallowed the lump in my throat and pulled her into a hug. "I know, honey. She shouldn't have taken you like she did." Her body slumped against mine, and her shoulders shook. "It's okay. Let it out." I rubbed her back, praying for her until she quieted.

"Mr. Troy said I'm going to live here." She wiped her nose on my shirt.

"Again, Ginny? I am not a Kleenex." I laughed. I leaned back and looked at her. "Yes, you're going to stay with me. Does that sound good?"

She nodded.

Sug, Mac, Troy, and Sierra joined us in a group hug.

Thank you, Lord. This crisis is over. My girl is safe.

Chapter 27

Ginny was determined to go back to school on Monday. With Thanksgiving break only days away, her classroom would be calm, predictable—exactly what we both needed. I was almost convinced it would work. Then my phone rang before we got out the door.

"Mrs. Johnson? This is Detective Sanford in Memphis. I've been talking with your daughter, Becky Johnson."

"Yes?"

"Well, it seems your daughter can go to rehab and avoid charges. It's up to you," he said.

I rocked back on my heels. Another decision. "Oh, okay. What do I need to do?" *Please don't make me come back to Memphis.*

"I need you to sign paperwork if you agree to her going to rehab."

I closed my eyes and shook my head. "Do I have to come there? I live in Virginia Beach."

"I'm aware. I believe you can coordinate this through your lawyers."

Thank God. "Thank you. That will work. I would much rather she go to rehab."

"She'll be here for a few days, detoxing. She has to do that before she can get into a place." He cleared his throat. "I wanted to tell you that I've had a few run-ins with your daughter. I took her to a rehab once, but then she was back on the street. I tried. I'm sorry."

My heart warmed. "No, don't be sorry. You're an answer to prayer. It's really up to her, you know?"

"Mhm."

"What's the difference between detox and rehab?" I asked.

"Detox is when they're getting off the drugs or alcohol. It's just about the physical side of addiction." He heaved a heavy sigh. "It's a good start, but she needs rehab where they'll help her deal with the other parts. You know, mental, behavioral."

"Thank you. I never understood all of that. Who sets up rehab?"

Tapping on computer keys came through the phone. "That's up to you." More tapping. "Okay, she can go to one here in Memphis—we have several good ones. I can recommend Serenity on Poplar here in Memphis." He read a few more names off a list. "Or she could go to one in Virginia."

I checked the clock on the stove. "Detective, I have to leave for school. I'm a teacher. But when I get home, I'll look into rehabs here and contact my lawyer, Mrs. Edwards."

"That's fine. One more thing you should know. Becky said that after she goes through rehab, she wants custody of her daughter. In my experience, that can happen."

"Thank you for letting me know." I hung up and shook my head. There was more work and more to pray about. Always something more with my daughter.

Drug rehab is expensive. I always assumed it was for anyone who needed it. Some insurance companies covered it, but Becky didn't have insurance.

After a long day at work, where I attempted to teach antsy third graders who were already anticipating Thanksgiving break, I called Mrs. Edwards. She provided information on local rehabilitation facilities for drug addicts and said she would contact Mr. Matthews in Tennessee about the paperwork.

I also called Maggie, hoping she would have insight into what I should do. I figured I would trade information for a home-cooked dinner and include Sugar and Mac as guests.

Mac arrived first. He pitched in and got four glasses of ice water while Ginny set the table. Sugar knocked and entered, carrying an apple pie for dessert.

I leaned over and sniffed it. "That smells amazing."

She set it on the counter. "Thanks. I think it'll taste good."

"I've never eaten anything you've made that doesn't taste good." I chuckled.

A knock sounded, and Sug answered the door. She and Maggie had spoken on the phone before and were chatting as they entered the kitchen. Mac came in from the backyard, where he'd been playing with Ollie.

He held up his hands like a surgeon. "I need to wash that stinky dog off my hands."

Maggie's lips twitched. "Hi, I'd shake your hand, but you look busy. I'm Maggie. I've heard a lot about you."

The tips of his ears reddened. He washed his hands and turned. "Nice to meet you." He shot me a look. "I didn't know you invited someone else, Kat." He grabbed another glass out of the cabinet and filled it. "Let me put this on the table."

When he left the room, Maggie winked. "He is cute," she whispered.

Sug and I giggled but straightened up when he returned to the kitchen.

He rubbed his hands together. "We ready to eat?"

"Let me dish the food." I got out five bowls and scooped up the noodles and sauce, handing them out as I filled them.

"I'll get the bread and butter." Sug winked at Maggie. "It's a staple around here."

Ginny smacked her lips. "I love buttered bread, Ms. Maggie. Grandma's psghetti is the best."

"Most times I make it, Mac is here." I gestured to him with my bowl.

He glared at me. "I contribute my presence and table-setting skills, Maggie. I'm a horrible cook."

"Maggie makes a great chili." I looked around to see if everyone had their food. "Let's all go sit down."

Ginny entertained us through supper. Conversation with Mac was stilted, and he seemed out of sorts. When Maggie excused herself to the bathroom, I leaned over to him.

"What's wrong?"

"Kat, what are you doing?" His normally bright blue eyes were stormy.

"What do you mean? I wanted to ask her about rehabs around here."

He shook his head and tipped his chin at Sug. "You in on this too?"

Sug fluttered her eyelashes. "I have no idea what you mean." She patted my arm. "My good friend here is just providing dinner for her friends."

Ginny looked between us. "You are all weird." She took a big bite of noodles. "Maggie is pretty, Mr. Mac. Don't you think so?"

Mac covered his face. "Y'all are not subtle."

"Shush, here she comes," I said.

Maggie pulled out her chair and sat. "So, Kat, what did you want to know?"

Mac left the room, snorting as he hurried down the hall.

"Is he okay?" Maggie frowned.

I chuckled. "Yes, he's fine. Probably choked on a noodle." I set my bowl in the kitchen and returned with a notepad and pen. "I need information on rehab. Becky can avoid jail time by going there, but I don't know anything about it."

"Gotcha. I can only share my experience with you. I was there maybe four times."

Ginny's eyes widened.

Maggie tapped her on the head. "Yes, sweetie, I am a recovering addict."

"I didn't know that." She looked Maggie up and down. "You don't look sick like my mom."

"Your mom's in a bad place right now. I quit drugs a number of years ago. It's not easy though."

"Can my mom do that?" Hope shone in her eyes.

"I hope so, honey. I sure hope so." Maggie turned to me. "What do you need to know?"

Sug tapped Ginny's arm. "Let's take Ollie out back for some exercise." She poked his belly with her foot. "He's getting chubby."

Ginny rubbed the dog's ears as they went outside. "Don't listen to her, buddy. She's just kidding."

Maggie and I talked about the best rehab options in the beach area. She also shared her experience in rehab with me.

"For the first two weeks or so, I hated everybody. I didn't want to be there. I was miserable without drugs. I made sure everyone, even my mom, knew I despised rehab and that I'd been forced to go." She made a face. "I resisted what they tried to tell me there. I guess that's why I went so many times."

"You were able to call your mom?" I didn't want to talk to Becky yet.

"Yes. Limited phone calls, but yes, I could call." Her mouth pinched to one side. "I made a total pest of myself, that's for sure."

"Can you help me with the pros and cons of having Becky here versus in Tennessee?"

"The way I see it, having her closer is better if you want to visit her and have her work toward being with Ginny," she said.

Mac came back in and sat at the table. "Troy said you'd mentioned him helping to raise Ginny."

"Yes, I think that would be a good idea. I don't want Becky to have custody." I shifted in my chair. So many big decisions to make.

"She still wants it? Custody?" Maggie shook her head. "It's amazing what she's come up with."

"That's what the detective in Memphis said. Knowing Becky, she does. When she's sober, she's a good mom." I shrugged.

Mac grimaced. "She hasn't been sober very often."

"True. It's so hard to know what the right thing is. Do I pray she gets clean and can keep Ginny? What's best for Ginny? It's a lot to decide." I fiddled with my napkin. "And I can't know what the future holds for any of us."

Maggie patted my hand. "It is a hard decision. But Kat, so many people love Ginny and are already strong forces in her life. I've seen how you are with her. What she needs is for her friends to help and provide her with positive role models. Good examples are so important for her. You can't wait for whatever Becky does to live your life."

I agreed. Ginny hadn't had a good role model in her mother. And yet, my granddaughter was already an amazing person with many wonderful character traits. I wanted to make sure she grew up to be everything she could be. I was so tired of waiting on Becky.

I patted my chest. "My health isn't the best. I don't want that to be a problem."

"Then working with Troy to raise Ginny might be best," she said.

My phone rang. Mac picked it up and checked the screen. He held it out to me. "Speak of the devil."

"Mac!" I swatted his arm, grabbed the cell from him, and pushed the speaker button. "Hello?"

"Mom, it's me. I want to go to rehab, and I want Ginny back." Becky's words came out in a defensive rush.

Becky wasn't budging on Ginny. "The detective told me that."

"Just so you know, that is my plan." Her voice turned flat but determined.

"Where are you going to rehab?" I looked at Maggie and Mac, raising my eyebrows.

"Wherever you set it up is fine."

"It's all on me?"

"You're the one who put me in jail." The sneer in her voice came through the line.

I sat back, anger rising over her words. Maggie made a face and motioned for me to hang up.

"I will let you know the plan." I punched the disconnect button.

"Bravo." Maggie clapped. "I know that was hard."

"She was ordering me around. She still doesn't take any responsibility for her actions." My heart broke for my child. Even as much as she drove me up the wall, I wanted her to be safe and healthy.

"It'll be a while for that to happen, Kat. She still has lots of drugs in her system," Maggie said.

"Well, that makes me want to keep her in Tennessee. As far away from Ginny and me as possible."

Mac stood. "I don't blame you there." He wandered into the kitchen. "Where's that pie Sugar brought?"

It took me over a week to arrange Becky's rehab. Maggie reminded me of the difference between detox, where the drugs get out of the addict's system, and rehab, where Becky could learn tools to adjust to a sober life.

I finally found a rehab in Virginia Beach that would take her on such short notice. I dipped into my savings and paid upfront for a six-week stay.

After I informed the Memphis police of what I'd arranged, Becky called. "If I'm going to rehab up there, you'll have to come get me."

"You want me to drive there and bring you back? Can't you take the bus?"

"I won't come unless you pick me up." My daughter's ugly side was showing.

I bit my lip. "Fine. Be ready to leave on Thursday. I'll pick you up."

"You have to come to 201 Poplar."

"Oh, I know where you are," I said.

Becky snorted. "This will be so fun."

I wasn't sure *fun* was the right word. Becky had grown more demanding since she'd been in jail. Each call from her held the same refrain—I sent her there and destroyed her life. I could tell from her tone that if I didn't get her and drag her to rehab, she wouldn't go. I don't know how she thought she'd get Ginny back, but her twisted mind seemed to think it could happen.

Sometimes, I wondered what she'd do if I left her at 201 Poplar. It was a tempting idea.

I left for Memphis on Wednesday morning. Sug had to work, so Ginny stayed with Mac and Sierra to attend school. I promised my friends I'd wear compression socks and take plenty of breaks. When I arrived at the hotel in Knoxville, I wanted to sleep for a week. I hadn't had any chest pains—no physical ones, anyway. However, the stress continued to rise, and my body pushed back. My head throbbed—the weight of all the decisions I'd made and would have to make overwhelmed me.

The headache I went to sleep with followed me to Memphis. The Criminal Justice Center looked as imposing as ever, but I signed the paperwork to have Becky released. I answered her questions, refusing to debate with her. Finally, she gave up on engaging me, curled up in the front seat, and slept. I heaved a sigh of relief, tossed back two more acetaminophen, and headed home. We stopped just east of Nashville to eat dinner and then drove to Knoxville.

"Is there any way you can drive some tomorrow?"

"I don't have a license, but sure." She switched on the radio and scanned for a station.

I rubbed my forehead. "No, that's okay. I'll be all right." I yawned and turned into the hotel's parking lot. "A good night's sleep will help."

We checked in and rode the elevator to the second floor. Becky opened the door, and I eased into a chair, propping my feet on the bed.

"Mom, your ankles are swollen." Becky pushed on my ankle, and the impression from her fingertip remained. "That shouldn't happen."

"They're uncomfortable, for sure."

"Here, lie on the bed and put this pillow under your feet so the swelling goes down." She helped me get situated and brought me a glass of water. "It's probably from driving so much." She shook her head. "You have heart problems too, right?"

I had a heart attack only a month ago. I didn't tell her. "Yeah, I do."

She shook her head and turned the lights out. "Get some sleep, Mom. Hopefully, they'll be better in the morning. I don't want you to stroke out on me."

Stroke out? I'd never thought about having a stroke. But watching Becky transform from being disagreeable to being watchful of me was fascinating. She was a good person. She had good traits. But those drugs sure did change her.

Chapter 28

I sensed something wrong in my body. My ankles usually didn't swell like they were, and I'd never had a headache last this long. I pushed through, and we arrived at the rehab late Friday afternoon. The older building, located in a less desirable part of town, was surrounded by a wrought-iron fence. It reminded me more of a psychiatric institution.

With Thanksgiving less than a week away, the rehab facility had turkeys and pumpkins displayed on the walls, along with signs indicating who could and couldn't visit and what they were allowed to bring into the building. It felt surreal to be there.

Becky didn't have any clothes or personal items, but they offered an all-in-one package, which I bought. I didn't think I could manage to go shopping for what she needed. I hugged her when I left.

Tears filled her eyes. She swiped them roughly. "This isn't my first rehab, but maybe this one will take."

"I hope so, honey. Truly, I do." I kissed her cheek and hurried to my car. I needed to get myself to the hospital. My chest clenched, and my vision wavered. I stared at my ankles—swollen, straining against my socks. My heart felt wrong, off, failing. I needed help—fast.

I parked at the hospital and dragged myself into the emergency room. When I told them my symptoms, they sat me in a wheelchair and rushed me to the back. After they took my vitals, they got me settled into one of the rooms.

When Dr. Thompson walked in, he shook his head. "Did you drive yourself here?"

"Dumb decision, but yes." I stared at my hands.

"Kat, I don't even know what to say." He checked my chart and ordered some blood work and scans. "You know the drill. You'll be here a bit. Is there anyone you need to call?"

I called Mac—he'd spend less time fussing at me than Sugar. And I wanted to check on Ginny.

"I knew you weren't up to that drive, Kat," he scolded me. "I'll let Sug know. And Maggie."

"You have Maggie's number?" I teased him, hoping it would distract him from my health.

"Why yes, I do, thank you very much. We met for coffee on Sunday afternoon."

"That's great, Mac. I'm happy for you."

"I know what you're doing, Kat. I'm still going to call them both and tattle on you." I imagined he was shaking his finger as he spoke.

"Ugh." I shifted in my hospital bed. "Tell Sug I need some clothes, please. And a toothbrush. And my favorite pillow."

"They're going to keep you? Is it that bad?"

"All this with Becky, plus the quick trip, didn't help. I'll be okay, Mac. I'm in the best place possible." I picked up the TV remote. "I'll get settled and call Ginny."

I wanted to wait until Dr. Thompson stopped by before speaking with Ginny. He'd tell me what to expect, and I could prepare her. On my last visit with him, he spoke of doing a heart catheterization. I didn't know for sure what that entailed, but if that's what he recommended, I would do it.

Dr. Thompson knocked on my door that evening.

"Twice in one day, Doc? That's not good."

He laid my chart at the end of my bed and sat beside me. "We need to do that heart cath I told you about. Looks like you may need a stent placed."

I rubbed my chest. "What's up with this heart of mine?"

"From what you told me, it's the stress affecting your health. You cannot make any more trips." He patted my leg. "None, Kat. I mean it. You're heading toward a major heart attack or a stroke. Now, you will need to be here for a couple of days to get things under control, and then we'll do the procedure. I plan to have you home for Thanksgiving."

"Okay." Another holiday that my health had messed up.

"I know you don't feel well. When I only get an 'okay' from you, it concerns me." He smiled.

"No, I really don't. Please fix me up." Tears welled in my eyes.

He laid my chart down and opened the door. "I'll do my best. For now, rest."

That was easier said than done. Machines whirred and beeped, nurses came and went, staff members requested information and consent, and people chatted in the hallway. It gave me time to think, though.

I wondered how Becky was doing and if she could stay clean. How long would she need to be sober before I could trust her? What would a judge say? She'd been clean before for several years, but I'd seen how that turned out.

My expectations were high. I didn't think Becky would meet them. I knew what expectations led to—premeditated resentment. I shouldn't have set Becky or myself up like that.

One day at a time, Maggie would say. She opened up about her struggles and admitted that she was just one drink or drug away from relapsing. She also said, "Once an addict, always an addict." I struggled to understand that concept.

Maybe I shouldn't, though. As stubborn as I was about doing everything possible to fix Becky and save her, I didn't take care of myself. Fixing other people and situations and not allowing God to lead me was my addiction.

The doctor scheduled my heart catheterization for Monday afternoon. Maggie came to visit on Sunday but refused to bring me a burger. Instead, I asked for a milkshake. She pulled a banana out of her purse.

"That's not what I asked for." I crossed my arms and pouted.

"Sorry, I can't keep a milkshake in my purse." She plumped my pillow and turned the television down. "You're a bit grumpy."

I gave her the stink eye. "You'd be grumpy too, stuck in here."

"Want to hear about Mac and me?" Her eyes lit up when she said his name.

"Yes, that sounds interesting." I motioned her closer and patted the bed. "Come sit by me and give me all the details."

She settled beside me. "We've been out twice. I really like him. He's fun and sweet."

"He's a good guy." I squeezed her hand. "I highly recommend him."

"I told him I'm a recovering addict." She twisted a ring on her finger. "I haven't heard from him since. I think he thought I had a family member who was an addict."

I was disappointed in Mac, but he'd come around. "Maggie, he's smart. Give him some time. He needs to get used to the idea."

When she left, I did some extra matchmaking and called Mac. "Hey there, how are you? I should be getting out of here by Wednesday."

"I can pick you up. Sugar is going to host Thanksgiving this year. She has it all planned out."

"Sounds good to me." I paused. "Want me to invite Maggie?"

"I wish you'd told me she was an addict." His words came out as a growl.

"Recovering."

"What?"

"She's a recovering addict. Addiction is a disease, Mac. And people do recover. But it's an ongoing thing."

"That's why she couldn't guarantee she'd never return to it." He wasn't asking me, so I kept quiet. He exhaled noisily. "I really like her."

"She likes you too."

"Becky keeps running through my head, though. I'll think about Thanksgiving, okay? I'm just not sure."

I understood what he was saying. Trusting an addict was taking a chance. But in all honesty, trusting anyone was, and I told him that. Then I asked to talk to Ginny.

"We've had Ollie and Red here at Mr. Mac's," she said.

"You have? I'm sure that's fun."

Ginny's giggle cheered me up. "I think it's fun, but I'm not sure Mr. Mac does. Oh, Mr. Troy's been over some. I really like him." She giggled again. "I think Ms. Sierra does too."

"She sure does. I'm glad you like him, sweetie." Troy and I agreed to wait for the DNA test results to tell Ginny he was her father. It made me happy that she liked being around him.

"How's my mom?" she asked.

"I haven't talked to her since I dropped her at rehab." It was a relief not to hear from Becky every day with some new problem.

"Oh, okay." Ginny hesitated. When she spoke again, her voice was husky. "Grandma, does it matter who I want to live with?"

"What do you mean?"

"I want to live with you and Ollie and Red." She sniffled. "I don't want to hurt my mom's feelings."

"Ginny, I want the very best for you. We're trying to work all that out."

"But Mr. Troy and Ms. Sierra were talking. They said Mom wants me back."

I wasn't sure how to answer her. This sweet child had to deal with so many grown-up problems and decisions. "Do you trust me, Ginny?"

"Yes." She blew her nose.

"I hope that was a tissue and not someone's shirt."

"No, it was a tissue. I do trust you, Grandma. I know you'll do the best thing."

I appreciated her confidence. I wished for the same faith in my ability to make the best decisions.

That night, before my heart catheterization and possible stent, I prayed for my health and the doctor, for Becky, my lost and hurting daughter. I included Ginny, Troy, and my friends. I vowed to do what was best for Ginny. Troy and I would learn to work together and parent her the best we could. Becky could be involved in Ginny's life, but only with supervision. She might never be entirely clean and capable of being a good mother. I wasn't willing to take any chances.

I also prayed that God would help me love all of these people in my life unconditionally. I'd gone from a simple, quiet, boring life to one full of friends and family. The drama overwhelmed me at times, but the rewards were amazing.

I could live with that.

Finding what I was thankful for on Thursday wasn't hard. The doctor released me on Wednesday afternoon as promised. Mac and Ginny drove me to Sug's on Thursday. I wasn't allowed to walk the few blocks there. I had to promise to sit with my feet up and rest.

Sug held onto me for a long time when she answered the door.

"I'm so glad to see you," she said in my ear. "I've been so worried." She leaned back and looked at my face. "You're pale, and you've lost weight. Come on in, and let's change that."

I linked arms with her. "The heart cath went great, and I only needed one stent."

"Only." She shook her head. "You're tossing those medical terms around like I understand what they mean."

"It means I'm still here and doing pretty well." I sat on the couch, propped my feet on the coffee table, and let them wait on me.

Ginny hovered close by, keeping an eye on me. She answered the door when the doorbell rang and came back chattering with Maggie.

Maggie leaned over and hugged me. "I'm so glad to see you."

"That's what I said." Sug pointed to me. "This woman will have a bionic heart at the rate she's going."

I held up my hand. "I have no intention of having any other procedures done."

"Good for you." Maggie stiffened when Mac entered the room. He walked straight to her, hugged her, and whispered in her ear. She relaxed and kissed his cheek.

"All good now?" I watched Mac head back to the kitchen.

Maggie wiped her eyes with the pads of her ring fingers. "I think so." She played with her necklace. "I hope so. I really like him."

"Mr. Mac has a girlfriend," Ginny sang.

Maggie and I laughed. The doorbell rang again, and Ginny skipped off to answer it.

"Grandma, look who's here." She entered the living room, holding hands with Shrimp and Beverly.

"Well, looky here." Shrimp hugged me. "You're a sight for sore eyes."

Beverly, leaning heavily on a cane, squeezed my hand. "You look good, Kat. We've been worried."

"I'm so glad y'all could come. It's been three years since we've all been together."

"And you've added new friends." Shrimp winked at me. "Ms. Loner here thought she didn't need all of us."

"Funny man." I rearranged myself on the couch. "I've learned a lot in the last few years, but before we talk about that,"—I pointed to Maggie—"this is my friend, Maggie."

Sierra and Troy wandered in and introduced themselves to Shrimp and Beverly. Beverly sat beside me, leaning her cane against the coffee table.

"What happened?" I asked.

"I had my knee replaced." She rubbed her right leg and knee. "The cane helps me balance. So, tell me all about you. Sug said you just got out of the hospital."

"Yesterday." I filled her in on my heart issues.

"And Becky's here in rehab?"

"Yes, she is. She's been there almost a week now." I leaned my head back against the sofa. "She wants Ginny back when she gets out."

She squeezed my hand. "That girl. She had it going for a while."

"She did. It's so frustrating." I described how she'd taken Ginny. "I don't think I'll ever be able to trust Becky again. She got clean and relapsed, left Ginny, and then abducted her. She can get clean. I know she can be a good mom." I glanced at Beverly. "But who knows how long that will take or if it will last."

"Any plans?"

"Actually, yes. I want permanent custody of Ginny, and I want Troy to help me raise her. Whether he lives in my house or we have joint custody. If Becky is clean, she can have visitation. That is my plan."

She patted my hand. "Good plan, good plan. I think you have this worked out."

I made a face. "I have to get everyone on board. Especially Becky."

"That'll be the tough part," she said.

I worried about Becky. She didn't call me when I was in the hospital, and I wasn't sure if she knew I'd been there. She probably thought I was ignoring her. If she was going through what Maggie told me about, she hated me now more than ever. I didn't mind that I hadn't heard from her. I didn't need that stress.

After our Thanksgiving feast, Troy stood and pulled Sierra up beside him. He held up his hand until we all quieted. "I, we, have an announcement." He wrapped his arms around Sierra. "We're getting married."

Ginny jumped up and down and hugged them both. Mac beamed and shouted, "Woo-hoo!"

Troy sat by me after all the congratulations. "You're okay with this?"

"I've seen the change in you. I'm happy for you and Sierra. And Ginny."

"Thank you. That means a lot." His look at Sierra reflected his love for her.

"You got a good one, for sure." I grinned.

"Yes, I did." He crossed his arms. "What should we do about Ginny?"

Troy and I talked for a while, and Sierra joined our discussion.

"I think joint custody is the way to go. That way, Ginny will be safe. Whether she's with you and Sierra or with me."

"What if the DNA test shows I'm not her father?"

I made a face. "We'll cross that bridge if it comes, but I don't think it'll be a problem."

"What about Becky?" Sierra asked.

"I've been thinking about that. I thought that when she gets out of rehab, I'd offer to let her live with me." I twisted the hem of my shirt.

"Hmm," Troy said. "You don't seem very sure about that."

"I don't know what else to do." I held up my palms, one higher than the other. "On the one hand, Ginny is safe. On the other hand, if Becky lives with me, it might keep her from abducting Ginny."

"It would let you keep an eye on her too," Sierra said.

"Can your health handle that stress?" Troy asked.

I raised one shoulder and dropped it. "That's the part I'm not sure of."

Chapter 29

Becky followed the pattern Maggie warned me about. She called Thanksgiving night after I got home from Sug's and ranted for ten minutes. I held the phone away from my ear, wishing I dared to hang up. But I figured she'd call back.

She finally wound down.

"Are you done?" I baited her. My happy Thanksgiving Day was ending on a sour note.

"Funny, Mom. You do remember that I'm in here because of you."

"Me? You're the one who kidnapped Ginny."

"I mean that I left you years ago." She grunted. "You don't remember the fight? You told me to leave. I was only sixteen. But I did what you asked." She added some choice words and hung up.

I shook my head. My memories were different. We had numerous screaming matches that I always thought were her fault.

Did I really tell her to leave?

"Come here, Ollie." We went out onto the front porch. Red followed and curled up on the footstool. Ginny was spending another night at Mac's, so it was just me and my mini-zoo.

I thought back to four and a half years ago, when Ginny and Becky first arrived. Some things had changed so much. Ginny had grown and matured. She'd also been through many awful things. Her mother's disregard for her safety and care had to leave deep wounds. She dealt with them well, but she was still a child. She needed counseling—someone who could help her more than I could.

My love couldn't fix her. Just like it could never fix Becky.

Did I really tell her to leave?

Becky flip-flopped between actively using drugs, going to rehab, and staying sober for several years. Now, she'd been arrested, detoxed in jail, and returned to rehab. I didn't know what would happen when she got out. She remained the loose cannon in the whole mix.

This felt familiar. Again, I reminded myself that I could not fix her. That depended on her. God would help her if she reached out to Him. She'd have to do the hard work. Her choice, not anything to do with me.

She left at sixteen. Did I remember wrong? Could it be my fault?

After Maggie pointed out how much I changed, I realized the truth. Years before, Sug told me I was in a rut and accused me of living a lonely, boring life. And she'd been right. I'd been content then—or at least thought I was.

Before Ginny came, I'd settled for less than a full life. Now, I had my Ginny and more friends than ever. And possibly, my daughter would be restored to the family. Even if that part didn't happen, I knew where she was for the moment.

That was the best it could be with an addict. I understood that now. My desires, my expectations, and even my hopes had to be set down. Put aside for my own sake.

I couldn't remember what happened during that last argument with Becky before she ran away. Knowing Sug and Mac would fuss at me, I drove to the lighthouse early the following day. I sat in the car—I wouldn't attempt to climb all of those steps—and thought back to when Becky was young, and I'd bring her to Cape Henry.

Joe and I lived near Fort Story until he died. Even after, I drove the three miles from Mom's to the lighthouse almost every week. Climbing 191 steps with a toddler was risky, but Becky loved the water, the view. I loved the hope—the world spread out before us, and the mystery beyond it. I tried to pass that on to her, just as I would later with Ginny.

The lighthouse comforted me now as it always did. It had stood for many years. I wanted to stand too. I would no longer live in the past or act as I had. If I were the one at fault and had told Becky to leave, I would own up to it. Take responsibility for it.

My heart may not have been as healthy as when Becky was a baby, but my will, knowledge, and faith were stronger than ever. I resolved to set aside my worries and anxiety. I prayed and asked God to help me, and I promised to let Him out of the box I'd kept Him in. I vowed to let Him lead. And I would apologize to Becky for my past behavior.

I didn't count on what that would look like.

I went to a family group meeting the following week. At my request, Maggie told everyone that Becky was in rehab, and I received many hugs. That night, we discussed applying what we learned in our meetings to our everyday lives and putting those principles into practice. I'd already seen how some of what I learned affected my relationships.

Letting go and releasing bitterness against Troy improved my life and his. Those changes were very apparent. What I learned, like acceptance, serenity, and even more about prayer, added richness to my life. With Becky in rehab, my anxiety lessened, and I could put her down and not pick up all of her problems again. But I was learning that circumstances couldn't dictate how I felt. Feelings shouldn't control me.

I shared my thoughts.

Roger's shoulders sagged. "I know that's true. I have learned a lot." He gestured to his wife. "We've learned a lot." She nodded. "But our son is still missing. We have no idea where he is. It's been months." He wiped tears from his eyes. "My feelings are all over the place, especially during Thanksgiving."

"Holidays are the worst when you have an addict," Tamara said.

"That's the truth. Sometimes I think I have PTSD," he said.

PTSD. Yep, that sounded right. I raised my hand. "Isn't that only for soldiers or people who experience horrific trauma?"

Todd chuckled. "Addiction falls under horrific trauma in my book."

"Mine too." Tamara nodded.

"Exactly. That's what we're feeling," Roger said wryly.

"That makes sense," I said. "Plus, Becky does something almost every holiday to mess it up."

Maggie got her cell phone. "I'm going to Google trauma." She read for a minute and then held up a finger. "Okay, this website on addiction says that substance abuse is often connected to other disorders—co-occurring disorders—like depression and other mental health issues. And PTSD." She read more, set her phone down, and made a circle with her hands. "It's like a domino effect for the addict. It goes in a circle. They have trauma and PTSD and self-medicate, which leads to behavior issues. And that cycles back to PTSD and substance abuse. Does that make sense?"

Everyone nodded.

Roger held up his phone. "Check this out." He cleared his throat and read, "Living with an addict or alcoholic causes constant stress and can affect a family member or loved one's mental health. This, plus fear and guilt, can lead to PTSD developing." He put down his phone. "So, the addict can have it, and we can too."

Todd raised his hand. "I'm not undermining what you both read. I think it's true. But I want to remind you that we can learn to work through these things. We may need to go outside of this group for professional counseling." He leaned his elbows on his knees. "This is why we started this group. To learn and help each other. To find peace and serenity. To be a resource and help us all find what we need to live with and love an addict."

When Ginny first came, I had been so bitter and resentful about dealing with Becky's problems. Ginny wasn't the problem, but Becky's expectation that I drop everything and do as she wanted made me angry and resentful. Four years later, I found myself in a different place. I liked it.

"Peace and serenity are the best," I said.

Everyone agreed.

Ginny and I were in the final weeks of school, preparing for Christmas break. Becky had called a few times from rehab, asking me to visit her. I didn't commit because dealing with her would take a lot of strength and endurance. Then, when she called on Tuesday night, she dropped a bomb.

"Mom, I wanted to tell you that I plan to go to a step-down unit after here. It's like a halfway house. I can work and pay a fee but still have meetings and accountability. What do you think about that? I leave here before the New Year and can go straight there."

Her words stunned me. I never thought that she would go beyond rehab. It never occurred to me that there were other options besides her coming home. I sat at the table, rubbing Ollie's ears, thinking about her words.

"I think that's a good idea. It sounds like a good setup for you and will give you more time for accountability, as you said." *And more time to stay sober.*

"I do want to get clean, Mom. I want to be a good mother. I miss Ginny, and I miss you," she said, her voice thick with emotion.

She meant what she said. Sober Becky desired things that addict Becky couldn't achieve. Years of her being gone with no word and her wishy-washy behavior with Ginny and me were proof of that. And how she deserted her daughter when Ginny needed her. They were all things I had to keep in mind. I couldn't afford to forget because I couldn't let my granddaughter get hurt again. It finally dawned on me that keeping Ginny safe wasn't about me.

Keeping her safe was about her. Not her mom. Not me.

Mac, Sug, Sierra, and Troy, whether or not he turned out to be Ginny's father, were all part of Ginny's life. Becky may have had her to herself for six years, but now Ginny was embedded in our lives, and we all loved her.

"Ginny is always safe with me. I hope you know that," I said.

"I do, Mom, and I appreciate everything you've done for her. I've let you down and broken her trust many times." She paused. "I'm really sorry."

I bit my lip to keep from lashing out. This wasn't the time for recrimination and anger. She hadn't called me about that. This seemed like a good time for me to apologize.

"You're right. This is something we can all work through." I paused and drew a deep breath, my heart racing. "You said something a while back. That it was my fault you left when you were a teenager."

"Oh, Mom." She sniffled. "I was just being mean."

"I don't know. I've been searching my memories. We fought a lot."

"True, we did." She chuckled.

I hesitated, but I knew I had to do this. To make my amends. "Well, I think you're right. I think I did tell you to leave. I'm very sorry."

"Thank you. I needed to hear that." Her words were a whisper.

The idea of Becky staying with me after she got out of rehab, or the halfway house, flashed through my mind again. What if I let her and Ginny live with me? Would that work? Could I do it? My focus stayed on keeping Ginny safe, but my health wasn't consistently good. I already had to be away from her because of hospital and doctor visits.

Then there was Becky, still an unknown. Possibly, probably, always an unknown. Did this idea come from me or from God? I'd have to think about it more and pray about it for a long time.

I'd wait before I mentioned my idea.

We said our goodbyes, and I hung up the phone. I sat at the table and lowered my head in prayer, visualizing placing all my thoughts and concerns at the feet of Jesus. They needed to stay there, and I couldn't pick them up again. It was time to stop trying to work things out on my own.

Time and again, I had done that—thinking I'd handed things over and then figuring out ways to deal with whatever happened. I didn't allow for any time or help from God. My norm was to do something, force it to work, and hope God would approve.

Time to change the norm.

School didn't end for Ginny until the Wednesday before Christmas, and I had to work in my classroom that Thursday and Friday.

Mac stopped by and leaned against the door frame. "Hi, you two."

I waved and continued to stare at my bulletin board.

"Hi, Mr. Mac." Ginny waved from the reading corner.

"What are you up to?" I stapled a border on the board.

"I'm cleaning up my room some before the holidays, so everything's ready when we return in January. How's it going in here?"

I looked around the room. Ginny sat on a bean bag chair in the reading corner and plucked another book off the bookshelf. She had straightened the shelves and prepared everything for the students' return in the new year.

I put the stapler down. "I think I'm about ready to leave for the day. I'll need to take some things home to grade and a few things to plan, but that's all."

"Have you talked to Troy today?" he asked.

"No, I haven't seen him. What's up?"

Mac stuck his hands in his pockets and jingled some change. "He said he wanted to talk to you." He rocked back on his heels. "I'm not sure why."

Ginny was reading her book and listening to us at the same time. I stepped closer to Mac and lowered my voice. "Everything okay?"

"I think so." His eyes twinkled. "Just get in touch with him, and he'll talk to you." He turned to go. "I'll see you soon. Bye, Ginny."

Ginny wiggled her fingers without glancing up from her book.

What did Troy have to tell me? The DNA test results were due. Had he gotten them back so soon?

I returned to my desk, packed my things in my tote bag, and grabbed my purse. "Hey Ginny, do you want to get some lunch, and we'll take it home?"

She hopped up and shoved the book back on the bookshelf. "I'd love to, Grandma. I'm starving." She rubbed her tummy.

I put my hand on top of her head. "I think you've grown again."

"I know. My toes touch the end of my shoes." We both looked down, and I could see her toes pushing against the edges of her sneakers. Her pants were above her ankles.

"I guess we need to go buy you some new clothes. Or," I paused and wiggled my eyebrows, "I could give you new jeans and shoes for Christmas."

"Ha-ha, Grandma. I don't think that's a good idea."

After lunch, we headed to the mall to do some shopping. Ginny found three pairs of jeans and a new pair of tennis shoes. I grabbed a couple of tops. It had been a while since I'd updated my wardrobe, and my winter clothes looked pretty shabby.

Once Ginny put her things away, she came into my room. "Hey, Grandma, did my mom call you the other day?"

"Yes, she did." I hung my new shirts on hangers.

She picked at her fingernails. "How is she?"

I turned. She hadn't asked about Becky in a while. "She seems to be doing well. You can't go see her. They won't let you into the rehab, but you can talk to her on the phone the next time she calls."

She leaned against the door jamb. "I'm not sure if I want to."

"That's okay. I don't always want to talk to her either. You're allowed your feelings."

"Yeah." She rapped the door frame with her knuckles and turned. "I'm not sure how I feel."

She walked away, and I covered my face, imagining how she felt and how her emotions must be flipping back and forth. My mother had been there for me up until she died. She helped care for Becky and loved me just as I was. I didn't have any frame of reference for what Ginny was experiencing. She needed someone besides me to talk to.

Chapter 30

I had no idea who to call to see Ginny. I started by making her an appointment with a pediatrician, and they managed to fit her in for a checkup on Friday. She balked at the idea. I didn't give her a choice.

When we arrived, she looked around the waiting room. "They're all little." Her lip curled.

I glanced around and saw she was right. The kids were toddlers and preschoolers, along with a couple of babies. Young moms. No grandmas and no fifth graders.

"Sorry, kiddo, this was who I called and who could fit you in."

She crossed her arms and sulked.

I stifled a giggle. When I first met Ginny, she had been so prickly. Hard to love on and challenging to get to know. She opened up over that first summer. At least after she'd run away to Sug's. I thought spending the school year with Mom and summers with Grandma was okay with her. She adjusted surprisingly quickly.

Now, she was almost twelve. Things were changing in her body as she approached puberty, and major changes had taken place in her life. She hadn't ever lived with me full-time. Her mom had always been in the background. As unreliable as Becky could be, she had picked her up every summer before school began.

After we saw the doctor and I set up counseling for her, I would talk to Sugar, Mac, Maggie, Troy, and Sierra, and let them know. Ginny needed all of us on her side, now more than ever.

A nurse called out, "Virginia Johnson." Ginny stood and waved me up.

"Come on. It's my turn." Her tone conveyed her disgust.

I leaned over and whispered, "Maybe you'll get a lollipop if you're good."

Her lips twitched. "That's wrong, Grandma. Just wrong." She shook her head.

The nurse weighed and measured her and took us to a room. I told her that Ginny hadn't had regular checkups in the past. She asked about immunizations and blood work, and Ginny backed up, hand on the doorknob.

"Um, no. No blood work." She shook her head like a bobble-head doll.

I put my hand on her back. "Do you know if you've had any shots?"

"Like what?" she asked.

We turned to the nurse, who read off her clipboard. "DTaP, MMR, polio. Things like that."

"I don't know." Ginny's face paled. "That's a lot of shots."

The nurse frowned. "Did you have a doctor in Tennessee?"

"I went to Dr. Rosa a few times."

"Okay." She wrote on her paper. "Let me try to find that doctor. Memphis area, right?"

"Yes," I said.

"Let's check into that before we draw blood or schedule shots." She opened the door. "The doctor will be right in."

Ginny frowned when the door closed. "That wasn't the doctor?"

"Nope." I patted the examination table. "Have a seat. She won't do anything you don't want her to. I promise." I sat in one of the extra chairs.

Dr. Fielding entered the room, a tablet and stylus in one hand. Ginny crossed her arms.

"Nice to meet you, Ginny." She pulled a rolling chair up and sat in it. "Tell me why you're here."

Ginny raised her eyebrows. "My grandma made me come."

Dr. Fielding turned to me. "Grandma?"

I nodded and explained the situation.

"Okay. Was her mother using drugs when she was pregnant?" The doctor made notes on her tablet.

"I don't know. I would imagine so, but I'm not sure."

She turned back to Ginny and touched her knee. "You've seen a lot, haven't you?"

Ginny's eyes filled with tears. She roughly swiped them away.

Dr. Fielding stood. "Let's get on with our exam, shall we? I'll explain what I'm doing before I do it. How does that sound?"

Ginny nodded. The doctor led her through each part of the physical, checking her ears, eyes, throat, and reflexes. She let Ginny listen to her own heart with the stethoscope.

When she finished writing her notes, I said, "Thank you. I also want to find a good counselor for Ginny."

She wrote on a notepad. "Good idea. Here, these are my top favorites for her age."

Ginny hopped off the table. "Can I have a lollipop?" She shot me a wink.

The doctor opened the door and pointed. "Head that way to check out and ask for one." She turned to me. "Good kid."

"She's amazing." I shook my head. "I don't know how, but she is one remarkable little girl."

She patted my shoulder. "Don't sell yourself short, Grandma. You're doing a great job."

Her words were the encouragement I needed.

After the appointment, we ran to the grocery store to pick up bread, lunch meat, and cheese. I grabbed some fruit to make a colorful fruit salad for a light supper. When we got home, we let Ollie inside. Ginny helped me in the kitchen, preparing the sandwiches while I cut up the fruit. Red came in, hissing Ollie out of the room, then circled our ankles, meowing and purring.

Ginny dropped a piece of cheese for her. Ollie barked from the doorway to the porch.

"You'll have to give him a bite of lunchmeat if Red gets cheese," I said. "He'll get jealous."

She walked over to Ollie and held up a piece of lunch meat. "Sit."

Ollie sat and woofed.

"Gentle." Ollie took the meat from her hand and licked her fingers to say thank you. She rewashed her hands and continued fixing our sandwiches.

"Thanks for washing your hands. Not sure I want Ollie slobber on my food."

"I don't either, Grandma. That doesn't sound very yummy." She giggled.

We took our sandwiches, fruit salad, and water out onto the porch, and I opened the windows to let in the cool December breeze. We dug into our picnic dinner.

Ginny coughed and took a sip of water. She coughed again, and I looked at her.

"Are you okay?"

"I'm not sure." Her voice sounded hoarse. "My mouth and throat feel funny." She put her hand on her neck. "It's like it's hard to breathe."

I forced myself to be calm. "Stay right here, honey. I'll find some medicine." I rushed from the room but stopped and turned back. "Ginny, don't eat anything else, okay?"

She nodded and covered her mouth as she continued to cough.

I grabbed the phone in the kitchen and called the emergency line. Then I went in search of the medicine we'd given her four years before. I found it in the same cabinet and hoped it would still work. Ginny swallowed the pill, and then I called Sug.

"It's happening again. Ginny's having an allergic reaction. I called 911 and gave her that antihistamine. I don't know where her EpiPen is."

"I'm coming right now," she said.

I unlocked the front door and hurried back to my girl. She lay her head on the table, her lips puffy and breathing wheezy. I rubbed her back lightly and whispered to her. Sirens sounded nearby. Sug burst through the front door, rushing to Ginny's side.

"The ambulance is almost here." She brushed Ginny's hair off her face. "Hang in there, kiddo. You'll be okay. I'll let the EMTs in. You stay with her," Sug said to me.

This was a repeat of four years before, with three EMTs plus a paramedic filing through my front door. One of the EMTs carried a black bag, and she checked Ginny's vitals. She talked Ginny through the procedure and started the IV without a flinch from my granddaughter.

"Thank you," I said when the EMT stood up.

"Let's get her to the hospital, Mom," she said.

"I'm her grandma, but I have temporary custody."

"That works." She waved to her coworkers. "Let's get this girl going, guys. Grandma, you can ride with us."

I held Ginny's hand until we arrived at the hospital, where I stepped aside to let the professionals take over. Sug met me in the waiting room, and I led her to Ginny. When the doctor came in, I told him about her previous reaction. I'd taken her to the allergist, but those tests were inconclusive. The emergency room doctor wrote down what I'd put in the fruit salad.

"The best I can think," I said, "is that she doesn't typically have pineapple. I added a can of that to what I'd cut up."

"That's probably the offender." He wrote notes in her chart. "I'm going to send her home with this prescription for antihistamines and an EpiPen. She can take the antihistamines for a couple of days, and I recommend she see that allergist again." He patted Ginny's foot. "You're a trooper, kiddo. You're going to be just fine."

Tears sprang to my eyes. My sweet girl had experienced a life-threatening reaction, and her mother had no idea. Ginny *was* a trooper. Did Becky have any idea what a great kid she had?

Ginny went to bed when we got home, exhausted from the medicine and her fear. I sank into the couch, and Sug brought me some sweet tea.

"Your food is still on the table. I'm going to clean it up." Sug peeked into the sunporch. "Looks like Red helped herself to some of the cheese from your sandwiches."

I covered my eyes. "I'm sure she did." I leaned my head back. "Will you let Ollie in when you're finished?"

Sug patted my shoulder. "Just rest, okay? I got the food and your zoo."

Troy needed to know what happened to Ginny, but I was exhausted. I figured another day wouldn't hurt, so after Sug cleaned my kitchen, I went to bed.

After church on Sunday, Ginny and I brought out the Christmas decorations. "I invited Mr. Mac, Ms. Sug, Ms. Sierra, and Mr. Troy over." I hoped to talk to Troy about Ginny's hospital trip and hear whatever he wanted to tell me.

"What about Ms. Maggie?"

"You're right. I keep forgetting. I'll call her and then put on a big pot of chili and bake some cornbread."

We dragged all the decorations down from upstairs. Ollie inspected them, sniffing and barking at the ornaments. Mac and Maggie picked up a tree from Harris Teeter at my request. It was bigger than the year before. Each time the needles poked Ollie's nose, he sneezed and shook his head.

When we finished, my living room looked like a Christmas wonderland. Each year, I added more ornaments, and with garland hanging around the room and the lights out front, I had a picture-perfect Christmas house.

I set the pot of chili on the table along with a basket of cornbread muffins, and bowls of shredded cheese, sour cream, and butter. While everyone fixed their food, I walked into the other room with Troy.

"I wanted to tell you what happened to Ginny." I filled him in on her trip to the hospital.

"Thanks for letting me know." He shuffled his feet.

"Mac said you had something to tell me?"

He pulled something from his pocket. "Yes, I do." He waved a piece of paper. "This confirms it. I'm Ginny's dad."

I hugged him. Behind us, Ginny squealed. She had her hands over her mouth. I grimaced. This wasn't how I wanted her to find out.

"Is it true, Mr. Troy? Are you my dad?" Ginny clutched her hands to her chest, and her face glowed. She turned to me. "Grandma? Are you sure?"

I held my arms out to her, and she ran in for a hug. Troy circled us with his arms.

"It's true, honey." I kissed her head.

"What do you think about that?" Troy leaned back and ruffled Ginny's hair.

Ginny did a little dance. "This is the best Christmas ever!"

What I'd imagined she would react like didn't compare to how she actually responded. Ginny was thrilled to have Troy as her father. Over the next few weeks, I would make sure she understood what that meant and that Troy and Sierra would be involved in her life.

When we were all seated, Mac raised a glass of water. "I'd like to make a toast. Here's to another Christmas together." He looked around the table, and his gaze rested on Maggie. I could see the love he had for her in his eyes. Maggie blushed, and we all raised our glasses. Whoops, cheers, and Ginny's "woo-hoo" filled the house.

"And here's to me having a dad!" Ginny thrust her glass of water in the air, sloshing some on the table. We cheered again, and I mopped up the spill.

I'd cleaned up the kitchen table and finished putting dishes away when my phone rang. All of my friends were there. Who could be calling on a Sunday evening?

"Mrs. Johnson? This is Doris at Samaritan House Rehab. I need to talk to you."

My stomach flipped, and I plopped into a chair. "Yes, this is Kat Johnson. What's going on?" I waved at my friends to be quiet.

Doris cleared her throat. "It seems your daughter, Becky, is missing."

"Missing? What do you mean? How could she be missing?" I pushed the speaker button on my phone.

Maggie sat by me and placed her hand on my back.

"Well, you know, she wasn't court-ordered here. She was free to leave," Doris said.

Actually, no, I didn't know that. I looked at Maggie. Sug took Ginny into the living room, and Troy and Sierra followed. "So she just walked out?" I asked.

"As far as we know." I could hear Doris flipping through papers. "It seems she was noticed missing ... let's see ... Friday night."

I sat back, covering my mouth with my hand. How could Becky have been missing for two days and no one told me?

Mac took a seat on the other side of me and squeezed my hand.

Maggie spent several minutes talking to Doris, who had no other information. Becky went missing Friday night. No one called me, and no one seemed to know where she had gone.

"The only positive is that Doris said Becky had made great strides in the program," Maggie said after we hung up. "Maybe she thought she was done?"

"She'd been talking about going to a halfway house." I rapped my knuckles on the table. "No, this is just another Becky stunt." I shook my head and looked at Mac. "Remember after Hurricane Dianna when you were so mad at her? And I said I didn't have a choice. It is what it is? Well, I'm over that. Becky has done enough damage. And this time, I'm going to tell her."

When I found her.

Chapter 31

I didn't know what to do about Becky or where to search for her. I called the First Precinct on Princess Anne Road. They took Becky's name and my number and said they'd call if she turned up. What else could I do? I couldn't believe she'd messed up another holiday. It was a trend for her.

Ginny had heard enough of the phone calls that I couldn't pretend everything was all right. She shrugged and said she wasn't surprised when I told her what her mother had done. My heart broke at how resigned she'd become to her mother's behavior. I reminded myself that this was all on Becky. We hadn't caused any of it.

With Christmas three days away, I still needed to purchase several more gifts. Monday morning, I dropped Ginny off at Sug's so I could finish up. Judging by the sneaky looks and the whispered comments between them as I left, they were working on a Christmas gift for me.

I stopped at the mall and visited some specialty shops for gifts for my friends. I visited Forbes for Ginny's favorite taffy and grabbed some for myself. I'd put some of hers in her stocking, but I stuck mine in my purse to munch on when I wanted.

At a local bookstore, I found a pretty journal and a nice pen that reminded me of Becky. Then, I spotted a small Bible I thought she would like. I purchased all three and had them gift-wrapped. On the gift tag, I wrote, "To my daughter, Becky, I hope you find the peace and joy you long for. Never forget how much I love you. Merry Christmas."

Even though I was mad at her, I also prayed she was safe and healthy and that we would see her on Christmas Day. Maybe she had a simple explanation for her disappearance. I could only hope.

Still, I knew better than to bank on that hope. I'd have her present ready if and when she showed up. Who knew when that might be?

After Ginny went to bed that night, I wrapped the rest of the gifts. Red liked to help by eating ribbon, and I had to make sure she didn't because it would come out one way or the other. Ollie stayed in the kitchen and whined. The cat intimidated him, and he hated it when I tied ribbons to his collar. It was like waving a red flag in front of her.

Ginny woke me early Christmas morning. She opened her stocking and unwrapped her presents, exclaiming over the things I'd gotten her and enjoying her taffy. She gave Ollie a rawhide bone, and Red got an empty box. Both animals looked quite content with their gifts.

"I have something for you, Grandma." Ginny clapped. "Ms. Sug will bring it to Mr. Mac's."

My contribution to Christmas dinner at Mac's was a tossed salad and dressing, green beans, and sweet potato casserole with brown sugar pecans. Sugar promised to bring homemade macaroni and cheese and a pumpkin pie, and Maggie volunteered to bring corn and rolls. Mac said he would make the turkey. We didn't agree until Sierra assured us she would help her dad.

Ginny and I bundled up and walked the short distance to Mac's place. She knocked twice and opened the door.

"Hey, y'all. How's that turkey doing?" I set my food on the island while Ginny tucked our presents under Mac's tree.

"The turkey looks great." Sierra winked. "Dad made it all by himself."

"Really? Beefing up on your cooking skills, Mac?"

Mac put his hand over his heart. "You wound me. I can cook."

Ginny cocked an eyebrow. "Not usually, Mr. Mac. Remember when I stayed over last time, and you burned my oatmeal?" She looked at me, shaking her head. "Really, how do you burn oatmeal?"

We all burst out laughing.

"Where's Troy? I figured he'd be here," I said.

Sierra put her hands on her hips. "I'm not sure. He stopped by earlier and said he had a couple of errands to run. He'll be back soon, I imagine."

Sug arrived. I took the casserole dish from her while she returned to her car for the pie. She brought in some gift bags and handed them to Ginny. Ginny cupped her hand and stood on her tiptoes to whisper in her ear. Sug whispered back, then shot me a wink.

After Maggie arrived, we waited for Troy for close to an hour before giving up and serving our turkey and fixings. Sierra's worry seeped over to all of us. Troy was a solid and dependable young man. Whatever he was doing must be important.

It amazed me how much my thoughts and feelings about him had changed. He'd shown time and time again that he had left the drug life behind and had moved forward. He owned his own business, and he doted on Sierra. They were both committed to helping raise Ginny. Now that the DNA results confirmed him as her father, we wanted to proceed with the custody hearing.

However, we needed to locate Becky to obtain her signature for the transfer of her parental rights. Could she have guessed what we'd intended? Maybe that's why she disappeared.

I looked around the table and marveled at the changes in my life. I'd gone from having only Sug as a friend to sitting at a table filled with laughter and love. Maggie and Troy showed us all how it looked to live with addiction and to overcome and move past it. It wasn't an easy task. Recovering addicts were some of the strongest people I knew.

Mac was my dear friend—Sug's and my "little brother," and I cherished his friendship. He'd worked through his doubts about Maggie and had fallen head over heels for her.

I looked at Sug, and she grinned. We'd been friends for so long that she could read my mind. She felt the same as I did about our expanded circle of family. She told me years ago that I was in a rut, and she was right. She might not admit it, but she had been in one too.

Sierra jumped when her cell phone rang. She answered. "It's Shrimp." She held out her phone. "He wants to tell us all Merry Christmas."

We took turns talking to Shrimp and Beverly. They were enjoying the holiday at their oldest daughter's house. Shrimp's story of addiction and recovery encouraged me. When I spoke with him, I told him about Becky's disappearance.

"I'm so sorry. I hope she turns up soon," he said.

"I do too." My wonderful meal settled like a rock in my stomach. Worrying about Becky always affected my physical health.

"Hang on," he said, "Beverly wants to talk to you."

"Hi, Kat, did I hear right? Becky's gone missing?"

I explained what the rehab told me and that we'd reported it to the police. "I have no idea where she is. She may have gone back to Tennessee, but I'm not sure she'd leave this area with Ginny being here."

"Now, I've been through this a few times over the years." Beverly cleared her throat. "I can imagine how you're feeling. Lost, confused, angry, worried. Your stomach is a mess, and your chest feels tight." She paused. "Kat, you have to lay this all down. It's already taken a toll on your heart. Worrying about your daughter now won't do you a hill of beans of good."

Beverly had a way with words, and I nodded even though she couldn't see me. "I know you're right. Thanks for the reminder."

"I've got more than a reminder, girl. Let's pray."

And then and there, she prayed for me, Becky, and Ginny. She didn't mince words, and she didn't try to control God or the situation. She prayed for peace and healing for all of us. She asked God to cover us with His protection. I could hear Shrimp in the background adding his own "Amens" and "That's right."

Tears ran down my face during her prayer. What an amazing gift God had blessed me with. These friends loved me unconditionally and were just as concerned for Ginny and me as they were with Becky.

I wiped my face. "Thank you, Beverly."

"You're welcome, my dear. Call me for prayer. Anytime."

"I will, I promise." I handed the phone to the next person and went to the bathroom to blow my nose and wash my face.

Before we could open presents, Sierra's phone rang again. She answered it, and her face turned pale.

Mac hurried to her. "Sierra? What's wrong?"

Sierra hung up the phone. "It's Troy, Dad. He's in the hospital."

Everyone started talking and asking questions. Mac held his hand up. "Tell us what he said."

Tears stained her cheeks, and her voice shook. "It wasn't him. It was the hospital. They said he'd been beaten severely, but he gave them my name and number. He's in the ICU and has to have surgery." Her voice broke. Mac folded her in his arms.

"Grandma?" Ginny tugged at my arm. "Is my dad going to be okay?"

My sweet girl. She already thought of Troy as her dad. "I don't know, sweetie. I hope so." I turned to Mac. "Y'all go. We'll clean up here and then join you at the hospital. Call if you can."

Maggie grabbed her purse. "I'll drive you two." The three of them rushed out the front door.

Sug and Ginny stared at me. "Okay, y'all. Let's clear this table. We'll put the food away and wash the dishes." I hugged Ginny and tipped her chin up. "Then we'll go see how your dad is."

She nodded, and we worked together to restore Mac's house to normal. We put the turkey and other food in the fridge, cleaned off the table, and left for the hospital.

Mac, Maggie, and Sierra were in the intensive care waiting room. Sierra curled up on a chair in the corner. Ginny sat beside her and lay her head on Sierra's shoulder.

"Any news?" I asked.

Mac shook his head. "Nothing, really. They've taken him for surgery. He has a broken leg."

"What in the world happened?" Sug asked. "Who beat him up?"

"We don't know yet. He was already in surgery when we got here." Sierra shifted in the hard chair. "No one told us anything."

We sat and waited. I watched the clock, and Ginny rotated between us, sitting on our laps.

The waiting room door opened, and a doctor in wrinkled scrubs entered. He looked around the room. "Sierra Walsh?"

We all stood.

"Which one of you is Sierra?" he said with a frown.

She raised a trembling hand.

Mac put his arm around his daughter. "How is Troy?"

The doctor kept his gaze on Sierra. "He's doing well. The surgery went fine. He's in recovery, and you can see him in thirty minutes or so. A nurse will come for you." A strange expression crossed his face. "Do you have any idea how this happened?"

"No." Sierra scuffed her foot across the linoleum. "He left while we were fixing Christmas dinner. He didn't say where he was going. He said he needed another present, but that's all."

"Well, the police will want to talk to him. They'll be here soon."

"Police?" I frowned. "Why would they want to talk to him?"

"They found Mr. Turner downtown in a place that, well ..." He removed his surgical cap and scratched his head.

Maggie spoke up. "Down by Birdneck and Southern?"

My mouth fell open. That area was in the news almost every night and was well-known for gang violence and drugs.

The doctor nodded. "I can't say much more. You'll have to talk to the police when they arrive."

He left the room, and Maggie turned to me. "I used to buy drugs in that area."

Sierra crossed her arms. "No way. He wasn't using. He told me he'd been clean for years."

"I know, honey. But all it takes is one slip." Maggie reached out for Sierra's hands.

"I don't believe you. There has to be another reason." She pulled away from Maggie and began to cry. Ginny joined her.

"My dad doesn't do drugs." Ginny stamped her foot. "He wouldn't do that."

The pain on both of their faces broke my heart. I couldn't imagine why Troy went to that area or who beat him up. He had stayed clean for so many years. Would he jeopardize his relationship with Sierra and his chances of being a father to Ginny? Maybe the pressure got to be too much for him.

The doors to the waiting room opened again, and two policemen entered. The younger, stockier one said, "Anyone here with a Mr. Turner?"

Sierra raised her hand. "I am."

Mac stood beside her and gestured around the room. "We all are."

Ginny stomped up to the policeman. "My dad doesn't do drugs anymore. Why are you here?"

Even Sierra cracked a smile at her insistence.

I stepped forward, my hand on Ginny's shoulder. "Can you tell us what happened, please? We're very worried about Troy."

"Let's sit down." The detective took a seat, his partner remaining by the door. He flipped open a notebook. "A woman called earlier today and said her name was Becky, but that's all she told us."

"Becky? She said that?" My daughter willingly called the police?

"Yes." He frowned. "Do you know her?"

Did I know her? Oh, could I tell him stories. "She's my daughter."

"Ah." He consulted his notes. "She told her name and said a man was down off Birdneck, and he'd been beaten and injured."

"Did she give any other information?" Mac asked.

"Was she there?" I jumped in. Could they have found her? I squeezed Ginny to me while we waited for his answer.

"I'm sorry, but we found him alone, right where she told us to look. We called for an ambulance, and they brought him here. I spoke to the doctor, and we need to interview Mr. Turner when he gets out of recovery."

Ginny piped up. "Will you tell him I love him?"

The policeman standing by the door stepped forward and crouched to her level. "Yes, honey, we will."

Sympathy showed in his eyes. These men thought Troy had been buying drugs, and it went wrong. Why did Becky call it in? For that matter, why was Troy with Becky? I shook my head, trying to shake away all the bad memories and the awful images in my mind. Truth. I would focus on the truth.

"Will he be arrested?" I hated to ask in front of Ginny.

"It's not a crime to be beaten up, ma'am," the first detective said. "We want to question him about what happened. We've been trying to find the gang members who deal drugs in that area. It's an ongoing investigation." He hesitated before continuing, "We're hoping he can give us names."

Sierra sat back. "He won't know anything. He doesn't use drugs anymore."

"Yes, ma'am." He rubbed his hand down his face. "But we do need to speak to him."

Waiting for news and for Troy to wake up seemed to take hours. Just before midnight, a nurse came in asking for Sierra. She stood.

"Come with me, please. Mr. Turner is asking for you."

Both detectives hurried to the door. "We need to see him first."

"Really? I can't see him?" Sierra's face drooped.

"I'm sorry, miss. We'll come get you after we talk to him." The detectives followed the nurse out.

We returned to our seats. Ginny curled up on a bench, and I found a blanket to cover her, thankful she could sleep.

"Sierra, I don't believe he was buying drugs." I swallowed, my throat dry and scratchy. "I know what Maggie said is true. It just takes one slip-up. But there's more to this than what we're imagining. Don't give up."

She nodded and swiped tears from her cheeks. She brought her knees up and hugged them.

Thirty minutes passed, and the door opened again. A nurse waved to Sierra. "Come on, honey. Your turn now."

She stood and held out her hand to Mac. "Dad, will you go with me?" He hopped up, and they followed the nurse.

"I wish the police knew more about Becky." I fidgeted in my chair. Where was my daughter, and why had Troy been with her?

Sug blew out a quiet breath. "I do too. I wonder why Troy was with her."

"I think he went to find her. I don't know what he found, but obviously, he got the raw end of the deal."

Maggie joined our conversation. "I think you're probably right, Kat. No one mentioned that he had drugs on him or in his system. Just that he'd been beaten and had a broken leg. I imagine they would have told us if he'd been using." She hung her head and whispered, "I hope he hasn't been."

It wasn't long before Mac and Sierra returned to the waiting room. Sierra had been crying but looked more relaxed than when she'd left to see him.

I hugged her. "How is he?"

"He's going to be fine, Ms. Kat." She leaned hard on me. This night had taken a toll on the girl. "He wasn't buying drugs. He told me, and when the nurse came in, she confirmed there were no drugs in his system. He looks awful, though. He has black eyes, and his nose is crooked now. They broke his leg with a bat." She shuddered.

"What was he doing there?"

"Let's sit over here." Mac pointed to the other side of the room, away from where Ginny slept.

"Okay." Mac rubbed his hands on his pants. "There were no drugs in his system, and Troy could speak. He's missing a few teeth, and as Sierra said, he has two black eyes, a broken nose, and a broken leg. The doctor reset his leg, and his nose has been set and taped."

"Why was he with Becky?" I asked.

He raised his hand. "I'm getting to that. He left this afternoon,"—he peered at the clock on the wall—"well, yesterday afternoon, to find Becky. He had already searched for her in other well-known drug areas. He wanted to bring her home as a gift for you." Mac looked at me.

My breath caught, and I clasped my hand over my heart. "Oh, that boy."

"I know." Mac shook his head. "Good intentions, but it didn't serve him well. He found Becky. She's back to using and living on the street." He leaned forward and put his hand on my knee. "I'm so, so sorry, Kat."

I closed my eyes. My heart felt like lead. Heavy, unmoving. Sug took my hand, and Maggie put her arm around me. "We've got you, my friend," Maggie whispered.

I choked back a sob. "So what happened to Troy?" I asked after several minutes. Sug handed me a tissue, and I wiped my nose. "Who beat him up? Why did they break his leg?"

"Becky was buying drugs when he found her," Sierra said. "He said he yelled at her, and she ran, but the guys she was buying from must have thought he was a cop, and they beat him up."

"Becky must have hidden and watched." Mac patted my knee. "Then she called the police."

Sierra tipped her head, eyes shining. "She saved his life, Kat."

Chapter 32

Becky had been doing so well in rehab, but the drugs called her back to the streets. After learning from our family group and seeing Maggie and Troy live recovered lives, I understood that recovery was possible, but also a day-to-day choice. It wasn't something that someone decided and then never went back on. It was hard work. Tough work. And Becky couldn't seem to quit.

We headed home. Mac carried Ginny inside and tucked her into her bed. Presents would have to wait. I thanked him, locked the front door, and crawled into my bed. What felt like seconds later, Ginny shook my shoulder.

"How's my dad, Grandma?"

I blinked. "Can you back up a bit?" She stepped back, and I pushed myself up in the bed. I brushed my hair back with my hands and wiped my face. "Is it morning?"

"It's almost lunchtime." She put her hands on her hips. "You slept really late."

"We didn't get home until two this morning." I stretched and yawned. I patted the bed for her to snuggle beside me. "Your dad is going to be okay. He got hurt pretty badly and has a broken leg, but the doctor fixed it. He'll be home by tomorrow, I think."

She turned to face me. "What happened, though? He wasn't using drugs, was he?"

"Oh no, honey. He wasn't." I hesitated. I hated to tell her about her mother. I held her close to my side. "He found your mom, sweetie. She's back on the streets, using drugs. Troy found her, and the people with her beat him up."

Ginny clung to me and sobbed. I held her and whispered words of comfort. She had a lot to take in, and she'd already been through so much.

She wiped her face, and I handed her a tissue. Then, I told her what Becky had done. "Your mom called the police after your dad got hurt. She saved his life, Ginny."

"She did? Wow, that's pretty awesome, isn't it?"

"It sure is, honey. It sure is." I snuggled her to my side.

After a while, I got up and fixed brunch. We hadn't eaten since Mac's Christmas dinner the night before. Both of us dug into our scrambled eggs, toast, and bacon.

Ginny drank the last of her orange juice and wiped her mouth with her hand. "When will we open the presents at Mr. Mac's?"

"I'm not sure. Let's call him and see when your dad is coming home."

Mac answered on the first ring. "Sierra went to see Troy. Sounds like he'll be released tomorrow."

"Wow, that's amazing." Ginny nudged me. "Ginny wants me to ask when we'll open presents." She tugged on my sleeve and whispered in my ear. "She wants to see Troy too. Can we come over tomorrow when he gets home?"

"I think that will work," Mac said. "He's going to stay here while he recovers. He'll be on crutches for several weeks, and Sierra can help him more easily here. I'll call you when she brings him home."

Ginny talked about her mom intermittently throughout the day. I'd never seen her so open about her feelings. What she'd gone through in her young life made her more mature than most kids her age.

She understood that Becky's choice to return to drugs had nothing to do with us. Her mom was trapped, and even though she sincerely loved her daughter and me, she couldn't seem to break the pattern of using drugs.

This young girl continued to teach me.

"How did you get so smart?" I asked her that evening. We were eating spaghetti and buttered bread—comfort food for both of us.

She pointed her fork at me. "You taught me, Grandma." She dug into her bowl and twirled noodles around her fork. Before taking a bite, she said, "Remember when you read that Serenity Prayer to me?"

I nodded and recited it with her. "God, grant me the serenity to accept the things I cannot change, courage to change the things I can, and the wisdom to know the difference."

"And you told me about accepting my mom for who she was, not for who I wanted her to be." She set her fork down and covered my hand with hers. "It's time to do that, Grandma. I think we have to get used to her being how she is and try to love her anyway."

Serenity, courage, and wisdom. With God, Ginny, and my friends, I could do this.

Lots of tears flowed when we arrived at Mac's and saw Troy. Ginny traced the bruises on his face. "That looks really sore."

Troy held her hand. "Very." He shifted his leg. "This cast isn't fun, either." He tugged Ginny's hair. "I'm sorry I messed up Christmas."

"You didn't, Daddy. I'm just glad you're okay."

Troy turned to me. "I wanted to bring Becky for Christmas."

"I know. That was really sweet. But very stupid." I shook my finger. "Don't ever do anything like that again."

He grimaced. "I won't. I promise. This was enough for me." He gestured down his body.

Ginny snuggled beside Troy. "Can we open presents now?"

"I wondered when you would ask," Mac said.

"Grandma said we could today."

"Yes, we can." I held out my hand. "Help me pass them out?"

We took our time giving out the gifts and opening them. I wanted to savor this day with my family and friends—no need to rush. Even Ginny took her time. When no other presents were under the tree, Ginny cupped her hand over her mouth and whispered in Sugar's ear.

"It's behind the tree." Sug pointed. "I hid it back there."

Ginny reached behind the tree and pulled out a square wrapped box.

Troy tipped his head, eyebrows furrowed. "What's that? Who is it for?"

Ginny stood in front of me and held out the present. "This is for you. I made it." Her eyes sparkled. She glanced at Sugar. "Ms. Sug helped me."

"Thank you." I hugged it to my chest. "It's even more special because you made it."

She waved her hand. "Go on, open it."

Everyone chuckled at her expression and commanding tone.

I tore the paper and opened the box. Nestled in white tissue paper, I found a painting of a dove holding a heart in its beak. It was framed in light-colored wood. Across the bottom of the painting, Ginny had printed "Serenity."

"Peace, love, and serenity, Grandma," she said. "Like I told you yesterday. To always remind us."

And everyone cried.

Troy and Sierra decided to get married on Valentine's Day. Planning went into high gear, with Sugar driving us all crazy and making her lists. She had a list for the food, decorations, attendants, and reception. She appointed herself the wedding planner and assigned me to handle the flowers.

Like I had any idea what to do about them.

I called Sierra. "Sug is driving me nuts. She put me in charge of the flowers for your wedding. What kind do you want?" I clicked my pen and got ready to write.

"Um," she cleared her throat. "I have no idea. I still have to buy my dress."

"It's February first, Sierra." My voice ended on a high, panicked note.

"Please don't tell Ms. Sug," she whispered.

"I'm afraid of her right now too. Okay, here's what we're going to do. Tomorrow is Saturday. I'll pick you up in the morning, and we'll find a dress and decide on flowers. Sound good?"

She heaved a relieved sigh. "Yes, thank you. My mom hasn't been able to help at all. I thought she would ..."

Poor girl. I never asked about her mom, but from the few comments she made, I gathered she wasn't thrilled that Sierra had gotten close to Mac.

"It's okay. We'll do it. See you tomorrow," I said.

Ginny chose to stay at Mac's and hang out with her dad. They got along so well. The more I was with Troy, the more I liked him and appreciated the man he'd become. He had turned his life around with the help of rehab, a sponsor, and his faith. And he was outspoken about the need for all three. Ginny would learn so much from him.

Sierra climbed into my car and buckled her seatbelt. "What's the plan?"

"What's your budget?" I buckled and backed out of the driveway.

Her lips twitched. "Cheap."

"I understand. Might as well start at the mall. Let's see what they have before we brave one of those bridal specialty stores."

She only tried on two dresses before she found the perfect one. When she modeled it for me, tears filled my eyes. "You're stunning." I circled my finger. "Spin once more."

The dress—sweetheart neckline, long sleeves, fitted bodice—flowed to the floor with a short train. "It's perfect. Made just for you."

She clasped her hands under her chin. "I love it. But I'm scared to see the price tag." She turned. "Will you check it?"

I peeked at the price and swallowed. This amazing dress was beyond her budget. "Here's the thing. I'm going to pay for the dress." I hugged her. "My gift to you and Troy."

"Thank you, Mrs. Kat. Thank you." Her eyes shone with tears.

"You're welcome, honey. Your dad will argue with me, but he can pay for other things. Like flowers." I grinned.

I waved her off to change and texted Mac about the dress. He sent back a "thumbs up." When Sierra brought out the dress, I sent her to the lingerie section. "Find something for your wedding night."

She blushed the sweetest pink and scurried off while I paid, and the saleswoman bagged the wedding gown.

"Can you hold this while we finish shopping?" I asked.

She nodded, and I headed to find Sierra. I found her holding a beautiful white nightgown and a sheer robe. "What do you think?" she asked.

"Beautiful. Troy will love it." I laughed at the face she made. "Pay for that, and we'll go find a florist."

Having her wedding on Valentine's Day meant that flowers were more expensive than usual. Sierra picked a bouquet of white carnations with three white roses—one for her, one for Troy, and one for Ginny—surrounded by baby's breath and white satin.

"I want Ginny as my junior bridesmaid." She closed her eyes. "I can just see her in a red dress, with a white bow at the waist, holding a small bouquet of white carnations."

We ordered both bouquets and boutonnieres for Troy and Mac, as well as a corsage for Sierra's mother.

"I want another one just like that," she told the florist.

"Who is that for?" I asked.

She hugged me. "You, of course."

Sierra and Troy had a beautiful wedding. I found a dress for Ginny just like Sierra described. Mac gave his daughter away and then stood in as Troy's best man. Shrimp and Beverly couldn't come but sent a present and a card.

Sug nudged my shoulder during the ceremony. "Great job on the flowers."

"Thank you." I grinned. "Wonder who will get married next?"

We both watched Mac and Maggie at the rehearsal dinner the night before. Wedding fever was in the air. Mac stared at Maggie throughout the ceremony, and Troy had to shake his arm when it was time for him to pass over Sierra's wedding ring.

The audience giggled, and Mac blushed. As soon as the reception started, I found him. "Distracted?"

He grabbed a plate and loaded it with food, averting his eyes. "I have no idea what you mean."

Sierra joined us and kissed his cheek. She pointed. "Maggie is over there, Dad."

He turned and headed her way without saying another word. Sierra and I giggled.

"He is head over heels for her," she said.

I tipped my chin. "What's it like with your mom here?"

"They spoke last night and were cordial." Sierra picked up a carrot stick and munched on it. "I'm the only thing they have in common." She made a face. "At least they were nice to each other."

"True." I got a plate and filled it. "Go join your husband."

Sierra blushed and hurried off. Ginny joined me and grabbed a strawberry off my plate.

"Hey." I held my plate higher. "Mitts off. Find your own." She pretended to pout, and I handed her my plate. "Fine, I'll get a new one."

Ginny giggled and licked her fingers. "This was fun. Think Mr. Mac and Ms. Maggie will get married soon?"

Straight from the mouth of babes.

Becky hovered in the back of my mind. Wherever I went, I looked for her. On the streets, in the stores. I kept hoping she'd show up to reassure me that she was okay. I prayed for her every day and worked hard to leave her in God's hands. He knew her better than I did and loved her even more.

I struggled sometimes. My thoughts often strayed to Becky and her issues. Days would pass when I was sucked down into the pit of worry and unanswered questions. Then I'd get sick and tired of being sick and tired, and I would call Maggie or spend time outside in the fresh air. For me, staying in the midst of God's plan wasn't always easy.

A week after Troy and Sierra's wedding, someone knocked on my front door. I opened the door to find Becky on the porch. For a moment, I simply stared at her. *She's here, she's okay.*

I reached out. "Hi, honey. How are you?"

She stepped back. "Can we sit out here?" She perched on the end of one of the rockers.

I sat on the other, studying her. She was thinner, her skin sallow, her hair dirty. "How are you?"

She bobbed her head, her eyes cast down.

"Becky?"

"Would you mind if I stopped by and saw Ginny sometimes?" The words rushed out of her mouth. She held up her hand. "I'll sit out here. I just want to see her. And you."

I blinked. "I'd like that. I think Ginny would too. But I have a rule."

Becky tipped her head. "What?"

"When you come here, you have to be sober to see Ginny." I kept my gaze on her face.

She nodded. "Yes, I can do that."

I patted my knees and stood. "Want me to go get her?"

"Yes, please."

I found Ginny out back with Ollie. I told her that her mom was on the porch. While they talked, I fixed two peanut butter and jelly sandwiches.

I stuck them in a plastic bag and added a box of vanilla wafers, an apple, and a water bottle.

I carried it out front and handed it to Becky. "Is there anything else you need me to put in there?"

Her mouth pulled to the side. "Do you have an extra bar of soap?"

I hurried back inside before she could see the tears in my eyes. I had taken care of her for years, feeding her, keeping her clean, and ensuring she had nice clothes to wear. And now she wanted a simple bar of soap. I wiped my eyes, grabbed the soap, a washcloth, and a hand towel, and stuffed them in her bag. At the last minute, I tucked the Bible and journal I bought her for Christmas into it too.

I handed her the bag and kissed her cheek. "We're almost always home on the weekends. Stop by anytime."

She cried when she left us.

Our family group now included three more couples and a single dad. We shared our pain, discussed our thoughts, and celebrated when any of us had breakthroughs. At our next meeting, I told them that Becky had shown up.

"It was an answer to prayer," I said. "A reminder that God is still watching out for her."

Maggie beamed. "He is faithful."

I could only nod.

Finding peace, serenity, and joy was a journey. One Ginny reminded me of almost daily. As we left for school each morning, she'd tap the painting she'd given me. "Serenity today, Grandma," she would say.

Chapter 33

E pilogue
Seven years later

I opened the door and hollered, "Ginny, are you ready?"

"I'm coming!" She appeared at the top of the steps. "What do you think?"

"Come on down here, kiddo. Let me see you in your graduation gown. I want to take pictures before we leave." Ollie wandered in from Ginny's old bedroom. She slept upstairs now, but he had taken to sleeping beside her old bed. His old doggie joints didn't let him climb stairs anymore.

She tromped down the steps, her heels clacking on the wood. I stepped back, and she twirled for me. Ollie barked.

Tears filled my eyes at the sight of my granddaughter. Now taller than me, her beauty shone from the inside out. Her hair had darkened over the last few years and was shiny and bright. Her eyes reflected her love for me. I took her hand. "Gorgeous, simply gorgeous."

She blushed. "Dad, Sierra, and the girls are meeting us at the field. Mr. Mac, Maggie, and Sug are too. Let's get going."

Ollie sniffed the hem of her gown and woofed again. Red stood on the top stair and meowed. Ollie barked at her. He'd grown a bit braver in his old age.

I had Ginny stand by the picture she'd painted and given me for Christmas, the one when Troy had been beaten up.

"Peace, love, and serenity, Grandma," she said now. "To always remind us."

After I snapped several pictures, Ginny posed on the front porch for a couple more. "Do you want to run up to the beach too?" I asked.

We put Ollie on a leash and walked to the end of the road. I strolled behind her, clicking pictures as she went up the steps. She turned on the top step and looked toward me, backlit by the soft afternoon sunshine.

"Come on, you two!" She waved for Ollie and me to follow her.

I clicked away, in awe of her. She planned to move out in August to live on campus at Old Dominion. I felt sad to see her leave, but thrilled that she would be only forty minutes away.

The winter after Becky returned to the streets had been tough for us all, especially Ginny. She started middle school the next fall, and the kids teased her about having an addict for a mom and living with her grandma. I spoke with the principal several times. Troy and Sug stayed on top of her about her actions and attitude. Troy patiently described how addiction changed everyone, while Sug talked to her about not having a mother. Ginny saw her counselor, and for a while, she took medication.

We were all determined not to let her slip through the cracks.

In her sophomore year in high school, Ginny turned a corner. Sometimes Becky showed up at the house, and Ginny practiced what she had told me to do—let her go in every way. It was hard, but she managed to do it. She became a role model for all of us.

Today, we were celebrating Ginny's high school graduation. She'd finished in the top five of her class. I planned to teach for a few more years before retiring. Sierra and Troy's twin girls just turned two, and we seized every chance to have them stay overnight. I enjoyed being Grandma to them and wanted to spend more years with my family and friends. My heart had stabilized since that Christmas night so many years ago. I saw my cardiologist and walked almost every day. Letting Becky go and sticking with family group meetings kept the stress in check.

"Come on, Grandma," Ginny repeated. She looked at her phone. "We need to leave soon."

We took pictures on the beach and headed back to put Ollie inside. The ceremony started at four, but Ginny wanted to arrive early.

I kept hoping Becky would show up. We never knew what she would do. Over the last seven years, she appeared at odd times. Nothing regular, and never on a holiday. She'd sit on the porch, sometimes not speaking, and I'd pack her sandwiches. I bought some inexpensive drawstring bags to stuff toiletries and food into.

Ginny climbed into the driver's seat of her new-to-her car, an early graduation present from Troy and Sierra. She rolled the passenger window down. "Are you ready, Grandma?"

"I'm coming. I'm coming." I looked at my watch. "I don't think we'll be late. It's only three."

"I know." She waited for me to buckle my seatbelt. "Bradley is meeting me there. He said he has a present for me."

"Oh. Did he decide if he's going into the Navy?"

She shook her head. "No, he's not. He's going to ODU." She winked. "Just like me."

Ginny started dating Bradley in tenth grade. He was a good kid, and he recently asked Troy and me if he could give Ginny a promise ring today. I couldn't wait to see her face, but I planned to protect his secret.

"You'll enjoy that."

She turned into the school parking lot. "Do you think Mom will come today?"

"You never know." I couldn't promise her anything about her mom.

"Yeah, true." We had learned to love Becky as she was, without wanting more. Or at least trying not to. Sometimes, I had to remind myself of everything I'd learned about addiction. It wasn't a one-and-done thing. It was often day-to-day.

We got out of the car, and Ginny shaded her eyes, scanning for her boyfriend.

"There he is." She turned, hugged me, and kissed my cheek. "I love you, Grandma. I'll be with Bradley, and then I have to join my class."

I hugged her hard. "Have fun, baby." I forced a teary smile. I walked to the field and found seats in the stands. Sugar joined me, fanning herself with her program.

"Can you believe our sweet girl is graduating?" she asked.

"Nope. It seems like just yesterday she showed up with Becky."

"Think she'll come today?" Sugar wiped her forehead with a tissue.

I shrugged. "No matter what, this will be a good day."

She nudged me with her shoulder. "Yes, it will be."

Troy, Sierra, and their twins joined us, and we waited for the ceremony to begin.

"Dad and Maggie better get here soon, or they're going to miss it," Sierra said, checking her watch.

"Oh, they'll be here." I had so many secrets to keep. Maggie had called the night before and told me she was pregnant again. She and Mac married only a year after Troy and Sierra and were on baby number three. They planned to announce it to everyone after the graduation ceremony.

The two of them squeezed in beside us as "Pomp and Circumstance" began to play.

"Sorry we're late." Maggie leaned into me and rubbed her stomach. "The babysitter arrived on time, but I seem to have all-day sickness."

"Shush." Sug flapped her hand at us. "Here she comes."

Ginny walked by us, giving a little wave. As she passed, movement at the fence around the field caught my eye.

My hand went to my mouth.

Sug elbowed me. "What's wrong?"

I pointed, and she gasped.

"What is it?" Mac said. He followed my finger. "Becky, oh wow. She came."

Tears flowed. I raised my hand, and Becky waved back. I motioned for her to come up into the stands. As she got closer, I saw she wore a faded dress and her hair was brushed. She trudged in front of everyone and up the concrete steps to us.

I stood and hugged her. "I'm so glad you're here."

Becky waved at our group. "Hey, y'all." She scooted in beside me. "Look at our girl out there, Mom. Just look at her." She turned to me. "That's your doing, you know."

"Oh, Becky." I hugged her again. "That's all of us. You, me, Troy, Sierra, Mac, Maggie, and Sugar. We all had a hand in raising our girl. Thank you for bringing Ginny to me all those years ago."

Ginny may have come into my life unexpectedly, but she brought family, friends, and light with her. Where would I be without her?

Acknowledgements

I am deeply grateful to the family group I am honored to walk alongside. Your shared experiences, quiet wisdom, and steady presence remind me that I am not alone, even in the moments when life feels overwhelming. Through your love, steadfast hope, courage, and encouragement, you show me what it means to keep showing up—one day at a time—with honesty and compassion.

In listening and being listened to, I learned the power of letting go, of focusing on my own growth, and of trusting that healing unfolds in its own time. Your willingness to speak truth, offer support without judgment, and hold space for both pain and progress has shaped me more than you know. Thank you for the strength you model, the hope you carry, and the grace you extend so freely.

About the author

Jen Dodrill brings inspiration and hope to life through the pages of her books, telling heartfelt stories that shine in both good and challenging times. A mother of five and a proud grandma, she writes family-focused cozy mysteries, romantic suspense, and women's fiction—fueled by her love of reading and all things coffee.

Learn more at jendodrillwrites.com, and connect with Jen on Facebook, Instagram, and Pinterest @jendodrillwrites.

Also by Jen Dodrill

Find all of Jen Dodrill's books at: https://jendodrillwrites.com/books-by-jen-dodrill/

Birds Alive! - **An Empty-nesters Cozy Mystery, Book 1**

Peg—widow, mom blogger, and empty nester—is desperate for a new hobby. After a late-night blog post leaves her dedicated Mamma Birds followers fearful that she's closing her blog, she adopts a reader's suggestion and forms the Empty Nesters Birding Group. On their first outing overlooking beautiful Pensacola Bay, a birder dies from an allergic reaction to peanuts in the birdseed. Seed that should be peanut-free. A hurricane barrels toward the Gulf Coast, and Peg's overbearing, animal-collecting, but well-meaning mother-in-law crashes Peg's empty nest. After the hurricane passes, Peg checks on her new birder friends and finds one wounded and dying. The assailant is still there and knocks Peg down a steep staircase. Stuck in a boot with a broken foot and still reeling from the two murders, Peg recruits a fellow birder and her mother-in-law to help solve the crime. She even teams up with the detective investigating the case, whose dimples draw her in a way she hasn't experienced in years.

Where's the Quetzal? – An Empty-Nesters Cozy Mystery, Book 2

Peg Howard has planned the perfect baby shower for her oldest daughter. But the return of Estelle and Roger Keaton disrupts her peace, reigniting old mysteries. A chance discovery of a centuries-old shipwreck sets off a chain of events, thrusting Peg and her friends into a perilous game of deception. As they unravel the mysteries surrounding a rare quetzal bird, they uncover a plot that threatens their very lives.
With Detective Marcus Sharp and her mother-in-law Hazel by her side, Peg races against time to solve the mystery. But as she digs deeper, she realizes that some truths are better left buried.

In a tale full of twists and turns, Peg confronts her deepest fears, facing an adversary more cunning and unexpected than anyone anticipated. Join Peg and her friends on a journey through intrigue and peril, where bonds of friendship and family may be their only salvation. Will they uncover the truth before it's too late, or will the past come back to haunt them all?

No Egrets – An Empty-nesters Cozy Mystery, Book 3

Life in Stone Creek Cove is never dull—especially when the neighborhood egrets suddenly go missing. Peg Howard and her mother-in-law, Hazel, find themselves "volunteered" to head up the search. But tracking missing birds soon tangles them in a nest of secrets—complete with neighborhood gossip, suspicious business deals, and a body in the creek. Between babysitting her grandson, wrangling her mischievous new puppy, and juggling two men who both want her heart, Peg already has her hands full. Add in a trail of cryptic clues and dangerous warnings from enemies who would rather Peg quit snooping, and things quickly spiral beyond missing wildlife.

As Peg and Hazel dig deeper, they uncover connections that reach far beyond their quiet Pensacola neighborhood. Every lead brings them closer to the truth—and closer to danger. Can Peg balance family, friendship, and romance while unraveling a mystery that could cost more than feathers?

No Egrets is a warm, witty cozy mystery about friendship, family, and the unexpected adventures that come with neighborhood drama and a dash of danger. Perfect for fans of small-town sleuths, quirky neighbors, and mysteries solved over coffee and conversation.

Trinity Sands Beach Club – Second Chances: Romance & Mysteries

What do a widow, a newly divorced woman, and a retired professor of art history have in common?

They all came to Trinity Sands Island to find a simple life without any entanglements. But instead, they are each confronted with a mystery and another chance at romance. Will they be brave enough to face the possible dangers of solving a mystery and losing their hearts?

This collection includes three novellas:

"SeaBreeze Obsession" by Jen Dodrill—Newly single Karah Halyard returns to her beach cottage and starts "SeaBreeze Designs," a business specializing in beach decor. But beneath the tentative peace of her life, unresolved feelings stir as she considers reconciling with her ex-husband, Gage, who is in town doing research. When a secret admirer confronts her on the beach, Karah defends herself and runs. That night, he's found dead. As she and Gage face a murder investigation, they must confront their past and unravel the mystery of the real killer. Can they solve the crime and reconcile their fractured relationship?

"Trinity Sands Treasure Hunt" by Sharon Carpenter—Retired art professor Claire Anderson inherited all of her uncle's worldly goods. Arriving at his Trinity Sands Beach Club bungalow, she faces the daunting task of sorting through the boxes and bags that he left behind. When someone tries to break in and steal seemingly worthless items, Claire calls Chief of Security, Ben Hastings and sparks fly. Claire and Ben realize all is not as it seems when they set out to discover who is targeting the house. In their search for answers, will the attraction between Claire and Ben deepen into real treasure?

"Searching for Serenity" by Deborah Sprinkle—Grace Caldwell hasn't been to their beach house since her husband passed away three years ago. Her grief has kept her from moving forward with her life. But, when a letter arrives from her friend, Serenity James, saying something strange is going on at the Beach Club, Grace decides it's time to head south. However, when she arrives, Serenity has disappeared, and no one knows where she is. Detective Peter Young gets involved and, as Grace and he work together, a mutual attraction blossoms—one that takes Grace by surprise.

Will Grace find love again while solving the mystery behind Serenity's disappearance?

www.ingramcontent.com/pod-product-compliance
Lightning Source LLC
LaVergne TN
LVHW021221080526
838199LV00089B/5495